WHAT READERS HAVE SAID...

"My daughter and I both loved it! Will be on the lookout for a series."

– Candice, USA

"I loved this book, and I hope the author writes another one. As a Harry Potter fan, this is the first book to match it!!"

– Alyssa, USA

"Excellent book for teens! My son loves it and said it's a must read. Everybody buy!"

– Mary, USA

"I purchased this book for my two boys, ages 9 & 10. They had fun reading the book and talking about it with each other, which was exactly what I wanted. I like it when they're excited about reading material!"

– Rancho, USA

Also by Jonathan Gatsby

The Wars Between Angels and Gods: Forced into Heaven's War

Coming Soon

World War III: Nationberg, Gatsby, and the Execution Camp

Coming Soon

Jonathan Gatsby

The Beasts and the 4 Demigods

The Wars between Angels and Gods: Book One

SECOND EDITION

978-1-7361769-0-0

Second edition hardcover published by Gatsby & Noel (Jonathan D Dunham)

December 2nd 2020, Fairbanks, Alaska, United States of America

Cover Art by Ricky Gunawan Book Cover Art

www.facebook.com/rickyillustrator

Editing and Interior Design by Emily Gleeson Editorial

www.facebook.com/emilygleesoneditorial

First published by Gatsby & Noel August 10 2019

Cover Designer: Gerald Paar Editor: Margaret Gaspers Formatted by: Belinda Wright

The BEASTS and the 4 DEMIGODS

JONATHAN GATSBY

GATSBY'S REVELATIONS

DANGER:

THIS IS THE BOOK OF THE WARS
BETWEEN ANGELS & GODS
Do Not Read Past This Point

ONE

Police stood in front of Martin Luther King High School as students made their way inside. John was heading towards the main entrance, where every student was required to walk through the metal detectors. It was a freezing cold morning, despite being October. The drop in temperature coming out of summer made the chill feel like mid-winter.

John begrudgingly paused as a few cars passed by. The thumping of bass rattled the sidewalk as one revved its engine, its windows rolled down and gangster-rap music blaring from its stereo. John shook his head. Blatantly displaying your money like that was also a good way to become a target for robbers. He stood patiently until the road was clear for him to cross and join the long entrance line that wound out to the road—still there even though he was forty-five minutes late.

The high school was located on the southside of Chicago, Illinois, in a gang infested area. The streets were filled with trash and clutter and dotted with abandoned buildings, and the homelessness rate was at an all-time high. The southside of Chicago was a breeding ground for misery and liquor stores, and felt as though it lacked the attractions of its northside and popular downtown counterparts. Gangs and drugs were taking over, and it seemed as though it was only the devout religious that managed to keep separate.

The devout religious and John and his mom.

Homeless teens were becoming a devastating trend, growing with the rise of drug-addled parents and intra-family gang involvement. John was fortunate. He was happy in his home life with his mom, despite living in the dead center of the ganglands that were fast becoming the norm. He had all he needed, with his big TV and good ramen noodles. Content to watch from the edges of Chicago's sadness, John held fast to the intricate culture that set it apart.

He stood on the sidewalk watching the car that was blasting its music slowly drive by, making sure to not take his eyes off its passengers—not even for a second. It takes nine months to create life but less than a second to take it away. This was a lesson John knew very well from the rough crowds that he had grown accustomed to hanging around as he grew up, and though he was not in a gang himself, he was acquaintances with many members of various outfits.

The three guys and the girl in the car were clearly not high schoolers. They were most likely there to sell drugs or to catch one of their rivals off guard. They stared at John with dangerous, menacing looks on their faces. As they crawled past, he could see their eyes were ablaze with the adrenaline rush of the kills that earned them street credit and acceptance within their crew. Their brows were arched in anger, though he didn't know what they had to be angry about.

John did not turn his head, but instead, reached behind his back as if he had a gun, though he knew he did not. Fortunately, they passed without incident, and within fifteen minutes, John was walking through his classroom door into Mrs Norton's class. They were already reading, so John took his seat quietly and opened his book, *The War of the Gods*.

Marcus, his friend, was sitting across the room and John nodded his head at him in greeting. Marcus mouthed, "what's up?" back, returning the nod before turning back to his book to follow along. John did the same. He just had to find out exactly what page they were on.

"People of Greece! Oh, how we have been suffering at the hands of Zeus—for far too long now," Mrs Norton read as the class silently listened. Most classes were loud and had no structure, but Mrs Norton's class was always well behaved, mostly because she had gained their respect by treating them like human beings rather than trash like the majority of the teachers.

John rocked his tall frame back in his seat as Mrs Norton's soothing voice and the absorbing tale drew him right into the story…

TWO

"Zeus is not a god, just an immortal who lacks morals and people skills," spoke a scrawny man from the village platform. The man was distraught because, just two days prior, Zeus had attacked his family in retaliation for cursing his name. He had attacked the man's wife and killed his twelve-year-old son. The man looked to be on the brink of starvation, and had dust in his beard and a scar that ran across his right eye. He wobbled on unsteady legs, but spoke on with a strength he looked not to possess.

"Zeus is insecure and has turned on even his own family, constantly battling his mother, attempting to erase her from existence. He has declared a new law! Any god caught aiding the humans will now be prosecuted as a criminal and will be dealt absolute punishment." The man rose to his full—somewhat diminutive—height, his arms raised toward his audience. "And, to show the gods and us humans that he means business, Zeus has used his own immediate family as an example. Poseidon has been sentenced to a life of imprisonment in an enchanted cave, and Athena has been sentenced to exile from Mt Olympus. Her memory has been stolen and her appearance altered so that there is no hope for her to gain help from the others!"

A large group of people began to crowd around the platform to hear the man speak. "He forces our women—and when they bear his children, he kills his own offspring. Sounds familiar, doesn't it? Like father like son!" Worse! Kronos may have swallowed his children, but at least they lived on inside of him. Zeus is a killer! He's an adulterer! His wife has so starved him of love that, despite despising half-blooded children, he continues to come down to Earth and seduce our wives! Goddess Hera might be the Queen of Gods, but she is filth to allow this to continue!" The man seemed to grow larger, empowered by his own declaration.

A twittering wave spread throughout the restless audience. Some of them began to agree and egg him on, while others listened silently. They too, agreed, but were too scared to do so out loud in the open. Most just stood around to see if Zeus was going to retaliate, or whether he would continue to ignore him.

The man was not deterred.

"Hypocrite, coward, and sissy are words that I feel best describe Zeus," he said, gaze piercing the assembly.

"Zeus wouldn't last a day down here on Earth, picking on people as though he were a regular man."

"I'll bet that even now, with all of his powers, he wouldn't even dare fight his oldest son, Perseus, who has defied him more than once. He—aaaahh!" the man yelled, as startling electricity rained in lightning bolts from a clear and dazzling sky—it was broad daylight. The crowd broke into hysteria, running in every direction.

Nobody wanted to be hit.

The Earth beneath them split with a resounding crack, but the speaker refused to cower. For a moment, the sky looked to narrow, as it crushed in upon him, and his last breaths were wide-eyed and hurried. With a final rumble from the heavens, the lightning ceased and the man was dead—his audience was nowhere to be seen. Zeus smiled. "Humans," he said to himself. "They never learn."

He teleported home.

As Zeus stood alone on top of Mt Olympus, Hades appeared in the Great Hall. He looked like a crazed scientist who had finally snapped and gone into overdrive insanity. Anger was clearly etched across Hades' furrowing eyebrows and upon the blazing fire in his eyes.

The Great Hall was very large, with the ceiling more than a hundred feet above the ground. The entire height of Zeus' castle, set upon Mt Olympus, was over forty-seven thousand feet. The Earth was still one large mass of land, surrounded on all sides by water. The ceiling of the Great Hall was made entirely of bright and shiny diamonds and red rubies that spelled the words: *Zeus: King of the*

Gods. The walls were made of solid gold with more red rubies placed periodically along them. The windows were large with stained-glass images in each of them. On one side of the Great Hall, they were of the gods battling and defeating the giants. On the other side, they were of the gods defeating the titans. On the floor, the images were of Zeus, Hades, and Poseidon defeating their father, Kronos.

There were three very large, intricately designed, and gold-leafed chairs for each of the brothers to sit on and claim as his throne.

"Is it true, brother?" Hades asked, without even so much as a hello for the brother who he had—intentionally—not seen in person for centuries.

"Is what true?" Zeus responded as he sighed, showing his irritation at Hades' visit. Once every few centuries were still too many times for Zeus to see his brother, whom he greatly disliked.

"What do you want Hades? Why are you here?"

"Rumor has it that you have imprisoned our brother and banished Athena to live as a human on Earth with her memory erased. Rumor also has it that you've even changed her look, so nobody will recognize her." Hades was in love with Athena, even though she was his aunt. "I refuse to believe that you have turned into our father, Kronos, but from the looks of things, you are a mirror image." Hades stared Zeus down as he finished his sentence. Hades, unlike his brother Poseidon, never feared Zeus and couldn't care less about getting into a physical altercation with him. Zeus stared back at Hades for a minute before grinning.

"Of course it's true," Zeus said, smiling. "I am the Supreme Ruler of Mankind, and as you seem to forget, also the King of the Gods. Any god or mortal who opposes me, simply put, has to face the consequences." Zeus continued smiling, hoping to bait Hades into a fight.

"Has your mind become as dried as the dead grass? You are not the Supreme Ruler. You got your kingdom by killing our father—and with our help, might I add! — just like he became ruler by killing Grandfather Ouranos. Poseidon and I allowed you to rule up here because you freed us from the prison within our father. But you know! You know the prophecy as well as the rest of us, and although our ancestors split into sects upon Lucifer being cast into the bottomless pit, he will return—and he *will* rule again. We both know that when he returns, he will not take a back seat to you or any other. He couldn't, even if he wanted to."

"How does that prophecy go?" Zeus barely contained the smug smirk curling the corners of his mouth.

Hades scowled. "Either Lucifer will lead the fallen to victory, or he will lead them to defeat… But without Lucifer holding the reins… all who oppose The Creator will find themselves screaming in pain for an eternity from the Lake of Fire's unbearable heat."

"Oden, Rah, and Khaeo were wise to leave and start their own kingdoms." Zeus spoke, after allowing Hades to finish quoting the prophecy that Zeus had read many times.

"Prophecies can be manipulated, and I believe The Creator, as he is called by our forefathers, had that prophecy written in such a manner to keep us from launching our own war against him. The first war clearly showed that Lucifer does not know how to beat Him, so why not set it up for him to also be the leader in a second war?"

"You are a fool!" Hades shouted, his voice like the booming of a thousand thunderstorms. "That prophecy determines all of our fates and your stupidity is not going to be my downfall."

Zeus was glad that Hades' dislike for him kept him mostly confined to the underworld. A blue flame formed around Hades as Zeus stood to his feet with a conceited smile smug on his face. Zeus quickly formed a lightning bolt in his hands, but before he could throw it at his brother, Hades shot blue fire out of his hands directly at Zeus' heart, leaving multiple burn marks on his chest and knocking him off his feet and into the wall twenty feet behind him. Zeus and his brethren walked around at fifteen feet tall on Earth, but in their natural realm, they were free to stand their full height of sixty feet. The mere sight of them could kill a human, and the fight between them shook the mountain.

Zeus quickly recovered and threw bolt after bolt at Hades without even getting up. He launched them from right off the ground with ease.

Hades was hit in his arm and his face twisted in anger. "Argh!" he yelled as he grabbed his arm in pain and took cover, knocking over the dining table in the great dining hall of Olympus and hiding behind it. Every once in a while, Hades would come up from behind the table just long enough to shoot a fireball at Zeus.

"Enough!" Zeus finally yelled, after what seemed like hours. "No more powers. We settle this the old way."

"I'm perfectly fine with that!" Hades yelled from where he crouched. "Swear it first though."

"I swear on my existence that I will not use my powers!" Zeus roared.

Hades immediately stood to his feet. The look on his face was menacing. With a bulldog-like approach, he began to advance on Zeus. The moment Zeus was within arm's length, he began to swing powerful blows at him. Though Hades was stronger, Zeus was more skilled and easily slipped around Hades' punches, countering him and showering him with punches of his own.

"Ooohmp…" Zeus groaned, as Hades slipped under one of his punches, picked him up by his ankles, and slammed him hard on the ground. Zeus tried to recover, but before he could, Hades slammed him again, and then again, and over and over until Zeus was barely conscious. Zeus considered using his powers, but the consequences of breaking the oath he made would have him completely wiped out of existence.

Zeus mustered up all the strength he could and focused his mind on getting his hands to the floor in front of his head. As Zeus' body swung heavily one more time, he blocked his head from hitting the ground again with his great and powerful forearms. The floor around him began to crack in a straight, solid line that looked similar to a lightning strike. Many cracks had spread across the ground, slathered in Zeus' golden blood.

Hades attempted to swing Zeus and slam him again, but Zeus, mustering up just a bit more strength, was able to resist by pulling his legs inwards towards his body. Hades did not like this and immediately tried to jump on top of him.

Zeus used his quick wit and instincts to roll out of the way and return to his feet. His legs were wobbly. He was weak, and Hades knew it. Hades advanced with speed. It was

a scary sight; even Zeus trembled at the pure look of destruction and devastation that seemed to surround his brother, who was determined to kill him.

He tackled Hades' legs and took him to the floor, ducking his head to avoid the swing of a wild hook. Zeus quickly jumped up instead of finishing the battle on the ground, which would have been to Hades' advantage. His brother followed suit—slow and languid in his movement. He looked at Zeus and said, "This is going nowhere, brother. Let us finish this in animal form, but no other magic, or we will be in the same position."

"Deal," Zeus said, as he took a deep breath, attempting to calm the increasingly fast beat of his heart. He quickly turned into a dragon, as did Hades. The two gnashed and clawed at each other for a little over an hour before the fight finally ended. A few of the other gods had gathered around to watch the battle. Hera watched, hoping that for once Zeus would be put in his place. None of the other gods could beat him in a fight. Only Poseidon and Hades had enough power and strength, but Poseidon avoided battles with both of his brothers at all cost—for the sake of peace.

Finally, it was over. Zeus sat on the floor against the wall, injured, while Hades fled back to the underworld, barely alive. Zeus was tired after the fight and wanted to rest and heal up, but he knew better and decided to find out if Hades would try again to kill him. He straightened himself up and disappeared.

"Sister Fates!" Zeus yelled, as he appeared on Mt Oglophious, a stony mountain shrouded in mist with monsters guarding the bottom on all sides. Not a root nor blade of grass ever grew there. The three Sister Fates slowly walked towards Zeus. They looked like dirty cloths that had been used to wipe up vomit and excrement, and their hair looked like a mop-head that had been used over and over for hundred years and never once cleaned out. They had no facial features—no eyes, no noses, no mouths… Just one eye between them that they each took turns holding when it was their turn to speak.

Zeus looked on with disgust. "Tell me, great and ever seeing Sisters; will my brother Hades try to kill me?"

"You must first pay a toll," the oldest and ugliest Sister told Zeus, holding out her hand to receive payment and sticking out her snake-like tongue. Zeus felt his stomach twist and fought hard against retching at the implication. He quickly handed the eldest of The Sisters the bag of gold and then dug in his pockets for extra to give them.

"Hades will attempt to attack you tonight in your bedchambers. If you are there, lying in your bed, he will succeed and imprison you as you have Poseidon. But, if you curse your bed with the same trap that you used to entrap Poseidon, victory will be yours." The Middle Sister, who was nearly as ugly, spoke.

"Good," Zeus said. "Then I will curse the bed and when Hades appears; I will imprison him with Poseidon in the Cave of Misery for all eternity." A smile spread across his face as a feeling of incredible invincibility began to creep into his heart.

"The other gods will not be happy about this!" The Youngest Sister shouted. "And they shall war with you, and you will find yourself alone, ruling on Olympus."

As Zeus looked upon her, hate for the three Sister Fates filled him.

Oh, if I could just find a way to steal their powers, I would have no more need for these three hags and could banish them to some distant galaxy far away, he thought.

Zeus, without another word, teleported himself back to Mt Olympus to his impressive bedchambers. The walls,

like those in the Great Hall, were made from diamonds, rubies, and gold. The ceiling was created in the image of the universe, which Zeus longed to travel. The Asgardians were the only sect of fallen angels allowed to travel the galaxy—at least to other planets and realms within the Milky Way solar system—by using a bridge designed with dark magic, long before even the angels had been made. Oden bargained

a deal with Michael that granted them access to the bridges that dwelt within the Milky Way Galaxy. They were not allowed access to any realms or planets in any other solar system in the universe.

Upon the top of his bed, Zeus formed an image of himself and cursed it with the same curse he used to imprison Poseidon. After he set the curse, the fake Zeus lay sound asleep on the bed, snoring and all. The real Zeus had nothing to do but wait. He laid uncomfortably, hidden under the bed, waiting for his brother to appear. It seemed as though time was standing still. Anxious and impatient, Zeus was almost ready to give up and crawl out from under the bed.

"I wish The Fates had been more specific about the time that he was coming," he said out loud from under the bed, talking to himself in frustration. Just as he finished his sentence, Hades appeared in the bedchamber, holding a dagger engulfed in blue flames. Hades was surrounded by a blue flame as well, which happened when he became upset.

He cautiously made his way towards Zeus' bed, careful not to make any noises, knowing that the slightest squeak could ruin the whole plan. With his breath held, he rose from the ground until he towered above his brother. Blue light cast ghostly shadows across the room, and it became difficult to sense what movement was real and what was not. He couldn't afford to waste any time.

Swoosh! Hades' blade struck the fake Zeus in the center of his chest. Immediately, a mist began to rise from the fake Zeus. Hades was confused for a second as it surrounded him—a swirl formed under his feet. He tried to escape, but it worked as quicksand, dragging Hades in.

Hades screamed for help, as he had no idea what was happening to him. When he was down to his neck in the shifting ground, the real Zeus crawled out from the other side of the bed. He stood at a distance, smiling and nodding in triumph as Hades disappeared into the murky trap.

Landing with a cold thud against rock, Hades clambered to his feet the moment the strange substance let him go. "Bastard!" he yelled, at the top of his lungs. Poseidon, who had been sound asleep against the cave wall, jumped into the air. His eyes flashed open and he was ready to defend himself.

"Hades?" Poseidon gasped as he ran to his brother. "Have you come to rescue me from this dreadful place?"

Hades shook his head. "Zeus got me too," he said, face curled in disgust. "He tricked me, and now, I am a prisoner down here as you are." Hades looked around the cave. There were no doors and no way out. It was no bigger than a small bedroom and it was pure solid rock—there were no beds or any soft places for rest. There certainly wasn't anything to give away its position beneath Poseidon's ocean castle.

"Noooo!" Poseidon screamed, as he broke into frustrated tears, hitting his knees hard on the ground. He couldn't take anymore as it dawned on him that he would never escape from the prison in which Zeus so cleverly trapped him three weeks prior. “I wish he’d killed me instead! I’d prefer death than to stay here another day. You kill me!” Poseidon turned to his brother as he begged.

“Get a hold of yourself,” Hades calmly replied, shaking his head. “The other gods will come for us. I know they will. You know death isn’t possible. Not really. We can’t die, brother. We always re-form.”

THREE

Young Hercules was nineteen years old. With his head hung low, he watched another lightning storm from the distance, his eyes filled with sadness. He wanted to protect the humans, but how could he protect them from his own father? It seemed impossible.

Hercules was extraordinarily strong, but hadn't learned to fight and wouldn't stand a chance against the mighty Zeus. The youngster turned and continued his trudging journey away from civilization. He couldn't bear to watch another human being killed by his father, who was completely crazed and extremely paranoid—obsessed with protecting his position as Head God.

Hercules traveled far, to a remote place known in the present day as Sparta. It was a place where no humans had ever stepped foot, and the land was lush with caves, trees and whispering grass. The unbothered wildlife was plentiful, and it wasn't too far from the ocean. It was indeed divine.

There has to be a good cave around here, Hercules thought to himself. He searched until nightfall for a suitable place to sleep, but the first few caves he came across were filled with insects and Hercules, who was petrified of spiders, didn't want to chance being bitten. He wound up sleeping outside, using one of the trees he pulled up as wood for a fire to keep him warm.

The next morning, Hercules resumed his search. Caves were plenty but none quite to his liking. As he sat down to rest, taking a refreshing gulp from his water container, he spotted the largest cave entrance that he had ever seen. It was shining high up on the rocks, only made visible by the glinting sun. Throwing his water to the ground, Hercules began to climb. Parts of the rocky cliff stood at least a few thousand feet above the ground and it was extremely steep. Several times, Hercules nearly fell. It was a long and tiring effort.

About three-quarters of the way up, he began to wonder if he had imagined the entrance, because it had looked as if it were no more than twenty feet off the ground. With a shrug, he continued his trek, and by the time he reached the top, he was lathered in sweat. Expecting yet another disappointment, Hercules could barely contain his glee when he at last discovered the entry. To his surprise, the cave had been decorated and filled with workable furniture. The sight of a kitchen made his stomach rumble, but he was distracted by the sparkling walls and ceilings. They glittered as if they were birthed from fool's gold and diamonds. "What the…?" Hercules cursed, believing he was alone. He jumped when a shuffling noise came from the depths of the cave.

"For someone set on living outdoors, you sure are picky," a voice sounded from the shadows. The voice cackled in a loud laugh.

"Grandma!" Hercules said with excitement as he recognized his grandma Gaia's voice.

Gaia, even though at war with Zeus, always took care of her grandson, who still was learning to live on his own. Hercules didn't know how to hunt, fish, or even cook. All he had was his untrained strength, and he was in extremely bad shape to be on his own.

"Yes, dear, it's me." Gaia said, laughing. In her human form, she was a beautiful brunette with eyes that shimmered in spirited greens and blues and browns. "What on Earth are you doing way out here?"

"I had to get away from the people… and dad's lightning storms. Nobody in town will do business with me, and no one will hire me. I've tried fishing boats, farmers, welders, and offices. It is as if I am an outlaw just because I am the son of Zeus. I didn't think there'd be anyone here…" he trailed off in contemplation.

"You know your brother, Perseus, was rejected by the people too, when they found out that he was Zeus' son?" Gaia reached out to comfort her grandson, hands betraying none of her age. "Since he lacked your strength, the humans were able to bully him. They beat him with whips when they were mad at Zeus, and raced each other on horseback while dragging poor Perseus behind, with his legs bound together. They even burnt down his house—with his human father in it."

"And still he saved them?" Hercules asked in complete befuddlement.

"It was a tough road for Perseus." Gaia said, nodding. "He was hated, just like you are, and not because of something he did but because of his father's sins."

Hercules listened closely as his grandmother spoke.

"The people thought that by hurting Zeus' son, they were hurting Zeus. But Zeus cared nothing for Perseus and allowed the torture day after day. But the day he stood against Zeus… I remember that day." Gaia sighed. "That was the day the people's hatred turned into praise.

"On that day, he became a hero in the people's eyes—and Hercules, believe me when I say this—that's what the people need right now. Your brother was a pushover at first. He could not fight. He had no strength or special powers—that is until I had him trained in the arts of fighting, just as I did your father.

"I combed the Earth, gathering materials to make weapons for Perseus. I made him flying shoes, an impenetrable shield, a special sword made from unicorn hair and titanium—sharpened on the fingertips of death. This sword is the only one that can kill a god, except the one they used on Kronos."

Hercules pictured the events in his head as Gaia told him the story. He had never met Perseus, but he began to hope to not only meet him but to also spend time with him—as brothers—someday.

"I want to be a hero for the people," Hercules interrupted, just as Gaia began to speak again. "How do I become a hero?"

She turned to him with a small smile. "Are you sure about that? The training is hard and—"

"Yes, I want to be a hero," Hercules insisted, with a broad grin splitting his face. He could already see himself fighting off the gods, and having the love of the people instead of their hate. *And, the girls…* Hercules thought. *I'll be the number one ladies' man in town.*

"Okay." His grandmother relented easily. "I will have you trained. But you must promise to devote yourself to your training, always give your all."

"I do," Hercules quickly responded, squirming impatiently beneath her sharp gaze.

After placing enchantments on the cave to keep Zeus from seeing in, Gaia left for The East, to find the trainer of warriors, Turally. Turally had trained Zeus, Achilles, Perseus, and many other great warriors. Out of everyone Turally had trained so far, none had possessed the strength of young Hercules, not even his father, Zeus.

FOUR

What in the devil's name is going on?" Zeus bellowed from his throne. His youngest son had disappeared from the universe and was nowhere to be found, despite their connection. Zeus had a connection with all his sons; he could sense where they were at any moment.

"You," Zeus said furiously to one of his scouts. "Search the underworld and tell me if Hercules has been killed. Don't mess it up!"

He didn't care much for Hercules, but feared Gaia was hiding him, as she hid Zeus himself from his father. *I must find him*, Zeus thought. *Right now, I can easily defeat him, but with a little training and his strength at full power, Hercules would be a tough match for me. Gaia knows this.*

Zeus was nervous, and he yelled at one of the captains of his army. "Find Turally—my trainer! And take the army with you. I want him dead before the sun sets tonight!"

The captain—and the soldiers under his command—quickly marched away to carry out their mission. It wasn't long before they were marching loudly onto Turally's property—drums rolling and trumpets blasting.

"Turally, you have three minutes to come out!" the captain of Zeus' army yelled, glancing around at his troops as the music silenced. Nothing happened.

"I said come out!" the captain yelled after another minute, the scowl on his face growing quickly as his fingers rubbed at the loose button on his jacket. The captain waited for the three minutes, but when there was still no response, he sent his strongest platoon in to bring the offender out.

"It's empty!" a soldier yelled as he stepped out of the house. "There's no one there!"

The captain raged for hours, and insisted they wait. He ignored the rumbling of his empty stomach as he stalked the camp, slapping the backs of the heads of any soldier brave enough to complain.

They waited for three days, but Turally never came. Gaia had already taken him to the cave to train Hercules.

FIVE

Despite his strength, Hercules was clumsy. The swing, miss, tumble-across-the-room sequence was beginning to take its toll on the wizened trainer.

"Listen, Hercules," Turally said at the beginning of the fourth day. "Fighting is less about strength and more about technique. Being able to throw your weight around will do you no good if you can't find enough coordination to hit your target. Let's try something." He maneuvered Hercules' limbs until his awkward student was standing on one leg. "I want you to practice like this," he said. "On one leg, to help you learn to balance."

Hercules didn't see how practicing on one leg would help his coordination, but followed the instructions anyway.

He spent three weeks straight learning to balance his weight on one leg. When he had finally managed it, Turally had Gaia turn part of the cave into a staircase, and for almost a year, all Hercules time was spent on conditioning.

It was the same schedule every day. As soon as he woke up, he would start his training—running up and down the stairs until he was blue in the face, doing more push-ups than he could count, and crunching through enough sit ups to make him quiver. There were jumping jacks and knee highs, weightlifts, and handstands. In time, Hercules was able to balance upside down on a single finger. He liked the workout routines, but was anxious to learn how to fight.

"Mr Turally, I can't do this anymore," Hercules told his trainer. The Hercules who stood before Turally, bouncing from one foot to the other, was no longer a scrawny, wimpy looking kid. He was big—gigantic even—and muscular. He stood eight feet tall and his golden hair gleamed as it ruffled in the breeze.

"Can't do what?" Turally asked. Turally knew what he was going to say. Hercules had been grumbling for months about wanting him to teach him to fight.

"I'm not learning any fighting skills; all I'm doing is this constant conditioning." Hercules tried to keep the whine from his voice.

"You have to be in shape if you want to fight, my boy," Turally replied.

"But I am in shape. I can run across the whole of Greece and back! You've seen me do it! My legs are strong, and I can throw rocks from Earth right up into space and hit the moon. Remember when Gaia told you that I had to stop doing that because it was creating craters? My arms are strong, and my stamina is excellent. Please! Let's get to the fighting! I'm begging you, please." Hercules pleaded with Turally, almost on his knees.

Turally cocked his head and pondered for a moment.

"Okay," he said. "We start in half an hour. Be back here on time, or you'll owe me seven thousand push-ups."

"Yes sir." Hercules was excited. He was finally going to start his fight training. Twenty minutes later, when Turally returned with training equipment, Hercules was there to greet him. Not keen on the idea of seven thousand push-ups, he had spent his break in the cave.

"Here," Turally said to Hercules as he handed him a scroll. "This scroll contains all the punches you'll be learning. They're numbered from one to sixteen." He crossed his arms and tapped his foot, making his expectations clear. He gave the young demigod a few minutes to think before he turned to leave. He paused at the entryway. "Do you have any questions?"

Hercules shook his head, but the confusion on his face made Turally chuckle. "As of right now, you are on an even tighter schedule. As well as your usual conditioning work, you'll have boxing, wrestling, and martial arts training. In the afternoons, you'll be expected to practice your swordsmanship, stick fighting, and knife fighting. Your stealth training will begin after dinner, followed by intensive archery and—"

"Won't it be dark then? How will I see?" Hercules asked, interrupting his instructor.

"You'll find a way," Turally responded, a glimmer of glee dancing behind his eyes.

What have I done? thought Hercules as he tried to imagine piercing targets in the dark. He hadn't even managed to picture an arrow before Turally spoke again.

"When you're finished with your lessons, you'll meditate until nine," he said. "Then you must go to bed and sleep so that you're well rested for the next day."

Hercules stood still, dumbfounded.

"Enjoy the rest of your day today and have that list memorized by practice tomorrow." Turally walked away.

The very next morning, Turally woke Hercules by pouring a bucket of spiders onto him. Hercules jumped out of bed, screeching and swinging his heavy arms wildly in an effort to remove the eight-legged offenders.

"What the hell was that for?" he yelled furiously. The look upon his face would have put fear in even Arachne herself. His glare burned like a great fire in the wilderness in the midst of the night. His eyebrows shot up and his voice became as cold as the icebergs surrounding Antarctica.

"What would you have done if I had gotten bitten and died?" he exclaimed, still searching his body for any remaining creatures.

Turally just laughed. "You must have no weaknesses, Hercules, because your enemies will find them and use them against you. All they need to do is throw a spider at you, and you'll be defeated! It just won't do.

"Are you forgetting that the mother spider still exists?"

Hercules flushed in shame, but nodded to acknowledge that he was very aware that Arachne was still around. Originally a mortal girl who was extremely good at weaving, Arachne had been turned into a giant, poisonous spider by Athena. Athena had stolen one of her art pieces and Arachne had spoken out against her, enraging the goddess.

"Nothing to be embarrassed about Hercules," the trainer amended. "We all have weaknesses and fears. Zeus himself was afraid of the dark! Gaia had to leave a few torches burning, otherwise Zeus would have a panic attack in the dead of night."

"I know how the story ends," said Hercules, downcast. "Zeus overcame his fears in order to become stronger."

"No, he did not!" Turally interrupted. "That is why you will be training in the dark. Your father is still afraid! He is scared of the shadows… and he is claustrophobic," he said with a sardonic smile. "These are weaknesses that you can use against him."

Hercules perked up a bit at hearing he had a chance at beating Zeus, natural love for his father outweighed by anger and excitement. The thought of beating any god by itself was intoxicating, but to the idea of beating the King of the Gods was incomparable. It was almost too much excitement for young Hercules.

SIX

Theofolees rushed home. Darkness had fallen early, and the cold had become unbearable. Black clouds were forming across the sky, obscuring the sun and reducing his vision to nearly nothing. He stepped into his house expecting to find his wife, Martha, building a fire, but the fire was already roaring and a strange woman sat in his personal chair. She was fair with shiny, umber brown hair that hung low against her waistline. Though she was neither beautiful nor ugly, her hazel-green eyes brimmed with a magical glow, and Theofolees couldn't help but to stare at her nude form.

The loud rattling of thunder broke Theofolees from his shock, reminding him why he had rushed home. He yelled for his wife.

"Martha!"

"Theofolees, what are you doing home so early?" Martha asked, caught completely off guard by her husband's early return from work. She rushed into their living room to usher the woman into another. As much as Martha wanted to help her, she wasn't going to leave a naked woman around her husband.

Their house, though not a mansion, was very nicely built. Hundreds of large boulders had been plastered together with sticky mud, and the windows were lined with gems and seashells.

Theofolees glanced at the sky through an open window. By the look of the clouds, Zeus was preparing to hit them with yet another lightning storm—he must be mad with the humans again. *Hopefully not* too *mad*, he thought. At times, when he was completely infuriated, Zeus' lightning storms would last for hours and kill many.

"Who was that naked woman, wrapped in my blanket?" Theofolees asked his wife.

"I found her lying naked on the road." Martha softly spoke, with a worried look on her face. "She has no memory of who she is or where she comes from. I think we should let her stay here until we can find out who she is," Martha finished as she stood in the doorway, blocking her husband's view of where the woman was dressing. Martha remained silent as she patiently waited for an answer. "Well," he began. "I don't think we have enough food, let alone enough room for another."

His voice wavered at Martha's pleading look, and he caved immediately. "Okay, okay," he said. "She can stay, but find her some clothes!"

"Thank you!" Martha cried, ignoring his gruff scowl as she leapt up to hug him.

During the storm, they hid under the wooden dining table as Theofolees and his wife always did. The lightning seemed to strike every few seconds and the sky lit up in brilliant flashes. The storm was over within minutes, but it left a firestorm of ruin in its wake. The trees on the right side of the house were burning and Theofolees had to rush over and over to the well, seventy-five feet west of the house. He ran for twenty minutes straight before he was able to extinguish the blazes, and even then, a grayish-white smoke billowed high into the night sky in torment. Ash rained from the heavens, and the entire surrounding forest smelled of smoke, despite the small size of the fire. Zeus' lightning burned hot.

Theofolees had half a mind to check on his neighbors, but Martha convinced him to stay home and help her get their guest settled in. It was an extremely long night for Theofolees. After the woman went to bed, she kept screaming in her sleep, yelling for Zeus to spare Poseidon and to imprison her instead. It seemed like hours passed before she stopped. Just as Theofolees finally began to drift off, there was a knock at the door.

"What now?" Theofolees swore as he got out of bed. "If it's not one thing, it's another." He opened the door and was shocked to see his neighbor's thirteen-year-old daughter standing there alone in the middle of the night, rosy cheeks glowing in the moonlight.

"Have you lost your mind, child?" Theofolees asked as he snatched her into his house, scanning the area carefully. "Don't you know that the monsters—thrust upon us by the gods to contain us—prowl these forests in the night, eating any humans they find out past the midnight hour?"

"I know," the girl said, tugging at loose strands of golden hair. "But I would have been in as much danger staying in my house as I was traveling alone this night. My family is dead and I am left alone. The skreltroy monster would have sensed their death and sensed my life force and would have come for me if I had stayed there! Don't you see?" The girl, whose name was Brittany, began to cry into her hands. At just thirteen she was tall for her age, but with her brown eyes wet with tears and her dark skin obscured by long brown hair, she looked every bit the child that she was.

"Ostopholee is dead?" Theofolees asked Brittany, his voice cracking even as he reached out to wrap an arm around her.

"Yes, my dad, my mom, my two sisters, and my Uncle Alexander are all dead. I am the only one that is left." Brittany's face scrunched up as she fought back more tears. She bit her lip, but she couldn't stop the tears from raining down her cheeks. She remembered her father telling her that when tears come from heartbreak, there is no fighting them. Heartbreak is an invisible force that wrenches the gut like nothing else in the world. She'd always imagined it to be like being dead and alive at the same time.

She'd been right.

"Oh my, please sit down, dear child! I am grieved to hear such terrible news… Martha—Martha, please come here quickly!" Theofolees yelled, only betraying his panic in the quiver of his fingers drawing soothing circles across the young girl's back.

Martha was quick to come. Her hair was unruly from sleep, and it fell from its tie as she almost broke into a run. She saw Brittany sitting on the living room chair and turned to her husband.

"Her entire family is dead," Theofolees said to Martha, giving a stiff nod towards Brittany. Unable to contain his grief any longer, Theofolees left them alone the moment his wife took their charge into her arms. He needed a moment to mourn his friend and neighbor.

Neither Theofolees nor Martha got any sleep that night.

The following morning, Theofolees took Brittany home to bury her family. After sending her away to grab her things, he dug shallow graves for each member, heaving at the workload and the smell. He paused as he heard Brittany's gasping sobs. She'd stepped outside just in time to watch him deposit what was left of her family into holes that should have been too small for humans: The skreltroy had definitely feasted on her family members through the night. Some were half eaten, while others were stripped entirely of flesh—eaten down to the bone. When at last she stopped crying, Theofolees suggested Brittany say a few words over her parents' final resting place.

"I will miss you as long as I live," she said through her sobs. "And I will always remember the good times but not the bad. You raised me to be a lady, and I will do my best to make you proud. I will finish school, and I will stay safe with Theofolees until the time I marry." She tried to continue but a fresh wave of grief clutched at her heart and brough with it more tears.

Theofolees held his goddaughter in an attempt to comfort her the best he could. As she cried, he too said his piece. The last words for his friends were few but sincere.

"Old friend, I swear to you that I will raise your daughter as my own. I will help her with her schooling, feed her, and clothe her as if she were mine. I am sad to see you gone, after all these years we have known each other, and I will miss you. I won't make any promises—except that I will do my best. Goodbye my old friend." With those words, Theofolees broke free from Brittany and threw the last bit of dirt on each grave.

"Let's go home," he said, taking her dirt-stained hand in his.

Seven

After the storm, Zeus retired to his chambers. Hera, unable to face her husband any longer, was in bed asleep. She hated everything about him; he was cruel and violent, and was unfaithful. Even worse than his scandalous escapades with human women was his affair with a goddess—The Harlot.

I won't be here much longer, Hera thought. *By morning, I will be gone from Mt Olympus, never to return*. She had it all worked out. She would hide among the humans, disguised as one of them, work a human job, and marry a human man. She would live without using her powers so that Zeus and his spies would not be able to find her.

As the night ended and morning took its place, Hera stole into the dawn and left Mt Olympus. When Zeus opened his eyes and turned over in his bed, as he did every morning, he found himself alone for the first time. At first, he assumed that Hera had gone out. When she didn't return by midday, Zeus tried to focus on her location but found that he could not find her. Hera had cast a spell to hide herself from him, and all the gods of Olympus. Zeus searched the castle in case she was there, hiding in one of the extra chambers or hidden rooms.

She was nowhere to be found.

Zeus had all his servants scour the Earth and the sky for her, but she had vanished. Zeus vowed that if he ever found her, he would inflict the worst torment he could imagine upon her for all eternity, and in his rage, he unleashed another mighty storm.

*****

For the first few days, Hera remained homeless, and refusing to use her powers, the once Queen of the Gods even resorted to stealing food. She searched diligently for a job, but it seemed that no business could afford to hire her. After a week of searching, Hera gave up on employment and went to hide in the mountains.

A goddess dying of starvation? Hera thought, when she could no longer ignore her stomach. Who has ever heard of such a thing?

But Hera would welcome death so long as it kept her from Zeus.

As she walked through the countryside, loneliness settled in and a dark depression threatened to overcome her. Enrobed in gray mountain fog and with a crushing weight on her shoulders, she began to long for the re-forming that marked a death of an immortal. After so much time to live, it was their greatest misunderstanding—the gods still assumed that a re-forming was much the same as dying.

"Life as a human is unbearable," Hera said to herself. "No wonder they're always crying and complaining."

Weak from hunger after days without food, the temptation to use just a little bit of power was overwhelming. Her stomach hurt, and she was sleeping more and more. Finally, after three days straight of not eating, Hera caved into her hunger and discomfort and conjured a fire out of thin air. Its crackling flames helped to keep her warm, and she was finally able to cook herself a hot meal. Hera knew that it was a risk, but also knew that it had become desperate—use her powers or die. Despite her melancholy, Hera was compelled by instinct to protect herself. After eating, she felt her strength begin to come back to her and the fog in her mind began to lift.

It became suddenly clear to her that, despite her personal dislike for the woman, she needed to find a way to warn Hercules' mother that Zeus was watching her. He had spies and soldiers who would take her prisoner on his command, in case Hercules ever surfaced. She had great value as a bargaining chip—there was little doubt that Hercules would surrender to protect his mother. Hera needed a way to warn her without being spotted.

After a much-needed night's rest, Hera set out on her trip back towards the town. It was the only way she would be able to find a way to accomplish her mission. It took her less than two days, and she hastily disguised herself once more—another dangerous use of magic. She took the form of a fly so that she would be able to fly around and not be noticed.

She flew at incredible speeds through the city of Thrace, towards the bungalow where Hercules' mother lived. As she flew, she scanned the area for spies but saw none. She knew that they wouldn't be out in the open; they would be hidden and in many forms. Some would be animals, and some would be disguised as trees or furniture. This made her plan extremely difficult.

How can I warn her without being caught? She wondered often, as she buzzed around and around the house, inspecting it for danger.

Everything seemed alright, but she was unsure of how to be certain without revealing herself. Poised on the windowsill, she sat in silent contemplation for a long time, and finally decided to leave a magical message on the blank piece of parchment she spotted on the kitchen table.

Hera waited for hours after she retreated, maintaining a good distance from the home and keeping watch with the perfect vision bestowed upon her as a goddess. She first grew frustrated, but when darkness began to fall and Hercules' mom still had not returned, the frustration turned to worry.

"Where could she be?" Hera mumbled to herself. Hera had initially made it no secret that she hated Hercules and his mother, but as time went on and her resentment of Zeus turned to anger, she had been forced to change her mind. Zeus had manipulated the woman—posing as her human husband—and it was no one's fault but his that a child was conceived.

Hera sent apologetic gifts over the years, to try and atone for all the times she tried to kill them both in jealousy, but they were unforgiving. She knew then, in her heart, that Hercules' mother hadn't come because she was afraid of walking into a trap. In a strange act of kindness, she decided there and then that she would take her fly form and keep watch over the house and its occupant.

She would keep them safe.

EIGHT

Turally had a hard time training Hercules, but on the morning of his three-hundred-and-seventieth day, he smiled. He picked up the pieces of the training plan he'd arranged and re-arranged a hundred times and tossed them into the open fire sparking in the back corner of the cave.

"We've really had to wing it, haven't we?" he asked Hercules. "

"Yeah—but..." Hercules was unsure. "Is everything okay?" he asked, wondering if Turally was disappointed in him.

"Everything is perfect," Turally answered. "You see my boy, every fighter I have trained, I have trained differently. With you—it took me a while to see, but I understood. Because of your dyslexia, it can take you longer than others to learn new things…For a while I despaired. I see it now, though—it took you longer, but once you get it, you got it… and boy, have you got it!"

Hercules smiled. It was the first time Turally had ever complimented him. He knew he wasn't perfect, but he'd practiced his coordination and was ready to start with more—with the archery and sword fighting that he'd been forbidden to do until now.

That night, Hercules slept well. His bed was made of rock with silver-fir wood bundled on top of it, and covered with blankets woven by Gaia. Hercules was focused on the compliment, "Once I got it, I got it." Hercules said to himself out loud as he fell asleep.

Gaia watched him from in her Earthly state, not revealing herself, but quite happy that Hercules was enjoying his training. Gaia knew that things would not always be so pleasant for him, so she stayed, only her eyes lingering in the walls of the room, watching her grandson and enjoying the smile on his face.

Truthfully, Gaia didn't see how Hercules would make it past Arachne, let alone Zeus. Hercules was stronger, but he would still have his hands full against Zeus and his wicked lightning bolts. Gaia wanted to interfere and help Hercules herself, but Zeus' power had surpassed even hers, and she knew she could not. She couldn't help but sigh as she watched her grandson mutter in his sleep. It was a big ask for a boy.

*****

Zeus sent soldiers searching in every town to look for Hercules and Hera. His anger boiled over, and paranoia and betrayal tore at his mind. He began to watch the other gods constantly, accusing them of plotting his destruction. After Zeus attacked Hermes, gravely injuring him, things on Mt Olympus became unbearable. Fierce with rage about Hera leaving him in order to frolic about with Hercules, Zeus was prone to random fits of violence, throwing out lightning bolts that lit up the skies and scorched slashes in the ground.

Many of the gods of Greece abandoned Zeus and Mt Olympus. Some started their own sects, while others just went off and disappeared among the humans.

But Zeus was not done.

Those who left Olympus to set up kingdoms found themselves at war with the mighty king. Even though he was alone with only his army of soldiers to back him up, he defeated the new kingdoms one-by-one, causing the other gods to flee the lands.

NINE

When Athena woke the next morning, Martha and Theofolees were waiting in the living room for her, questions written in the lines of their faces.

"My dear," Martha began, gesturing for Athena to sit. "I want you to think about your past—try to remember *anything*… Last night you were screaming—screaming *Zeus* in your sleep, telling him to imprison you instead of Poseidon. Do you remember what your dream was about?"

Athena flushed and dropped her gaze to the ground.

"I wish I could," she started. "But I don't remember having a dream. I recognize the name, though—Zeus. I don't know why, but I feel like it should mean something to me."

"It should," Theofolees cut in. "He is the God of Lightning and the Head of the Gods."

"Oh, no, that's… that's wrong. That's what he wants you humans to think!" Athena interrupted automatically, her head snapping up as she rose to her feet. "None of us are really gods, we're angels—well, the offspring of angels…

"The Creator crowned Lucifer King of the Earth. It was… Lucifer became greedy for power. What he'd been given—it wasn't enough. He wanted to *be* God—to take over from The Creator. He led a revolt and ultimately fought a war *against* The Creator in an attempt to rule the universe. Earth would never be enough. But he failed. Lucifer and all who followed him lost, and were banished from heaven and confined to Earth." Athena gasped and clapped her shaky hands to her mouth, but there was no way to put the secrets she'd revealed back inside.

Theofolees and Martha stood speechless at the blasphemy spewing from the woman with no memory, and Brittany was staring as she laughed silently behind them.

Athena tried to stop but the words kept on coming. "Lucifer was cast into a bottomless pit for a thousand years—that was his punishment for leading the charge. It's almost up and… Zeus is no god, don't you worry… though he does wish he was." She couldn't help a tiny chuckle as she finished.

"Theofolees!" Martha gasped. "Theofolees!" She grabbed her husband's right arm suddenly and began to forcefully pull him into their room, seeking privacy.

"What are you doing?" Theofolees yelled, startled by his wife's sudden fervor. "I don't appreciate the way you've been treating me since that woman came along! You've been cutting off my sentences… dragging me around… demanding things of me—what the hell are you smiling at?"

Martha waited patiently, but could not hide her excited laughter.

Theofolees looked livid, but Martha placed her hand on his, urging him to relax.

"Do you know who that is?" she asked.

"Of course not. *She* doesn't even know who she is! That's what we've been trying to figure out, remember?" Theofolees frowned, confused, as Martha started to laugh even harder, shaking her head.

"Go have a look at the back of her neck and come straight back."

"You want me to do what?" Theofolees eyed his wife as if she were mad. "No! She'll think me strange."

Martha sighed and shook her head. "I'll distract her, so she doesn't notice. Just walk right on past and take a look at her neck."

Theofolees reluctantly agreed, and when Athena turned enough for him to see, he grasped his chest against the sudden stab, drawing in a deep breath. On the back of her neck was none other than the signet of the Goddess Athena. It was right there in front of him: a spear, a distaff, and a shield made out of goatskin with the head of Medusa attached to it. It was mesmerizing—so mesmerizing, in fact, that Theofolees jumped in fright when an ethereal voice settled upon them.

"She has to go now," the detached voice said. "Arachne, Athena's most vicious enemy, is on her way here. You all must go, for she will kill anyone she finds." The speaker materialized from a shimmer before them. "I come to protect you, though I won't take any of you by force, except the Goddess Athena."

"Who are you?" Martha asked as she trembled on the ground, bowing her head. Her skin rippled and she felt the weight in the air evaporate—she was surely in the presence of a real god.

"I am Gaia, mother of many of the gods, or as Athena has revealed, many of the angels."

"Wow," Martha whispered to herself.

"Gaia?" Theofolees asked. "Gaia… but… who is Lucifer?" his curiosity got the better of him and he sat down in a chair by the table, awaiting answers to his questions.

"Never you mind," Gaia snapped. "You're not supposed to know about us." Her voice was grating even as it tinkled over them; it was like white-hot knives slicing through flesh and lava coursing through veins all at once.

"I'm upset at Athena for having such loose lips," she continued. "I'm shocked at the depth of her knowledge."

"It's amazing!" Brittany exclaimed, having found her voice again quickly. "She's had her memory erased, but she still remembers! Without any help!"

"That isn't what I meant, child," Gaia rumbled. "She wasn't alive for the battle and we never speak of it, so how could she know?"

"Well, she is wisdom, isn't she?" Theofolees shook himself off and stared at Gaia. "If any of the gods could work it out, it would be the Goddess of Wisdom."

"Those are wise words for a human." Gaia complimented Theofolees. "You must decide what to do now. Arachne is no more than a day's journey away."

It wasn't much of a decision: a huge spider set on revenge or Gaia—who might even protect them.

"We will go with you," Theofolees declared without hesitation. He would rather take his chances with Gaia than be eaten alive by Arachne. Martha looked at Theofolees with concern twisting her smile, but she held her tongue. She knew she needed to trust her husband. Nothing was said and there was no magical swirl, but somehow, their house vanished. It was replaced immediately with an unfamiliar earthen space with stone walls and dirt beneath their feet.

"I created this space for Hercules to train in," Gaia said by way of explanation. "I call it Sparta, which in the Language of the Gods' means *fight to the death*."

"I have a question," Theofolees spoke up at last. The silence that had been stretched between them long after Gaia's tour was complete was finally broken. "If you aren't really gods but fallen angels, would it be offensive if we called you something like Gaia the Angel, or would you rather us still say Goddess Gaia?"

"Neither!" Gaia hissed, clearly agitated by Theofolees' bold assumptions. "You will call me only Gaia, as I have been called for millennia. For your safety, it's best that you forget the things you've heard today regarding our past. Sometimes it's safer to know nothing." Gaia's words were gentle, but carried an unmistakable threat. "Athena has shared too much in her crippled state. The memory loss that Zeus has cursed her with has made her a danger to us. I will have to begin undoing it immediately, though it will take time—months… maybe even years. But we need Athena at her full power and strength, with memory intact if we are going to beat Zeus. I will do whatever it takes."

They waited for Gaia to continue—for more cryptic information—but in the silence that followed her tirade, the Mother of Angels shimmered into nothingness once more.

"This is crazy," Martha finally spoke out after what seemed like an eternal silence.

"I know," Brittany said. "Gaia actually talked to us, and we've made friends with the Goddess Athena—she's my favorite by the way."

Athena smiled at the young girl's tenacity.

"I wouldn't put it that way," Theofolees said, eyeing the goddess warily. "When she remembers herself, she is more likely to kill us than to thank us."

"Either way, I can't wait to tell my friends about this!" Brittany squirmed as her face split into a wide grin. She paid little attention to Theofolees' words, causing him to scowl and shake his head.

“I know,” Martha said to Brittany, pacing the length of the cave. “This is exciting!”

Theofolees looked outraged that his wife was encouraging the younger girl and, in long, deliberate steps, he made his towards them.

“However,” Martha continued, wringing her hands for a moment and ignoring her husband’s glare. “I’m really referring to this crazy information about the gods, not a friendship with Athena—no offense,” she grimaced slightly, but the goddess did not appear upset. “Fallen angels! What if they’ve tricked us, just to give them more power; add strength for the next battle with The Creator?”

Theofolees snarled and ran a hand through his hair in exasperation. “Gaia said to forget about it—that it’s dangerous to know! And look, she’s right! You’re already talking about battles! I demand we leave it alone! Both of you—stop! Before you get us all killed.” Theofolees’ roar quieted into a whisper.

Ten

Turally and Hercules rushed into the cave room, swords drawn and ready to fight any monster or beast that Zeus sent their way. They spun around in shock and were struck almost dumb by what they saw. The space was occupied with two women, a small girl, and a gruff looking man.

"How did you get in here?" Turally said, so fiercely that even Hercules cowered just a little.

Martha stepped forward. "Gaia brought us here," she said, the edge in her voice betraying her nerves. "You see, we have been taking care of the Goddess Athena."

Although Hercules remained wary, Turally only scoffed. "You humans have been taking care of Athena?" He could barely keep himself from laughing. "And where is the goddess if you have been taking care of her, hmm?

How is it even possible—humans taking care of a powerful goddess? I don't believe it." Turally folded his arms across his chest, expecting the humans to have no answer.

Theofolees flung an arm out to protect his group as he spoke up first. "Well, first off, your Goddess Athena is right here." He was astounded at the conceit of the swordsman when he could not even see what was in front of him.

He continued, even as Turally raised his hand to speak. "Zeus erased her memory and cast her down to the Earth. My wife found her lying outside our house during one of his lightning storms."

Turally looked angered and taken aback but allowed Theofolees to carry on. "They are not gods. We found out from Athena, and even Gaia admitted it! They are angels! Fallen from heaven! They fought against God and were cast down here to Earth."

Turally's eyes got very wide. "You humans should not know such things," he said, a growl twisting his words into anger.

"That's what I've been trying to tell you! We know because of Athena! Look at the mark on her back. It's her signet, and the only people who bear the real signets are the gods themselves…"

"The gods and their offspring," Turally interrupted. "That is impressive, but still, it does not prove anything."

"It is," Gaia said, from somewhere they could not see. "And you, Theofolees! I told you to forget what you have heard because if anyone overhears you, you will wish you were never born!" The agitation in her voice grew until it felt like nails scraping skin and ice-cold water on teeth. "Tartarus heard you and wanted me to take you to him! I only asked him to wait because I need you for a mission! Consider yourself extremely lucky."

"A mission?" Theofolees repeated, the upward inflection in his voice marking him as cowardly.

"Wait a minute—" Hercules spoke for the first time. "Why have I been doing all this training if you're giving the first mission that comes up to someone else?"

Gaia materialized before them to comfort her grandson, who was clearly put out. "Hercules," she said. "Your time will come. You are not training for small missions, but to fight Zeus! We don't need him getting a hold of you before you are able to defeat him."

Hercules scowled, throwing the humans a vicious glare, but inside he was scared to death. He knew no matter how much training he went through, the battle against his father would be the fight of his life; the fight *for* his life.

Gaia refused to be sidetracked, and stepped forward to wrap boney fingers around Theofolees' trembling wrist. "Your job is not as life-threatening as you think, human. Calm yourself." Her words were soothing but her grip was firm. "All I need is for you to spend some time in the town—searching. You see, Hera has fled from Zeus, and is hiding there somewhere, in disguise. I can't sense her. It is… unusual. All you need to do is find what you do not recognize. She could be in any disguise; even look at the animals. An animal acting strangely could be Hera."

Theofolees was entranced by her stare but could not meet her eyes. She stepped closer, so that he could feel her breath against his face, and with one thin finger, forced him to look at her. “This is very important, human. Do not let anyone know what you are doing, because Zeus is paying close attention to everything now—he is trying to find Hera *and* Hercules.”

She left him in stunned silence when she turned to Turally. “We have a problem,” she said. “I know you need to train Hercules with spiders to prevent Zeus using them against him, but Arachne is in communication with him, and you know the spiders will report to her. I have destroyed all of your spiders, as they have already alerted Arachne to Athena’s presence. Without them, she will not be able to find her location, so she will be safe here now. I need to work on her memory, and on returning her to goddess form. Theofolees will continue my search for Hera.”

*****

Theofolees walked around town, not quite sure how to find Hera when Gaia and Zeus themselves were unable to. Concerned that he would be caught talking to animals, he focused on them for only a short time. As he searched, the sun mounted higher and higher, and he began to feel the draining heat quickly. He retreated to the hills, resting in the shade beneath a sprawling fig tree. He didn’t know if he was being watched by Gaia or not, but the break was much needed—he was exhausted.

"If I nap now, I can search later tonight when it's cooler and the streets are less crowded, and it will be easier to find Hera," Theofolees said out loud—in case Gaia was listening in on him.

"So, you seek Hera, do you?" came the sharp voice of a woman sitting up in the tree. Her clothes were filthy and shredded, exposing her concave stomach and dirty skin, and the sour, coppery smell of homeless need wafted from her.

"I do," Theofolees responded. "I'd ask you if you knew where she was, but I don't feel like going on any crazy wild goose chases at the present."

"Oh, I see." The woman swung from a creaking branch to face Theofolees. "Well, do you mind if I ask why you are looking for her?"

"It's not for me," he said slowly. "I'm looking on behalf of Gaia. And Hercules and Athena I suppose. The story is pretty crazy—even for people like you."

"Why would Gaia and Hercules be looking for me? And how did they find Athena?"

Theofolees, staring into the distance and fiddling with his shirt buttons, only half heard what she said so he answered without thought.

"Well, Athena was with me when Gaia appeared. We found Athena lying naked outside our house and, of course, we had no idea at the time who she was. The minute we

figured it out and said her name, Gaia appeared and took us all to a secret cave. She claimed that Arachne was on her way to our house to kill Athena—and us."

Theofolees stopped speaking and looked at the woman, awaiting her reaction. He was sure she would think him insane, but she looked as though she was taking it all in and analyzing the information she had just received.

Without so much as a warning, she changed her appearance right before his eyes.

She was beautiful.

Her long, dark hair cascaded to her waist, and her cheeks blushed brilliant pink. The lightning blue of her eyes sparkled like stars in the night, lighting her curvaceous figure with youth.

Hera.

"I am Queen Hera, the one you seek," she said, power radiating from her for a moment before she disappeared back into the skin of an urchin girl.

"Why the transformation?" Theofolees asked.

"Because Zeus searches for me day and night, and even in that brief second, the Lord of the Sky almost locked on my position. Take me to Gaia at once."

Theofolees looked taken aback at the demand. He wanted to say that a 'please' would be nice, but Hera's wrath was famous throughout Greece.

ELEVEN

Hercules stood in the doorway of the cave, enjoying the large raindrops as they trickled down the back of his neck on the warm day. Thunder sounded in the background and lightning was surely on its way. As the son of Zeus, Hercules had a natural love of storms, and they helped him to process the tumultuous thoughts in his head. Over and over he imagined the coming battle. Sometimes he won and sometimes he lost.

He dared not even imagine fighting Arachne, since he knew there was no way for him to beat her. She was faster than a cheetah and as strong as Zeus, and her giant pincers could pierce through a bronze shield. Her sticky web was a prison, and just one touch would immobilize her target so that they were unable to move—forced to wait anxiously for her to descend into a blood-sucking attack.

Athena settled beside him, a soothing hand resting upon his shoulder. "You are worried. I can see the battles taking place in your eyes. No hero's journey is an easy one, Hercules," she said. "But they all feel fear. The only difference is the heroes do whatever it takes to succeed, while the dead give up. I have a feeling that you will never get the opportunity to face Zeus at all..."

"Why do you say that?" Hercules thought she was indicating that Arachne would kill him first.

"The one-hundred-and-twenty-years Gabriel warned us about is at hand. Tomorrow will be exactly one-hundred-and-twenty-years from the day that The Creator said he would put an end to man—and to us angels for a time. If we angels don't unite, we will all be destroyed."

"When you say The Creator, do you mean Zeus?"

"No." Athena shook her head. "I refer to a higher power than any there has ever been—to the one that created Gaia, Oceanus and every angel and thing in existence…"

Hercules starred, too stunned to say anything. He felt as though he were trapped in a box with thousands of angry, poisonous spiders.

"So, the gods aren't the most powerful beings?"

"They are not even gods, but the angels who were banished from heaven after the war and cast down to Earth."

"Well, if the Greek gods are the outcast angels, wouldn't that make you guys the villains in this story?" Hercules asked.

"Yes, yes, I guess it would," Athena said, smiling.

"How do you remember all of that with your memory gone?" Hercules asked, his eyes were scrunched up as he attempted to understand all that had been said.

Gaia had restored Athena's memories before she talked with Hercules, and she remembered everything. Before Hercules could speak again, she was gone. Athena, with all of her memories back, knew it was time to leave. Nobody knew where she went, for she kept well hidden.

TWELVE

Zeus, once again, stood before the three Sister Fates. They had summoned him. Never in times past had the Sister Fates summoned Zeus. It rather made him a bit on edge about what kind of news could cause them to gift him a prophecy.

"Zeus, sit," the ugliest and oldest of the Three Fates instructed, voice firm.

"I'd rather stand," he said, jittery despite himself.

"So be it."

The Youngest Sister held the knowing eye and Zeus could feel it boring through him. "Three weeks from now the war begins…" she said. "Though it may take time, death reaches everyone—for death is the price of sin…

Angels on high versus angels below… From the Kings of the Earth, The Father soon retakes control."

Zeus' eyes widened. He started to speak, but the Sister wasn't done.

"Who can be trusted?" she continued, sending a shiver of icy thought through the air. "Neither Greek god nor their sons and daughters… Neither can any trust in man… To win this fight—for all to survive—they must fight this war hand in hand…

"Through floods, one shall be destroyed. This is not the finale. In just a short time, one shall rise, one shall die, and one shall be in chains. There will be wars in other places—all the heavens silent, as the next chapter is being written, day by day, page-by-page. One laughs as they find pleasure in hearing the shrill sounds of their enemies shrieking in pain. The war will last for ages, and is destined to soon begin. It will be a long, rugged, seemingly never-ending battle, fought on both sides to one's bitter end. The Gods of the Earth unite to defeat Michael and his angels in a war where there shall be no draw. One side has to lose while the other side chants victory for us all."

Zeus sat down, as The Sisters knew he would.

"What does this prophecy mean?" he asked in frustration. "Are Michael and his army going to attack us in three months?"

"It is forbidden for us to interfere. We have told you what we were told to tell you, and we can say no more," the Middle Sister said. With that, the three Sister Fates disappeared into the darkness and were gone, leaving Zeus with only questions. He grew bitter and angry, imagination running wild and drawing vivid paintings in his head.

They want my throne, do they? he thought. *Well, good luck*. Zeus returned to Olympus, where he now reigned alone, preparing for battle with Michael. He rubbed his temples and sighed. He had never met Michael—only read about him in scrolls. He had transformed those scrolls into the *Forbidden Book*, that no humans or demigods could read without severe consequences.

Zeus' thoughts were interrupted when Tartarus moved, and a presence shifted in the atmosphere. *But it couldn't be*, Zeus thought. His face tensed as his eyebrows raised, causing three lines to form across his forehead. *Ouranos is dead*. He had been slain by Kronos long before Zeus began his existence, so how come he felt his presence?

THIRTEEN

On Earth, Gaia and Hera also felt Tartarus move, and then felt the presence of Ouranos. Gaia feared what he might do, as there was no way he would not be seeking revenge. Gaia called to Zeus from Earth, but Zeus did not answer. Gaia worried for her son who, in his hatred and hope to be rid of her, was willing to risk his own safety. She shook her head, knowing she was unable to reach him.

"We need to free Hades and Poseidon from their prison," Hera said, breaking the tension immediately. Gaia was startled by Hera's arrival, but grateful for the timely interruption.

"Well Hera, I see Theofolees has succeeded," Gaia said. "And exactly how do we find them, do you think?"

Hera smiled wryly, a glimmer of gold appearing between her fingers. "This gold pen is the key that unlocks their prison, but we have two problems," she said. "One: only Zeus or one off his offspring can open it, and two: the doorway into the prison is in Poseidon's element. He who sets them free must be a child of Zeus, and able to survive under water."

"Well, we have a son of Zeus—" Gaia began.

"Who?" Hera looked astounded at the thought of Zeus having a child unknown to her.

"Hercules."

"Hercules is here?" Hera asked, eyes wide and brow deeply furrowed.

"Indeed," Gaia responded. "He's been here since I found him wandering in the woods."

"No." Hera shook her head, stepping away from Gaia. "We cannot send him alone. Zeus is looking for him—he wants him dead!"

Gaia released a long breath, running withered fingers over the bridge of her nose. "Well, then we must summon the other gods to see who can accompany him on this mission. If Hercules does not go, there will be dire consequences. The Creator plans to destroy man—and me in the process."

"What do you mean?" Hera asked.

"The Creator sent an angel—one of those still loyal to him—named Gabriel to Earth. Gabriel was sent to tell a man named Noah that he is going to flood the world.

Noah is building an ark—he's telling everyone that God is going to flood the Earth."

Hera closed her eyes in silent contemplation. "And what about us?" she asked after a moment.

"He didn't say, but I'm sure none will go unpunished."

"Is it… just us in Greece and Rome? Surely it's not everyone?" Hera leaned back against the wall of the cave, shocked by the vengeful revelation.

"I don't know," said Gaia. "But right now, the threat is on me, so let us focus and start preparing for what is to come. Ouranos is angry—we allowed him to die with Kronos… he will flood the Earth for The Creator happily." A wave of sadness shuttered her face. "Gabriel gave Noah a timeframe… It is short. We have maybe two weeks until the flooding begins."

"That's not a lot of time," Hera said, shuffling her feet and peering out of the cave's entrance.

"No, it is not. I know it's sudden, but I'll need you to gather the gods so that I may continue to prepare Hercules for his mission."

"Of course," Hera said with a sharp nod. Without another word, she disappeared into thin air and was gone.

Gaia, in human form, materialized next to Hercules during his archery lesson. "Nice shot," she said, approval in her smile. "I see you are quite the warrior now."

Hercules was no longer nerdy and wimpy, but strong and cocky. The difference that a little training had made to his personality was remarkable.

"Oh, that's nothing Grandma," Hercules said, giving Gaia a sideways glance and a head nod to let her know he was about to do something impressive.

Hercules took an apple from his pouch and threw it as hard as he could. He quickly retrieved an arrow from his archer's bag, pulled the bowstring back to near breaking point, and released. The arrow pierced the apple just before the it hit the gravitational field, forcing it into outer space.

The apple never re-entered the atmosphere.

"Very impressive." Gaia smiled. "Even Apollo isn't that good, and he is the best at archery—or he was the best."

"What's going on?" Hercules asked. He didn't know why she had come but in all the time he had been there practicing she had never interrupted his training.

"Well," Gaia began. "I know how badly you wanted a mission, and you know how hard I have been trying to keep you away from one."

"Yeah, I sure do." Hercules scowled, his voice trailing in wistful irritation. "Well, your time has come," Gaia said. "I have a treacherous mission for you. Your journey will be a tough one. You will face many trials, but you must complete it if we are to survive."

"What is it?" Hercules asked. He was curious, excited, scared. His voice quavered but its booming, deep bass sound leant him strength in his fear.

"We require you to free Poseidon and Hades," Gaia said, her voice leaving no room for reproach. Grandma or not, she was not to be argued with.

"Me?" Hercules asked, pointing to himself as if Gaia could have been talking to someone else, even though he was the only one present.

"Yes, you. You are the only known living demigod son of Zeus, and Zeus designed their prison so that only he or one of his demigod children could open it."

Hercules grinned. The knowledge that his mission didn't involve a giant spider was relieving. His thoughts raced as he imagined himself victorious. There would be statues made in his honor—feasts thrown! He was interrupted by the unexpected appearance of his stepmother.

"Gaia, you doom us all. You send this boy on a suicide mission, unsure if he is capable of bearing such a burden."

"Trust me," Gaia said, the corners of her eyes crinkling—knowing. "He is well trained."

Hera was not convinced. "Prove it," she said. "We can save him from death in a test, but we cannot interfere with any serious missions!"

Hercules couldn't decide whether Hera was trying to help him or make him look bad. She did always hate him and his mother. However, he was encouraged to learn that they could save him from a test.

Gaia sighed and reluctantly told Hera about the practice mission she had had Hercules complete. She called it The Twelve Labors, and he had faced an unbeatable lion and the great Atlas himself. When she let it slip that, despite his proficiency in the fighting and physical strength aspects, she had been forced to cheat and assist him with the three labors requiring wit, Hera interrupted. She was not impressed at all.

"He will not survive without your help on a mission, and you can't help him—lest you doom it! You already know this Gaia."

"I know the rule." Gaia snapped. "But we have no choice—we have limited time." She strode the length of the cave and back, muttering to herself. "He needs companions… the rule of thumb is that demigods should always travel in threes: in the past, it has always been their lucky number—"

"Athena has a daughter." Hera interrupted, resting a hand on Gaia's arm. "Poseidon has a child as well—a son, I think it is."

"The best way to find out will be to ask all the gods to present their children. Without their help, we'll use up the whole two weeks searching for them."

Gaia and Hera gathered the gods together for a meeting. So many attended that Gaia had to enhance the cave so everyone could fit.

"Time is short." She explained the situation as quickly as she could, skipping formalities in favor of information. I have put forth a mission for Hercules… As the son of Zeus, he is the only one who can release Poseidon and Hades from their prison! He needs help! We cannot interfere with a mission, but our children can—we need to know about your children. We wish to send a team of three demigods to free the brothers—"

"On a mission like this, I say we send six to double the chances of victory!" Aries shouted. "Let us be smart on this one. If The Creator beat our powerful ancestors, I'm not willing to bet on low numbers."

The cave swelled with hopeful pride as almost everyone raised their hands. They all hoped their children would be chosen. Gaia shook her head, chuckling softly as she scoped the room. "I should have known," she said.

Hera laughed. "Well, we have a lot to choose from."

"Not really," Gaia said. "We need one more. We have Poseidon's son, Athena's daughter, Hades' daughter, and Aries' son. Including Hercules, that makes five—not six."

Hera turned to those remaining. "Hephaestus, can your children use fire?"

"No." He sighed and shook his head.

"Janus, do your children have any powers?"

"Yes," Janus replied. "They can turn beings to dust by looking into their eyes, and they can read the stars and know the future." Janus puffed his chest up and looked around.

"Girls or boys?" Aphrodite asked.

"A girl," Janus replied.

"Too dangerous on a mission with boys of their age. We have enough girls already," Hera said, her eyes bright with mirth.

"I have a son." Aeolus, the Greek God of the Winds spoke up. "His powers are the same as mine—he can control the winds; his power is very strong."

Gaia cocked her head and eyed him for a moment. "It is settled then. We have our six," she said. "Now we must gather them. Aeolus, get your son! Hera, can I trust you to gather some without scaring them to death? We know how much you hate demigods."

Hera, tamed by the weight of the mission, shrugged. "Of course. You can count on me. I want to see this mission succeed just as much as anyone else. For a short time, I can put my hate for demigods away."

"Good then," Gaia said. "Find Athena's daughter. Aries, your son. I'll fetch Poseidon's and Hades' youngsters myself. Don't waste time convincing them. Find them and teleport them here immediately. We'll meet here soon." She disappeared from the room, followed by Aries and Aeolus. Hera was the last to leave.

In less than an hour, they were back in the cave and staring down a group of confused demigods.

"What's going on?" one of them asked. "Why have you brought me here? Let me guess, you need something, don't you? Never pay us any attention unless you need something from us."

"I've been calling on my father for months and he hasn't answered me. Now that he's in need, he wants to talk." Poseidon's son agreed with the first speaker, shaking his head in disgust. It took no more than a few seconds for him to realize Poseidon wasn't there.

"Where is he?" he asked.

"Before we answer your questions, mouthy son of Poseidon—" Gaia spoke with room-shaking force. "—

All of you introduce yourselves and say who your godly parent is, starting with you, son of Poseidon."

"I am Jeffrey, and I am the son of Poseidon." Jeffrey's skin was a glistening black that matched his short hair. "I am twenty years old." Despite his imposing figure and jaguar skin outfit, Jeffrey's voice was quiet—he was a loner, and not comfortable with the assembly.

"I am Athena's daughter, and my name is…" the girl hesitated and blushed as she scanned the crowd. She had never seen the gods before, and here, they were standing right in front of her. "Um, my name is Savannah, and I am twenty-one years old." She was tall and trim, and her brown eyes overflowed with wisdom and kindness. She turned to the girl beside her, eager to remove the focus from her.

"I am Kikilliana," she said, understanding. "My father is Hades, and I haven't heard from him in months either. I've searched the underworld, but he's not there." Her dark brown hair and light brown skin struck a stunning picture, matched only by her presence. Unlike the others, she spent a lot of time with her father, learning how to run the underworld in his absence. She'd been able to keep Zeus' soldiers from taking it while Hades had been missing. "I'm nineteen," she added, before the boy to her right cleared his throat and rested a comforting hand on her back, dwarfing her and showing his strength.

"I am the only living son of Aries, and my name is Gemini," he said. "I am honored to stand here before the gods." He spoke with humility and confidence, lacing a hand through his jet-black hair to keep it from flopping into his large, dark eyes. "I'm eighteen years old, and I'm developing a sword fighting style I've named *Samurai*," he said. "I spend my days teaching it to my Earthly family."

The room was quiet—awed by the young man. Gaia pointed to Hercules.

"I am Hercules," he said. "I am the only living son of Zeus. I am twenty years old." Hercules stood tall and it became evident how hard he'd been training. Even Gemini looked slight beside him. He smiled, allowing his enthusiasm to drift amongst them.

"I am the son of Aeolus," the smallest of them said, as Gaia pointed to him. After stating his father's name he was quiet and motionless for a moment.

"What is your name, and how old are you?" Gaia asked, with a withering stare.

"My name is Xavier, and I am eleven years old."

Gaia looked at the boy with pity.

"Aeolus, this is only a child," she scolded. "We cannot send him on such a dangerous mission."

"Only a child you say?" Aeolus was insulted. "Son, make this cave and mountain fly." Xavier looked nervous but with a flick of his hand and a deafening rumble, the entire mountain rose one hundred feet above the ground.

"Okay son, now put us back down." The mountain slowly floated down, landing on its foundations without so much as a puff of dust.

"Yes, he is only eleven," Aeolus said before patting his son firmly on the back. "But he's very powerful. I have been secretly training him since he was three."

"As you wish." Gaia was impressed with the boy. "He will do," she said.

"Wait! We have one more," Aphrodite yelled from the back of the room.

Aphrodite had gone off on a short mission of her own and had returned with her only daughter.

"What is this?" Gaia asked, her annoyance overcome with curiosity. She didn't know Aphrodite had a daughter.

"This is my daughter, Vanessa. She is thirteen and has great powers."

"Okay, let's see them then," Aries said, doubting the girl was as powerful as his son.

Aries watched on, but nothing happened. "I'm waiting." He tapped his foot rhythmically against the floor.

Everyone in the room gasped, eyes wide in awe as they stared at the place where Aries stood.

"What are you all looking at?" he demanded. What has she done?

The next second, everyone in the room disappeared. "Amazing!" Voices began to shout from what appeared to be an empty space. They reappeared before they could work out what Aphrodite's daughter had done.

"Very nice," Gaia said.

"That is nothing. Watch this." Aphrodite gestured toward her daughter.

Vanessa stepped forward and focused her eyes on Aries. She slowly batted her lashes at him three times. It appeared that nothing happened, but then Vanessa spoke.

"Fall in love with me," she whispered.

Aries rushed to her, bowing at her feet in rapture, with no hesitation.

"I love you!" he cried. "Be my wife! I'll do anything, just tell me what."

A bubble of raucous laughter ricocheted around the cave walls.

"Shut up!" Aries yelled, "I'll fight the lot of you. Why are you staring at her like that?" Aries yelled to Hercules.

Hercules looked around and then pointed at himself.

"Me?" Hercules asked in a confused voice.

"Yes, you. I shall kill you in combat."

"No, you won't." Vanessa said.

Aries stopped in his tracks. He had been walking towards Hercules with his sword drawn. Instead, his eyes sought Vanessa and his limbs carried him towards her of their own accord.

"You will give me your sword and slap yourself for such foolishness," she instructed.

Shockingly Aries obeyed. He walked up to Vanessa, handed her the sword, and slapped himself—hard.

"That is enough," Gaia barked. Vanessa batted her lashes slowly at Aries three more times and he came back to himself, not remembering a thing that he did while she was controlling him.

"How did you get my sword?" he yelled, snatching it back from the girl and sheathing it safely at his side. He didn't know what happened, but he knew he didn't like it.

"Oh, she'll do nicely. I don't think we need to worry about her with the boys," Hera said, laughing hysterically. Hera had never liked Aries.

"I want to see what powers the others have," Hermes said. "The two I have seen were more than impressive. Give us a show!"

"You." Hera pointed to Savannah. "What is yours?"

"Her power is quite simple, really," Gaia said. "All wise thoughts come from wisdom, correct?"

"This is true," the minor goddess, Klione, agreed.

"Savannah can read the thoughts of whomever she wants, whether the thought is wise or foolish, including in battle. She knows everything her opponent is about to do, even before the thoughts reach their minds. If she is lost, she can focus on the path and retrace the steps of everyone who took it before her, learning from their mistakes and what they did right, She can link up any device to the inventor's mind even if they are dead, and learn how to operate it. In combat, she is untouchable—she always has the advantage."

Savannah shyly smiled and gave a nervous half wave.

"Jeffrey, Poseidon's son, can control anything liquid," Gaia continued, unwilling to allow them to keep bickering. "He can create storms, hurricanes, tidal waves…" she trailed off. "He can even control the Earth's hot lava—anything in liquid form.

"Kikilliana can raise the dead and control monsters and ghosts. She can put everyone to sleep with the *Song of Slumber* she sings, and they will sleep for one hundred years before waking up.

"Hercules is stronger than Zeus himself. He's been reaching the moon with his rock tossing, and he's been trained in combat by the great Turally himself. They've worked on archery, hand to hand combat, wrestling, and various weapons use. And…" Gaia paused for a moment, her gaze finding Hercules'. "This sword I give him today can yield lightning, but only for Zeus and his offspring."

"So, we now have seven for the mission." Aeolus told the group. "You do what you have to," he said to the children. "But stay well fed and rested. Above all, you must work together."

The seven demigods stood in a circle, some confused as to what was going on, some upset, and Hercules excited and ready to get started. "Well, I guess we better get going," he said to the group as the last of the gods disappeared. The unlikely group of demigods slowly walked out of the cave.

FOURTEEN

Heavy and stiff from eighteen hours asleep, Poseidon stretched in his cave. He was bored out of his mind, but his heart was aflutter with the pounding anxiety that came with his imprisonment. In the time since Zeus had entrapped him, he had spent his days sleeping away time—there was nothing else that could be done. Hades, however, was always thinking—always pacing back and forth with his fingers roaming every inch of the walls—trying to find the weakness in Zeus' prison.

"Give up," Poseidon said, sprawling out on the ground with a heavy sigh. "There is nothing we can do." His voice quavered and the whiney tone bounced around the cavern.

"In a few weeks we will be too weak to be conscious if we don't eat, so, we must find a way out of this place!" Hades growled and continued his pacing.

Poseidon wanted to yell at the top of his lungs that there is no way out, but he couldn't. Hades was right. They were trapped in a prison with no food, and if they didn't eat within the next few weeks, they would be in trouble.

*****

Zeus snarled and ran his fingers through his wet hair as he shivered. Ouranos had released a light rain that drizzled its chilly fingers down to Earth, caressing Zeus' spine with gripping horror. The flashes of lightning that followed engulfed him in dread, and he began to slip into furious hysteria at the teasing. In his anger, Zeus struck back, sending lightning bolt after lightning bolt into the sky.

It was pointless.

Ouranos' laughter thundered from above and the storm stopped.

Zeus could not beat Ouranos alone.

He sat on his throne, eyes closed against the despair that threatened to swallow him. What could he do? He was Lord of the Sky, but Ouranos was the true God of the Sky and his powers far out-matched Zeus'.

Cloaked in self-pity, he crossed his arms before him and thought about all those who'd abandoned him in jealousy; about his mother, who wanted him dead.

Not for a moment did he consider his role in creating his current situation.

Although he knew the history of Gaia and Ouranos, the idea that Gaia had revived Ouranos just to get rid of him nestled deeply into his mind. It grew and grew until he could feel his head swell with it, and he roared in anger. "Oh, you are wrong mother!" he thundered, in a voice that shook the heavens. "I'll destroy Ouranos, as well as you and the others! Mark my words!"

*****

Gemini practiced his sword fighting while the others laid down to rest. The motions had to be perfect. He believed that the only way to be perfect was for a person to be one with their craft. Using the power of Chi, he practiced for hours every night, measuring the energy in his swing with a range of colors: red, blue, green, and burgundy. He had developed such control over energy that he was able to form fireballs with his hands and heal many ailments.

Cushioned by the luxuriously healthy green grass that extended for miles beyond their camp and into the distant tree-line, the group rested easily. They sought safety, and had agreed—after much debate—that an open field allowed them free view of enemies approaching. The temperature began to drop as the day faded and the sun disappeared over the distant horizon.

"Everyone stay aware! Nobody is to walk off on their own." Gemini was frustrated by the group's complacency when he returned. "There are many dangers in the night, and the minotaur is nearby. I can feel his presence. He's been following us since we left the cave. What do you call that place again, Hercules?"

"Sparta," Hercules responded, chest puffed in pride.

"How can you sense him?" Vanessa asked.

"Because the minotaur is his brother," Savannah answered for him.

"Wait, I thought you were the only living son of Aries?" Jeffrey asked, looking confused.

"I am, the minotaur is my half-brother. He is not alive but died many eons ago. He gifted Zeus with human flesh to eat, and my father killed him in battle—punishing him to roam the underworld eternally, eating only the flesh of expired humans."

"Hades released him though—to get under Zeus' skin. He is free to roam the Earth at night," Savannah interjected, eager to show her own knowledge. "Well, part of it was to get under Zeus' skin, the other part was to keep the humans living in fear," Savannah continued when she noticed Gemini was not speaking but watching her to see how much more she knew. "Hades hates that the humans respect Zeus more than him, especially with Hades being the oldest."

"Very good," Gemini said, nodding slowly. "You are very knowledgeable. You represent your mother well."

"Thank you," Savannah said, confidence blooming in the smile on her face.

"I will take first watch," said Gemini. "We're going to have to take turns—I fear the minotaur won't be the only one after us."

"Sounds good," Hercules said. Everyone agreed.

As everyone started searching for good areas to sleep, Savannah and Hercules stepped aside. Their shared fear of spiders was too intense to allow them to sleep while so exposed. Hercules' fear was primal, but the spiders were the mortal enemies of Savannah's mother, and she had grown accustomed to protecting herself. She drew a large bundle of mint leaves from her bag and settled herself beside the others, encircling herself with the leaves.

"What are you doing?" Xavier asked, overwhelmed with curiosity.

"Oh," Savannah said, blushing a little from embarrassment. "My mother is the reason spiders exist. She was challenged to a Spinster's Competition by a human. My mother cursed the human for her pride, and for thinking she was equal to the gods. The human was turned into a spider. Ever since, Arachne's spiders have attacked us children of Athena. Sometimes they kill us themselves; sometimes they wind you so tightly in their web that you cannot escape, to take you to Arachne herself. Legend has it that she feeds on you while you're still alive…"

Hercules watched intently from beneath the tree he'd been considering sleeping in. "Do you have any more leaves?" he asked, sure they'd be better than his plan.

"Yeah, I have more."

"Thank God." he said, flooded with relief. "I don't like spiders either. Could I possibly have some?" he made his way to Savannah's side.

"Sure," she said, smiling.

"No need for all that," Xavier announced as he summoned seven clouds out of the sky. The seven clouds lined up in a row, four feet above the Earth. Everyone looked at them in amazement.

"Nice!" Jeffrey yelled, unable to contain himself. He climbed onto the first cloud using the wispy staircase it had produced. The steps disappeared as soon as he was all the way on the cloud. Surprisingly, it held his weight. Vanessa was next to climb onto the cloud nearest to her.

"How does it feel, Vanessa?" asked Kikilliana.

"It feels amazing," she shouted down. "It's solid enough to hold your weight but also so soft! So comfortable and warm..."

"Nice!" Kikilliana responded.

Within seconds everyone was on a cloud and preparing to sleep. The clouds began to rise further.

"What is going on?" Jeffrey yelled.

"I'm raising the clouds away from the ground, to get us out of danger."

"What happens if we have to use the bathroom in the middle of the night?" Vanessa shouted.

"I didn't think about that," Xavier shouted back as the clouds began to lower back down towards the ground.

"I guess we'll still have to do those shifts after all," Jeffrey said, the clouds returning to their floating positions.

Gemini flipped out of his cloud and began his shift. For the first thirty minutes he practiced his swordsmanship, but intrigue got the best of him and he began to explore the area. At first it was easy to see the surrounding terrain, but as the sun slowly set and darkness fell, it became nearly impossible. Anticipating the sunset, Gemini had brought a torch along with him, and he lit it so that he could continue. He roamed the surrounds of their makeshift camp, noting the many paths begging for exploration. As his shift change drew near, he sighed and stifled a weary yawn—he would have to head back to camp.

This place is amazing, Gemini thought. *I hope we stay another day so I can explore more*.

He paused suddenly on his way back to camp. A ripple of cold washed over him and he crouched and scanned the area. As his eyes darted over the grasslands, he felt the eerie sensation of someone watching him. It burned into his back and set his nerves on edge; whatever was watching him was pure evil, and its intentions could not be good. His hand clutched the hilt of his sword at his side, and he swung the beam of torchlight from side to side, hoping to keep the evil away as he crept back to camp. His mind was racing, turning different possibilities over and over as he slunk closer to the ground. Their enemies were numerous—each one more dangerous than the last—and they came to life in his head, scattering his thoughts and crowding his brain. Heart pounding and ears rushing, he was silent until at last he was back in the camp.

FIFTEEN

"Okay class, close the books," Mrs Norton said, looking at the clock.

The students sighed. *The War of the Gods* was an enthralling book, and as always Mrs Norton ended on the best part—leaving them excited for their next class.

Mrs Norton was an elderly lady with white hair, who taught twelfth grade reading comprehension at the school.

John picked up his book and took it to the front of the room. His imagination was running wild.

Wow, he thought, *if only I could have powers like them. That would be awesome! I'd be superman—no... Wolverine! Incredible*.

"Hey, John!" Marcus yelled, jogging up behind him. "That book is awesome!"

"Yeah, it is, man."

"What class do you have next?" Marcus asked.

"Dang, I have math next." John ruffled through his bag, pulling out his schedule. "Eugh, I don't want to go… I hate fractions."

Marcus and John laughed together.

"You'll get it, man," Marcus said. "You just have to study extra hard."

John looked at Marcus and shook his head in disapproval of the words 'study hard.'

"Bro, if you're going to pass that class you need to study. Dude, this is embarrassing. You are in twelfth grade and still in pre-algebra. Look, after school, when I get done with basketball practice, I can help you study," Marcus told John, really wanting to help.

"No," John quickly replied. I'm good bro." He rolled his eyes and shook his head in disappointment to show Marcus that the conversation was becoming more irritating than interesting.

"Dude, if you don't pick your grades up, you'll end up getting held back, like Ho Young."

"Heck no, that will never happen, Ho Young is what, like twenty-six in the eleventh grade?" John snickered as they walked.

Marcus almost doubled over with mirth as he burst out laughing.

"Dude, did you hear what Ho Young said yesterday?" John asked.

There was a rustle of plastic and a tiny 'pop' sound as Marcus opened a Crystal Light drink that he'd pulled from his backpack. "No, what did he say?" he asked, smiling because he knew from experience that whatever it was, it was usually dumb and funny.

"Bro… Ho Young said that before the Indians became Mexicans, they were Egyptian." He chuckled, waiting for Marcus' reaction.

Marcus snorted and spat sticky Crystal Light everywhere as he held his stomach laughing.

Ho Young was an Asian kid; his last name was Kim. As a twenty-year-old senior, he was a bit older than the rest of the class, but he was still hoping to graduate. He had all kinds of theories about everything. He was constantly chattering, and his lively presence made him seem much larger than his thin five-foot-seven frame really was. He'd been held back a few times, but it didn't seem to matter. He was friendly and humble and super respectful to his teachers and coaches—he saluted them as though he were in the army—and most people just assumed he was a little slow, or that maybe he'd used some bad drugs that'd zapped some of his intelligence.

"Dude, look." Marcus said, a big grin spread across his square-headed face. John slowly turned his head to see. The schools in Chicago all had their hallways inside of buildings due to the snow and the very cold temperatures. The lockers in each hallway were a different color, depicting what year the students in that hallway were in: green for freshman, orange for sophomores, silver for juniors, and gold for seniors. The school didn't allow the display of red and blue colors, and that included the lockers. Technically, they were also banned from wearing red and blue, but no one who did ever got sent home like they were supposed to. Gangs wore their gang colors all day every day, and not a teacher or hall monitor said a word.

John saw what Marcus was pointing out. Just down the hall was the most beautiful girl in the school, Jasmine Turner. There was not a single boy in the school that didn't have a crush on her. A lot of the girls liked her as well, but luckily for the boys, Jasmine was straight. Everyone from Freshmen through to Seniors hoped to make Jasmine their girlfriend, and John and Marcus would often make bets on who would get the first date. With a quick glance at each other, they both took off after her in a sprint.

"Hey, Jasmine!" Marcus yelled, beating John to the punch. He was tall and muscular, and as always, dressed in his sweatpants and t-shirt, showing off his muscles. Jasmine didn't seem to notice.

"Um, hi, you okay?" she asked.

He tried to speak to her, but his words were coarse and airy as he was still trying to catch his breath.

John had started walking three steps into the race to make it look like he'd tricked Marcus into running. He knew Marcus was faster with his giraffe sized legs, and decided that lions didn't race giraffes, especially in front of Jasmine. Though not as tall as Marcus, John was still about five foot ten and fit—one of the school's best athletes, competing in boxing, basketball, and football.

"Hey, what's up?" he asked casually as he approached them with a lopsided grin. He found himself tripping over her name a little, as she'd only recently stopped using her legal name—Selene—and he still didn't know why.

She blushed a little and looked away, trying not to make eye contact. She ran her fingers through her long brown hair, the red and gold highlights shimmering as they moved. "You guys are so silly," she said, flashing a smile—as warm and as beautiful as a sunset over the beach.

"Thanks," John said, throwing a brief scowl over his shoulder at Marcus.

"Are you coming to class?" Jasmine asked, looking expectantly at John.

"Class? I have fifth period, math…"

"No, we have homeroom today." She watched as he worked it out. "It's first, second, third, fourth, and then we definitely have homeroom."

John turned and looked at Marcus, with his eyebrows raised. "Really, so you were going to just let me go to math, knowing we had homeroom next?"

"Honestly, I forgot bro. I was thinking about you having trouble with fractions and studying after school."

"You have trouble with fractions?" Jasmine asked, giving John a weirded-out look. "John, you know we learn fractions in middle school, right?"

He shrugged. "I had a bad teacher that year."

Marcus jogged a funny loop, unable to stop himself from laughing at his friend's misbegotten confidence.

Jasmine tried to be sympathetic, but John saw her wipe at a tear of laughter that had escaped despite her efforts.

"Really Marcus? Okay, I see how it is homie." John said, irritated.

"What? Marcus asked. He was confused at the sudden mood change.

"Bro, you know good and well that you just tried to throw me under the bus. It's all good though." John said, still a bit upset that Marcus had let Jasmine know that he had trouble with easy math.

"Oh, my bad bro."

"And no Jasmine," he said, sighing. "I don't have trouble with fractions. I just feel like they aren't needed in real life."

"I beg to differ," she said. "If you have one large pizza, and it's cut into eight pieces but there are thirteen of you, how would you cut the slices evenly, so everyone gets the same amount of pizza?" She folded her arms, waiting for his response.

"Easy, I take two slices for myself, and everyone else can share slices: two to a slice, six times two equals twelve. So, twelve people eating six slices would be two people to a slice." John smiled as he felt he'd given the perfect answer to the question. "Or, if I order another one, we all get two slices. See multiplication, addition, subtraction, and division are all you will ever need in life." John finished after seeing Jasmine give him The Look.

"Yeah, you need help, so let's set up a study group." Jasmine decided to put a stop to the bickering.

"I'm down," Marcus said, "When?"

"How about Friday night at my house?"

"Yeah, sure thing," John replied, "What time?"

"Does 7:30 p.m. work for everyone?"

They both agreed.

"Okay, it is settled. Now John, we need to get to class before the bell rings. I am not trying to get written up!"

"Okay, go to class then." John said with a smirk. "I'll just see you when I get there." Jasmine grabbed John by his ear jokingly and pulled him towards Marcus.

"Tell Marcus goodbye," she demanded.

"See you later bro," John said as they did their special bro handshake.

John and Jasmine made it to class and were in their seats just seconds before the bell rang. Though it was a long room, it wasn't a big class setting at all, with only twenty-six seats in total. It had all the makings of an ordinary classroom—there was a whiteboard with markers next to the teacher's desk and various books spread about the place—but there was an uninviting melancholy about it. The outside of the windows were darkened with spray painted gang signs, and you couldn't see in our out well at all. It felt… stuffy and miserable.

The teacher began to take the roll and most of them started to settle. He sighed as someone interrupted.

"Can I go to the bathroom?" It was Eugene, one of the best members of the football team—he'd been recruited by coaches when he was still in elementary school. He grinned at the teacher with a cocky toss of his head that made his thick braided hair spring into life, heavy and alluring against his dark skin.

"Yes, you may, Mr Bryant," the teacher said. "You may also return within a reasonable timeframe."

John laughed, as did a few of the other students. The teacher said that every time, and Eugene always came back with only a half an hour left in class.

"Thank you, sir," Eugene said respectfully as he climbed out of his chair, likely headed off somewhere to smoke weed with his friends.

Their teacher cleared his throat and continued. "Tobias Henry Spears."

"You know I'm here," Tobias laughed out loud. "Oh, I am always here… Perfect attendance—yup. Can you say that?" Tobias asked John as he laughed again.

"I would if it mattered in life," John muttered, fiddling with his pen. "You act like McDonalds is going to ask you for your school attendance records." The class laughed as the teacher looked over his clipboard, directly at John.

"Jonathan Dunham."

"Present." John said as he raised his hand, watching Jasmine with a guilty smirk on his face, indicating to her that he was mimicking her. He flinched and spun around further, barely catching Jasmine's grin as she pulled her hand back from his shoulder. She looked quite proud at having punched him so neatly.

When the roll call was finished, Mr Rosh, the teacher, returned to his desk. "You know what to do, just work on your assignments from other classes during this period."

John raised his hand immediately. "Yes, Mr Dunham?" Mr Rosh rubbed the bridge of his nose.

"All we do in this class is work on homework for other classes. This class literally is detention with a different name. You should just let us have free time instead."

"This class varies from detention, Mr Dunham. In detention you can't talk, in here you can. In detention you are there for half a day, or for a full day, and in here you only have to spend one and a half hours."

"Okay, so you named two things," John replied. "So, like I said, this is pretty much detention then."

John and Jasmine exploded into laughter along with the rest of the class.

Mr Rosh looked at John through his spectacles. He had a very pointed nose and was very skinny—he reminded John of the music teacher from Sleepy Hollow. The only difference was that Mr Rosh always wore brown sweaters and khakis, and instead of a ponytail, he slicked his hair back all greasy like, like Professor Snape from *Harry Potter*.

"Your opinion is duly noted," he said in an exaggerated drawl. "Okay class, get your homework out, and voices down."

"John, you already know he doesn't like you. Why do you always press the teacher's buttons?" Jasmine asked.

"Can't help it I guess," John replied, smirking.

"Okay, well pull out your fraction homework."

"Whoa, wait a minute, I thought we agreed to do that on Friday?"

"So, you want to do your homework that is due tomorrow on Friday?" Jasmine raised her eyebrows.

"No, I don't do homework, only class work. I don't spend seven hours in school to go home and do more schoolwork. Even without doing homework I have a two point three. Math is the only class I have an F in."

"Well, let's get that grade up because I don't date guys who get Fs in anything."

John pulled the out the math work, and his pen and paper, before Jasmine could even finish her sentence

"By the way, we aren't dating yet, so you better remember me doing this schoolwork for that cause. Consider it my first payment on your heart," John gave a cute smile as he said it.

"Not a romantic in the least I see," Jasmine said as she smiled back. "Consider that noted as your first *missed* payment on my heart."

Bing, bing, bing, bing. The bell sounded at the end of class. John and Jasmine were already ready to go. They walked down the hall together to Jasmine's locker.

"I could go for a strawberry-blueberry smoothie right now," John said.

"Me too, those are so good," Jasmine replied, handing him her books so she could easily open her locker.

"Hey guys!" Ho Young wandered around the corner.

"What's up Ho Young?" John asked.

"Not much, man, just ready to go home, but I got something I want to show you."

"Whoa there guy. I'm only into girls," John said laughing.

"Stop." Jasmine whined, nudging him.

"Hey, before I show you, I was wondering if you guys ever wondered why giants today are much slower than giants were a few thousand years ago?"

John stared at Ho Young with a frown, his forehead creased. Jasmine bit her lip to keep from laughing,

"Well… they are," Ho Young continued.

"Ho Young," John began, "How many giants do you know today?"

"Oh man," Ho Young said, excitedly, "I was on YouTube watching a giantess swimsuit model."

Marcus, who had just walked up, almost fell to the ground laughing. John and Jasmine exploded into laughter with him.

"Ho Young," John said again, in between raucous bursts of laughter. "Out of everything that you could have looked up on YouTube, you chose to look up a giantess swimsuit model?"

"Yeah, that and clones. You know, I feel like a lot of people today are clones, you know?"

"No, I'm afraid I don't," John replied, still laughing.

"Yeah man, it's crazy—they were cloning the dinosaurs back in the days when dinosaurs were alive. That's how they went extinct."

"How did they clone dinosaurs back in the day with no technology?" Jasmine asked. John was about to ask how they cloned dinosaurs back in the day with no *humans*, but Jasmine elbowed him in the ribs.

"Well," Ho Young looked around for a second and then offered a random salute, "I don't know. Ha ha. But hey, I really got to show you guys something."

Marcus, John, and Jasmine walked around the corner with Ho Young.

"Okay," Ho Young said as he led them into the maintenance area. The three of them followed him as he searched the area to make sure it was clear. "Can't have anyone see this," he said as he walked back towards them.

"What, do you have a gun?" John asked, a little worried that Ho Young had snapped.

"No, no, I have powers. Watch this!"

Without warning, Ho Young threw his arm forward. His hand was empty as he did it, but a ninja star stuck to the wall where he was aiming.

"What the hell?" John said, eyes wide. "How did you do that? Your hand was empty!"

"Oh, that's nothing, watch this."

Ho Young placed his hands in the air like he was holding a bow and arrow. He pulled back on an imaginary string and then let go. Again, there was nothing in his hands, but an arrow notched deep into the metal wall that he was aiming at.

"What in the universe!" Marcus yelled, jumping back and landing hard against the concrete wall, just as Jasmine ducked and screamed.

“Oh my God!” she said. “I’m scared. What’s happening?” She gripped John’s arm tightly.

“I don’t know,” he replied.” I’ll admit, it is a little creepy, but also pretty tight.”

“How did you discover you had powers?” Marcus asked, overcome with intense curiosity.

“Well,” Ho Young said, looking excited to finally have someone to tell. “I was dreaming, and in my dream, there were a bunch of camels, but there was this one that was different from the rest that actually *looked* like a camel.”

“Ho Young,” John said sighing into his hand and watching him the way he always did when Ho Young said something strange. “There were a bunch of camels, but only one of them looked like a camel?”

“Yeah man, it was crazy.”

“Ho Young,” John interrupted again. “If only one of them looked like a camel what did the rest look like?”

“You know man, I would say the other camels looked like zebras. Yeah, they looked like zebras, I guess.”

“Could they have been zebras?” John said doing all he could not to laugh.

“You know what? I was actually thinking that, like hey, what if they were zebras? Wow man, that is crazy!”

The nervous tension was broken as everyone laughed uproariously, staggering to keep their feet.

“Ah man, that was dumb wasn’t it?” Ho Young said, stepping back.” I say stuff sometimes, and it sounds different in my head, you know?”

"You're good, Ho Young, it was funny, it wasn't dumb." John said, "You're not dumb, don't ever think that. We laugh at each other all the time."

"Okay, you sure? Because, it does sound kind of dumb now that I think about it…"

"No, Ho Young," John said, still laughing, "Just finish the story."

"Okay, well, the camels, I mean zebras, were all in the water drinking. The camel that looked like a camel was in the middle."

John couldn't help it. He kept his laugh as quiet as he could, hoping Ho Young wouldn't notice, and explain the rest of the dream.

"Well, the camel started talking to me," he said. "He showed me the motions to use and told me to mentally see the end result, and that I would never miss." Ho Young stopped talking and just looked at everyone.

"That's tight," John said, pretty impressed.

"Yeah," Marcus said, "It is."

"I wouldn't show too many people though," Jasmine cautioned, watching him sympathetically. "People get scared at things they can't explain or don't understand."

"Yeah, that is true," Marcus agreed. "They would probably try to put you in a science lab and cut you open and investigate and stuff."

"Oh no, I don't want that!" Ho Young yelled. He stepped back from them all, suddenly wide-eyed, and began jogging in a circle—waving his hand frantically.

"Okay, well, don't show anyone else, but man, that is really cool," John chimed in with as soothing a voice as he could muster. By the time they left the maintenance room, everyone—including Ho Young—had started to calm down. Once they had sweet-talked their way past the friendly maintenance man, Mr Dicky, Ho Young wheeled around to face them in a fresh panic.

"I forgot!" he cried, shaking his head over and over. "I wasn't supposed to tell anyone. It's a secret!"

Marcus laughed. "I give up," he said quietly. Even Mr Dicky was chuckling as he continued into his office.

"Oh shoot!" John shouted suddenly. "The arrow is still in the wall, and the ninja star!"

"We have to go back and get them out before Mr Dicky sees them and thinks we did it, and we get expelled for vandalizing school property. My dad would kill me," Jasmine said, grabbing the top of her head.

"No, we can't. If we go back now that would be admitting we did it, and we would be expelled regardless because there is no way that he didn't see them by now." John said, thinking hard about ways to get them out of the trouble they might be facing.

"I'm sorry." Ho Young said. "I didn't mean to get everyone in trouble." As he spoke, he bowed to them.

John laughed, but not unkindly. "No, Ho Young, we all forgot about it. It's not your fault… I got it! We can say Ho Young took us in there to show us the arrow and the ninja star in the wall. We can say he discovered them while wandering in there. They would definitely believe that." He shot a quick glance at Ho Young, hoping he didn't think he was insulting him.

"Yeah, I think that'll work," Marcus said. Jasmine nodded too.

Sure enough, before they could get off the school property, they all were called into the principal's office, and they all stuck to the story as planned. The vice principal wanted to give them detention, but the head principal stepped in. They couldn't get detention for something there was no proof that they did. The four of them left to go their separate ways after school. Jasmine went home and Marcus and John went to basketball practice.

Ho Young went to the park to grab some sleep. Jasmine was the only one who knew he was homeless, and had been for a long time.

*****

"Okay, class. Books open to chapter thirteen," Mrs Norton said in fourth period the next day. There was a rustling of bags and a ruffle of paper as the class pulled out their assigned copies of *The War of the Gods*. Marcus and John sat on opposite sides of the classroom in assigned seats. They'd started the year sitting together, but by the second week, Mrs Norton discovered that separating them would probably be in everyone's best interest.

There were only a few kids in the class who didn't like the book, so they were ready to read quickly. They enjoyed being transported into the world of the gods—who wouldn't enjoy a book about having superpowers?

"Okay! Pens out, papers out, and remember, if you hear anything important, jot it down." Mrs Norton smiled. "Okay, here I go…"

SIXTEEN

Gemini reached the campground but even though he did his shift change with Kikilliana, he stayed up. Something wasn't right, and he felt it in the pit of his stomach. Something bad was coming.

"No!" Savannah screamed as she abruptly jumped up in the air, waking suddenly. It must have been around six in the morning because the sun had not yet risen but the darkness had already faded away into a grayish blue, making way for a beautiful sunrise.

"Everybody!" she called loudly, making sure they were awake. "Get on the clouds, now. Xavior! Get us out of here fast." Savannah finished yelling as she quickly stood to her feet and clambered onto her cloud. She frantically surveyed their surroundings, hoping that the panic in her voice would be enough to get everyone moving.

It was and despite their confusion, they all did as she ordered without complaint.

Gemini and Kikilliana were last to jump onto their clouds, and as soon as they were aboard, Xavior raised the clouds rapidly and then sped them off across the sky. When the startled group of demigods looked down, all they could see for miles were thousands of creeping, crawling spiders of all sizes. It seemed that over the course of Kikilliana's shift, they had been carefully surrounding the camp, getting ready to make their move. A short distance away, still running towards them, was a giant black widow spider.

It was Arachne herself.

She was the size of a two-story house and fear spread through all seven of the demigods as they looked at one another. Hercules grimaced. *How the hell does Gaia expect me to defeat her?* He thought. *It'd be a suicide mission.*

"Hang on!" Xavior shouted as he moved them faster and raised them higher. Arachne was much faster than Xavior had anticipated and had nearly caught up to them. As the clouds sped up, slowly, their view of Arachne became more and more distant, until she disappeared altogether.

The clouds carried the group long and far. Nobody knew where they were going except Xavior, and he only decided to land when rain began pelting down from the sky in large, sharp drops. They were about fifteen miles out of the nearest town.

"You know, we're right next to Athens," Gemini said, looking fearful as he wrung his hands. "You landed us as close to my brother as you possibly could. Athens is his home base. Tonight, he will come after us. He senses our presence even now." He glared at Xavior.

"He can't take us all," Xavior said, "Or even one of us. We're too powerful."

"Oh yeah, he is definitely coming," Savannah added. The minute Gemini mentioned the minotaur being close, she'd focused her energy upon him, and could see the plans he'd made before they arrived. "He knew already that we would be here on this day," she continued.

"How?" Kikilliana asked, confused. "Can he see what happens in the future?"

"No," Gemini responded. "He can't see the future, which is why it baffles me as to how he knew we would be here when we didn't even know *we* were coming here!"

"He went to the Sister Fates," Savannah said angrily as she mentally retraced the minotaur's steps.

"How?" Hercules asked. "They're on our side. Why would they betray us?"

"For money and power. Ouranos promised them safety and more power if they sided with him."

Vanessa, who was listening to the exchange and tugging at a loose thread on her shirt, interrupted. "But why would they believe he would do that for them if they know the future? Unless..." She paused for a second, eyes widening in fear and worry lines creasing her face. She didn't have to say the rest—the group had already figured it out.

If The Fates switched sides, that means their side must end up losing.

"So, there isn't a point to this mission then, if we already know we're going to lose," Hercules said downheartedly. "We might as well all go home."

"No," Savannah said, with a tear in her eye. "We must continue. If we give up, the gods will take it out on us and our families. And monsters, like Arachne, already have our scent and will hunt us until we and all of our families are dead!" Her voice quavered. "Besides, our mission isn't to fight the war, just to free Poseidon and Hades." She stopped to think on this for a moment, the others left waiting on bated breath. "So… maybe they lose the war against The Creator and Ouranos, but we succeed!"

Hercules wanted to argue, but he couldn't. Hera was his evil stepmother, and he knew how vengeful she was.

By now, the group was drenched. "Let's hightail it to town and get dried off." Xavior flew just above them, using the winds to keep him in the air. Just as the sun began to rise and they reached the edge of town, they were greeted by an array of soldiers.

"State your business in Athens," the centurion demanded. Had the seven youngsters not been demigods and very powerful, they might have been scared at the sight of the fierce soldiers. Athens was a new town—very small—but it was growing fast because of the bountiful harvest of vegetables, fruit, and wildlife. Families could hunt every day and not have to worry about running out of food.

"I am Hercules, the son of Zeus—from Sparta," Hercules declared, towering over the four centurions. He picked up a boulder the size of a baby elephant and threw it into space, causing the centurions to back away in fear.

"I am Vanessa, daughter of Aphrodite," Vanessa said, making on of the guards disappear, causing the rest of them to cower and bow.

"And I—" Xavior began.

"No more!" one guard yelled. "We are under Athens' Demigods' rule. The people think our newly appointed king is in charge, but he's not!" He looked dejected; forlorn. "Your people are! They torment us day and night with their unnatural powers."

"What?" Vanessa asked, confused. "Take us to them," she said as she batted her eyes three times at the guards, placing them under her will.

The guards led them towards the center of Athens. Just before they stepped through the entrance of a dark tunnel, Savannah stopped them short.

"Hercules! Wield your sword and light this tunnel up with lightning bolts," she commanded.

"What?" Hercules said, unsure what was happening.

"Hurry!" Savannah yelled.

Hercules quickly removed his sword and filled the tunnel with lightning bolts—just in time. Something had been rushing towards them, only halted by the flickering electric current. It lay on the ground, electrocuted.

"They knew we were here and were going to try and kill us in this tunnel. This is Arethmus, the son of the goddess,

Nike. She is the goddess of sports and victories—the one who creates all the wars and battles on Earth. She hates draws; believes one side must always win.

"There are seventeen of them and they have a legion of forty thousand centurions under their command." Savannah told the group.

"Are their powers greater than ours?" Kikilliana asked, wiping sweat from her brow with the back of her hand and taking a step closer to Xavior.

"I don't know, but his powers were nowhere near as great as anyone in our group. All he could do was go super-fast and disappear into shadows."

"So… should we stay and fight or move along?" Xavior asked, looking at the group.

"I say let's move along before they make the decision for us." Gemini squared his shoulders and spoke loudly to the group, claiming leadership.

"We can't leave," Savannah murmured, eyes locked onto the form on the ground. "They're hiding something very important. Arethmus knew about it, but not what it was exactly, only the top elect of their group know what it is."

"Well then," Hercules said. "How do find out?"

"First," Gemini said, looking at Hercules. "We come up with a plan. We are about to be outnumbered big time."

"Okay," Hercules agreed. "Can't argue with that. So… what's the plan then?" He looked hopeful.

Xavior shot him a sideways look, muttering under his breath about 'dumb questions'.

"We've got to come up with the plan first," Xavior said, clapping Hercules on the shoulder as he laughed out loud. Hercules flushed pink with embarrassment when a few of the others laughed too.

"If we fight," Savannah said, "those demigods will want to see what our powers are before they risk putting themselves in harm's way… and they'll work as a team, so we'll have to separate them from each other."

"Agreed," Gemini said. "Hercules—," he rounded on him. "Do you think you can take the soldiers out while we work on the demigods?"

"Yeah," Hercules said, nodding enthusiastically. He was excited that the others thought him capable of such a great task.

"Here," Gemini said as he swung in a circle and pulled a huge shield from mid-air. He wielded it easily, even though it was easily six feet long and four feet wide. "You'll need that to deflect their arrows."

"Wow, thanks." Hercules sucked in a deep breath, taking the shield with awe. It was gold, and the ruby at the center was shaped like a lightning bolt. The outer edges were beautifully crafted from diamond, and razor-sharp.

"One swipe with this and you can cut a statue down," Gemini told Hercules, his chest puffed with pride.

"How did you do that?" asked Hercules.

"Well, I can will weapons into being just by thinking of them," Gemini said, a satisfied smile tugging at his mouth. "Now," he said, guiding them all back to the task at hand. "We're going to have to rely on Savannah's insight to beat seventeen demigods. They have powers just like us and outnumber us big time which puts the odds in their favor."

Savannah focused her mind on the other set of demigods that they were to face. To the others, it looked like she had fallen asleep on her feet, eyes glazed over. She snapped them shut, and when she opened them again, the trance was over and she began to tell the group about what the Athenian demigods were planning on doing.

"So, they plan to come out in three groups. Five in the first group; five in the second group. I assumed they would have sent seven out in the last group, but one demigod will stay out of the fight. As for the demigods fighting, they'll start out by sending their soldiers out first in four separate legions of three hundred. Are you sure you can handle that?" She paused to glance at Hercules, but intercepted his thought before he could speak and carried on.

"They plan to watch how we form our ranks and how we fight. Are we wild or do we fight together? If we make it past the soldiers and the three sets of Athenian demigods, the one remaining will flee to write their story if they fail." She stopped for a moment, allowing her words room to sink in. "Their powers are mediocre for the most part, but there are many I am unable to see for some reason, so we'll have to be very careful."

"Is the one staying behind going to take what they're hiding with them when they leave?" Hercules asked.

Savannah nodded her head. "Yup, I'm afraid that we have to get to that last demigod quickly, before he or she disappears with important information."

"Okay then… how do we do that?" Hercules asked in a defeated voice. He felt the mission was looking impossible.

"Well, since I can foresee what that person will do, we can figure out what powers they plan to use. I will have to go, and I might need Vanessa. My powers are limited, but if she can make us invisible, they won't see us coming—and she can control them once we've got them trapped." Savannah's eyes slipped out of focus again for a second, without warning.

"I hate when she does that," Xavior said. "I keep feeling like she's going to get stuck in a trance one day and not come back."

"Yeah, it creeps me out a bit, too," Jeffrey agreed, deftly poking Savannah in the arm to see if it brought her back to the present.

Savannah snapped back from her trance.

"It's a he!"

"Who's a he?" Hercules asked. Everyone in the group swiveled towards Savannah. She'd shouted very loudly, and they had to know what had her riled up.

"The one staying behind." She rushed through the words, wanting to get the worst part of the news out of the way as quickly as possible. "He has great powers," she said, her tone imploring them to understand the magnitude of her declaration. She turned to Vanessa and grabbed her arm. “If you don’t get him under your control, we’re in trouble,” Savannah said, worry oozing from her every pore.

“What are his powers?” Xavior asked.

“He can freeze people because he is the son of Klione, the minor Goddess of Winter. The snowballs that he shoots from his hands are dangerous—if they touch you, they’ll turn you into a lifeless snowman.”

Gemini looked up at this. “Maybe I should go,” he said. “I can shoot fire… it makes sense.”

“No,” Savannah said, sighing. “It must be Vanessa and myself. I don’t know why, but I know it’s the right combination for the job.”

Xavior couldn’t help himself. “No, he said, crossing his arms. “You may be fine with that plan, but what if something happens to Vanessa?”

“Xavior!” Savannah noticed Vanessa’s creeping blush and stared at him. “I see,” she said, smiling from ear to ear as Vanessa’s face turned red.

Savannah had intercepted his thoughts, and she knew why he had objected. Xavior thought Vanessa was the most beautiful creation in existence; he was in love with her, and had been since he first laid eyes on her in the cave where they’d been given their mission.

“It’s okay.” Vanessa smiled through her blush, turning shyly towards Xavior. “I took this mission knowing the danger, but thank you for wanting to protect me.” She averted her eyes nervously, but Savannah caught what she was thinking. mind.

"Nice," Savannah said out loud, and then realizing everyone heard her, quickly apologized. "Sorry!"

"What's going on?" For once, Gemini looked lost.

"Oh, nothing," Savannah said—too quickly.

"Why don't I believe you?" Hercules asked, his curiosity piqued.

Luckily, Jeffrey was focused on the battle. "Let's get back to the plan," he said, not interested in being sidetracked.

"Yes, I agree." Savannah said. "I—I can see more of their powers now. I don't know why I couldn't earlier… but Jeffrey… you need to avoid the one that can control dirt. A run in with that one wouldn't work in your favor—mixing the dirt with your water… it would become mud and he could control it—use it against you. He's tall," she halted for a moment, searching deeper. "Tall, black hair, a little overweight… Look out for him."

Even while Jeffrey was processing the news, Savannah continued. She listed the other demigods whose powers she'd found—one became a giant, one turned to solid gold and became impenetrable, and another turned into a massive wolf. She suggested that Hercules tackle the gold and addressed Gemini personally. "You should take this one," she said, referring to her current focus. "He can shoot lasers from his fingertips and his bare feet can be turned into metal blades."

Gemini thought to ask questions, but Savannah continued. "Kikilliana, now we know this information, can you summon soldiers from the underworld to fight the centurions? Because Hercules is going to be needed in this fight…"

Kikilliana nodded. "Yeah, I can."

"Xavior, can you pin the first group to the ground with gravity? Don't… don't kill them… just enough so they can't use their powers?"

"Sure thing," he replied. "I can do that."

Vanessa blushed once more from the corner of the room, but nobody saw her. She was amazed by Xavior and his power; awed by how quiet and humble he was with it. She found a spot to lay down and allowed herself a moment to imagine what life would be like if he was her boyfriend. She was used to boys hitting on her because of her beauty, but she'd never liked anyone back before. Yet, here she was falling for someone that she barely knew.

They all got little to no rest that night. Though they went to bed early, they were kept awake by excitement and fear. This would be the first battle they would face as a group, and for some, their first battle ever. The stars filled the night sky, shedding dim light across the land. The moon shone large and bright. Some of them, including Xavior, began to beg their godly parents to protect them through the battle. Most of them, though, did not fully grasp the depth of the danger they were in, despite the warnings from the gods. Those who did were anxious. Now that death was in arms reach, they very much felt his presence. They were afraid, wondering if they might be killed during the battle. Vanessa thought of Xavior and she was afraid for him, too, just as he feared for her.

Their fretful night was quickly swallowed by morning, and the sound of a bullhorn signified the arrival of the Athenian demigods and their soldiers.

"It's time," Savannah whispered into the dawn, as all seven of them jolted awake. "It's time."

SEVENTEEN

For a moment, Savannah felt as though she might stagger under the weight of their responsibility. Her stomach lurched and her legs felt like bread mixture. She had never been in a battle before, and the sound of the bullhorn that so loudly scorched the air made her want to run—to run far away, and continue on their journey without ever finding out what the other demigods were hiding from them.

Running wasn't an option, so she stood her ground, addressing the others.

"Do you remember the plan?" Her voice trembled when she spoke, and she tried hard to pull herself together. Jeffrey, noticing the stream of sweat trickling down the side of her face, reached out and laid a hand on her shoulder.

"I will die tomorrow before I ever let anything happen to you," he said, and although she didn't mean to, Savannah saw inside his thoughts that it was the truth.

In the hours before the fight, everyone's emotions had intensified. They had only just met, but everyone seemed to be connecting—falling faster for each other than perhaps they should. Maybe it was the threat of looming danger or maybe it was just comfort found in those like them, but they all found themselves in need of love.

They stood before Savannah and nodded in an indication that they remembered the plan. When, slowly, they marched their way towards the battle ground, only Hercules carried weaponry: his sword, and the shield that Gemini had created for him. The apparent leader of the soldiers met them on the battlefield, and though they did not know anything about military ranking, they knew he was the one who the demigods trusted to speak on their behalf. The rest of the soldiers stayed back, arranged about the desert-like terrain. There were no trees, no grass, not even a lake—just dirt.

"The gods will be gracious to you if you surrender now," the commander told the group. His face split into a broad smile and he cocked his head boastfully when he saw that only one of them carried a weapon. "That is the gods' only offer."

They think the demigods are actual *gods*, Savannah thought, as the commander continued.

"Quite frankly, I hope you stay. Killing scum like you is just like breathing. We do it without trying." He laughed at his own joke.

Without a word, Hercules grabbed the commander by the breast plate with one arm and threw him over the entire Athenian army of twelve hundred soldiers. The soldiers all stared in awe, their faces crumpling in fear, but they marched on towards the group, keeping their ranks nice and tight. With the throwing of the commander, the battle had begun.

"Everyone step back now," Xavior ordered the group as the soldiers closed in on them. All seven demigods were on edge with their every nerve alight with the intensity of the moment. As six of the seven stepped back, Xavior conjured a mist, waving his hand so that it stretched throughout the air and blinded the opposing demigods from seeing what was about to happen to the soldiers.

"Nice," Vanessa said, admiring his handiwork. The clouds completely covered the Athenian soldiers.

"Um, I just threw a guy over the top of twelve hundred soldiers. I'm just saying, I think mine was pretty impressive too," Hercules said, feeling a bit annoyed that Xavior got a compliment and he didn't.

Savannah laughed, "Hercules, trust me, nobody missed your throw. It was extremely impressive, but we need to focus now."

"Oh, sorry," Hercules said, feeling a bit sheepish for expressing his ego.

Kikilliana stepped forward, her eyes clouded with heart-wrenching expression. Her hair was wild, crackling with emotion as it was blown back off her shoulders and into the air by a wind that seemed only meant for her. She raised her hands as the soldiers met her with a volley of arrows, but Hercules rushed to shield her as Xavior formed a wind barrier between the arrows and their group. The arrows hit Hercules' shield and shattered on impact, and he grinned. Gemini's impenetrable creation was perfect.

Hercules' thanks were silenced as he saw the faces of his friends. Their expressions changed rapidly, eyes widening into terror and mouths open in shock. He turned, bracing to fight, and then he saw it too—felt the rumble beneath his feet. The ground had opened up and thousands of skeleton soldiers, still dressed in full military uniform, were crawling out of the Earth, their long, bony fingers clawing at the ledge as they made their way to the battleground above.

A deafening roar split the awed silence and Hercules turned to see a legion of dinosaurs and saber-toothed tigers advancing on the Athenian soldiers. The dust began to settle, floating embers cooling into ash, and he managed to duck just in time to avoid being knocked over by the wing of a pterodactyl as it dove towards the retreating soldiers.

There was no battle.

It was a complete and utter massacre. Both groups of demigods watched as a T-Rex scooped up a group of soldiers and chewed them into bits as though they were as soft as celery stalks.

It was over before it even started, and the opposing demigods were left with no choice but to watch on as the bloodbath continued, looking solemnly around their group. The boy in ripped shorts found Kikilliana across the divide and met her gaze with a furious glare. The message was clear—they'd be after her first. They exchanged glances, and sent the first wave of five out to fight.

"The first wave is walking towards us!" Savannah shouted, pointing in the direction of the opposing demigods. She was on edge and a tense energy radiated from her, her expression splintered and crazed by all she was seeing.

"You guys go," Hercules said, gesturing towards Savannah and Vanessa. "We got this, but we need you guys to get to the one holding onto whatever they're hiding."

"Okay." Vanessa nodded. "Let's go." The air shimmered and warped around them as she made both herself and Savannah disappear. Their invisibility did not go unnoticed by the Athenian demigods, and they paused for a moment before they were ordered to continue forwards.

Gemini readied himself to take the lead when Vanessa and Savannah had gone. "Okay Jeffrey," he said, "Your guy isn't with this group, so you're free to overtake them with water. Can you handle that?" He fidgeted a moment. "I figure we can drown them. We want to handle these guys using as few of our powers as possible, so the Athenians can't form a game plan."

"Um, I think we are underestimating our opponents," Kikilliana said, her voice rising in anger. "I'm sure Jeffrey is very powerful, but sending him alone is ridiculous—it's way too dangerous."

"You heard Savannah telling us about their powers… And Jeffrey can literally handle this first group by himself by drowning all of them." Hercules interrupted, eager to get moving.

"It's not a problem," Jeffrey said, watching the five demigods still slowly approaching, holding their ranks. He smiled at Kikilliana in thanks before he walked out to meet them. He could feel all the water of the Earth, sloshing and swirling as though it were at his fingertips. There was a lot.

"Wait a minute," Hercules said to Gemini, "Over there—that one to the far left, isn't he the one Savannah said Jeffrey can't fight? Yeah, look, he has the black hair!"

"That's exactly why I said not to send him alone!" Kikilliana snapped, arms folded in a display of attitude.

Gemini cursed. "Shoot, get out there. Jeffrey's powers won't work on him," he said with pure urgency in his voice, ignoring Kikilliana's comment

Hercules began to sprint and, within seconds, he had run one hundred yards, catching up to Jeffrey.

"What's up, man?" Jeffrey looked concerned. "I thought you guys wanted me to get this alone…"

"Yeah, but see the black hair on that guy over there?"

Jeffrey squinted his eyes, but they were too far away for him to see anything other than shapes.

"Sorry man, I can't see that far."

"Well, the demigod with the black hair is on the far left. Your powers won't work against him. We may need each other's help to defeat him."

"I definitely appreciate that," Jeffrey said, laughing to himself in a grateful way. It took around nine minutes for both parties to meet each other in the middle. When at last they reached their opponents, it seemed the Athenians wanted to talk.

"What do you guys want?" One of them stepped forward to speak. "We know there are two more of you out here; we saw them disappear." He wore a cloth to give him modesty, no shirt, and some sort of tribal markings on his chest. His ponytail whipped around when he spoke. He would've looked fierce, had Hercules not been standing there beside him.

"We are on a mission for the gods, our parents," Hercules spoke. "I am Hercules, son of Zeus."

"Really, your name is Hercules is it?" Another of the Athenians spoke up. "I have heard of you. They say you're very powerful."

"But also very clumsy," the man in black pants threw in, to insult Hercules.

"That was before I went to train with Turally," Hercules said, staring them down, mouth twisted in spite.

"Don't care. I'm Cavelli," the man in black pants proudly declared. "My mom was Medusa."

"Enough talk," Hercules bellowed, angrily enough that even Jeffrey jumped back. "Let's settle this the old school way, me versus you. If you win, we will surrender.

If we win, you will surrender. Otherwise, many demigods will die today." Hercules' face was bright with ferocity.

Cavelli stared at Hercules for a moment, wondering if it was a good idea to accept his challenge. When he remembered he couldn't be hurt by much of anything, he slowly reached out his hand and shook Hercules' in a deal.

"Now swear by an unbreakable curse." Hercules made one final request to make everything official.

"I swear by the unbreakable curse."

"Go back, Jeffrey, and tell the group what's going on."

Jeffrey nodded and turned on his heel.

"You lot, go back and tell the rest of the group about the deal, and tell them to be ready to make these mediocre excuses for demigods our slaves." Cavelli laughed as he finished speaking.

The Athenians looked confident as they walked back to their awaiting group.

*****

"What do you mean he made a deal? He can't do that." Gemini growled. "We already have a plan."

"Well, that plan is on hold because they used an unbreakable curse—if either of them break it, or we interfere, all involved will be sent to Tartarus by the gods. It is the written Law of the Gods and cannot be broken." Kikilliana said, disgusted at Hercules for putting the whole group at risk, but not willing to go to Tartarus.

*****

Hercules and Cavelli circled each other for a second, before Cavelli turned to solid gold and attacked. Hercules dodged his first punch, which was surprisingly fast, and when Cavelli moved into a roundhouse kick, Hercules caught his feet and threw him at least a mile away.

Hercules was hoping that would be the end of the fight, but Cavelli quickly got up off the ground and began running back towards him. When he had finally recovered the distance, he launched, limbs flying.

He threw a fast combo at Hercules, but Hercules dodged it and leaned into the punch. Cavelli's next move—a well-timed uppercut—caught Hercules right on the button and he stumbled backwards, chin burning with pain. His head felt like it was going to explode; like he'd been stepped on by an elephant.

Okay, Hercules thought. *He is fast and strong, but I know I'm faster—time to use my speed.*

Hercules threw punches thick and fast at Cavelli as the two groups of demigods watched closely. Their fates depended on this fight. Ducking under a left-handed punch, Hercules caught Cavelli by the arm and threw him again—further this time.

After the long trek back, Cavelli stood again in front of Hercules, breathing hard with sweat dripping down his gold-covered face. His legs wobbled and Hercules noticed how tired he was. Hercules smiled before taunting him.

"Give up yet?" he asked, grinning at the nearly beaten Cavelli.

"Oh, it's just beginning," Cavelli replied angrily.

He drop-kicked Hercules with a frontal kick right in the gut. Hercules folded over, holding his stomach, and Cavelli continued to kick him, hard. Within no time, Hercules had blood frothing from his mouth and flowing from his forehead. He was eventually able to roll away and get up, dazed and stumbling.

"C'mon!" Kikilliana yelled, not wanting to become a slave. Hercules was too far away to hear her, but she continued to yell in spite of the distance. "C'mon Hercules!"

Cavelli threw two jabs and a straight right hand at Hercules' face, and Hercules threw a long range left hook over it. Just like he did in training with Turally, he pivoted around his opponent, grabbing him by the waist and slamming him headfirst into the ground. Hercules pulled his sword from its sheath and summoned the lightning, trembling with the effort.

Cavelli was defenseless. Gold attracted lightning and he quivered and glowed with the pulsing electricity. After the fifth strike, Cavelli threw his hands up and yelled, "No more. I surrender!"

The Athenian demigods were furious.

"We will never serve you, Greek scum!" one of the Athenian demigods spat. In his fury, he summoned the Earth to his will, a barely contained snarl distorting his face. It was as though the ground softened and began to suck the Greek demigods into the Earth. Xavior, thinking quickly, used the wind to pick them all up from the ground.

"It's a good thing you didn't attack them back," an amused voice said. It was Hera, descending upon them. With a wave of her hand, the Athenian demigods all disappeared. Hercules and the others stared in bewilderment, not sure what was happening or what Hera had done with the others.

"What's going to happen to them?" Hercules asked, sincerely concerned.

"Well, they broke an unbreakable curse, so they will be sent to Tartarus, won't they?" Hera smiled as she spoke. It was no secret to most that Hera didn't much like demigods, and she punished them every chance she could get. This opportunity seemed a special treat for her.

"Oh," Hercules replied, not willing to say anymore, at risk of ending up back on Hera's bad side.

"Where are the other two?" Hera asked, looking around for Vanessa and Savannah. Though she didn't know it, the gods were unable to sense Vanessa's presence when she called on her invisibility.

"They went to go find the one that stayed behind, so they could get from him whatever the Athenians didn't want us to find."

Hera looked at them all, trying to decide whether or not she should tell them what the Athenian demigods were hiding. If they sought it out and read it, the Law of Origin would require the sacrifice of the lives of any demigod that opened the book.

"Well, I guess you'd eventually find out anyway," Hera finally said, after a moment of thinking to herself. "The Athenian demigods found a sacred book—the only one of its kind that contains our true history; it describes in detail the family bloodlines. Not just of us, but also of the gods outside our realm, and those we do not speak of—by contract."

"Other realms?" Xavior scratched his head. "This is getting really complicated and confusing."

"I won't explain it now," Hera said. "It takes too long, and you dim wits probably still wouldn't understand it."

As Hera spoke, Savannah and Vanessa appeared in the midst of the group.

"Could you at least summon the book for us then, Oh Mighty Hera, so we can at least try to understand it?" Savannah asked. She knew what they were talking about, because she had been keeping track of the group's thoughts to make sure they were all alive.

"I can," Hera said. "But at a cost. One of you must perform twelve labors for me when this mission is over." Nobody raised their hand to volunteer because Hera was looking right at Hercules.

"Wait a minute," Hercules proclaimed. "Why me? I thought we'd made amends, and you weren't going to mess with my mom or me anymore?"

"That was before you got my only son sent to Tartarus." Calm and joy and hate all fought for their place on Hera's face at this.

Hercules sat speechless. He didn't have time to be worrying about Hera attacking he and his mother again. "Fine, I'll do it," he said, standing back on his feet with pure hatred etched across his face. He held out his hand as he finished speaking.

"Oh, I am sorry my dear little boy, but I do not shake hands with bastard sons." Hera laughed to herself as if she had said something funny.

"That's perfectly alright, because I don't shake the hands of scarlet women either," Hercules hissed in anger.

Hera began to rise in height and the sky began to darken. Xavior wasted no time. No way was he going to let Hera attack his teammate because they defeated her son. He pulled at gravity, twisting it so that it pinned down only Hera. Her screams were sharp and penetrating, and Hercules' hands leapt to his ears. Jeffrey, trying to stop the screaming, caused water to rise from the ground and began shooting it into Hera's wailing mouth.

Unable to scream and unable to move, Hera lay on the ground motionless, pretending to be dead. The demigods stopped and stepped back.

"Is she dead?" Xavior asked, fear shadowing his eyes. Stress lines stretched across his face, even though he was only eleven years old.

What would the other gods do once they found out that they had killed the Queen of the Gods—the Goddess, Queen Hera. That is, if they didn't already know. His thoughts raced and his palms began to sweat.

"I don't know," Hercules responded, not taking his eyes off Hera, "But this isn't good. I need to call on my grandma, Gaia. She will protect us."

"No, Hercules!" Savannah yelled. "Do not call any of the gods. This has never happened before, and as close as you and your Gaia are, we don't know how she will react to one of her own kind being killed by demigods."

"Wait, I thought the gods couldn't be killed?" Jeffrey asked, after considering the matter over and over in his head.

"They can't," Kikilliana said, peering nervously at Hera. "I don't know what's happened, but I can assure you, she's not dead." As Kikilliana finished speaking, she and the others found themselves hanging upside down in the air. Kikilliana reached down and pulled her shirt up from covering her face so that she could see what was happening.

"My turn," Hera said, standing to her feet with the most vicious grin Kikilliana had ever seen. Hera's words dripped with hatred and malice. Xavior nearly wet himself—he was beyond scared. Hera was a goddess, and nobody would save them from being killed.

"No, it is my turn." Another voice surrounded them, booming from every direction.

Gaia had come to the rescue.

"I will not have you hurting what little chance we have to beat Ouranos." Gaia raised her arms and the Earth split once more, dragging Hera down and trapping her very quickly.

"Grandma!" Hercules yelled, fearing Gaia would leave before he could speak.

"Yes, Hercules?" Gaia responded.

"Hera made a deal with us," he said. "She requires twelve more labors from me at the end of this mission—for the book we need from the Athenian demigods. If you get me the book, would that break our deal and set me free?"

"I am afraid not, dear grandchild. Any deal made between a god and a mortal is ever-binding, and no other god can interfere without consequences."

"I understand," Hercules replied. "Can we at least get the book?" He cast his eyes downward, unsure how Gaia would react. She didn't speak again, but at Hercules' feet lay a book with the words History of the Gods inscribed on it. It was a plain brown book with plain paper pages. It was very thick, and more than Hercules wanted to read.

"Here you go, Savannah." He tossed the book to the one person in the group that would read and understand every word, and love doing it.

Savannah nodded her head, "We might as well stay here one more night. We have a full day ahead of us, but I know Xavior has to be tired after doing so much today, and you must be exhausted as well," she said quickly as she looked at Hercules. "You saved us with that deal. Nobody was hurt today because of your bravery and pride."

Hercules grinned, "Thanks Savannah."

"You're very welcome." She offered him a small smile, her head bowed to hide the pink flush of her cheeks.

"I can't believe you used your power on Hera," said Vanessa. "That was great! You actually overpowered one of the most powerful goddesses! And for quite a while."

Xavior smiled. He felt good inside. Because he did—he used his powers against Hera, the Queen of the Gods, and he ousted her. He had Hera pinned to the Earth and completely powerless.

Vanessa walked next to Xavior. "You did really well. I feel safe with you here."

"Safe?" he asked. "You can make yourself invisible and control people. I feel safe with you." They both laughed and continued on behind the others, side by side.

EIGHTEEN

Gaia convened with the other gods. "This is not good," she said. "Hera has intervened with the mission, and as you all know, that means dire consequences. Sister Fates, tell us something of the future, for this war now depends on it."

"It matters not what we say, nor," the Middle Sister said, "whether Hera had interfered or not. We are going to lose this war, but there is still a chance that this will not be the end. The demigods will free Poseidon and Hades. Gaia, I am afraid it will not be in your time frame. You will spend some time in Tartarus before Lucifer returns from his prison in the bottomless pit to free you and everyone else for a second war against The Creator."

"So, I'm not going to make it." Gaia looked sad for the first time in a long time.

"I am afraid I cannot give you details, but know this war is not what it seems or where it seems. It is very important that Hades and Poseidon are still freed. Ouranos, after showing Zeus who is more powerful, has formed an allegiance with him now, and they will work together to bring you down."

"I am confused. You say the war is not where it seems, but if the war is against us gods and Ouranos and Zeus, how do we not know where the war is when we are in it?"

"You shall soon see," the Oldest Sister answered.

Fear wove itself into Gaia's contemplative expression.

"That which was from the beginning is beginning to self-destruct. This is the last part of the first prophecy, from The Creator," the Oldest Sister continued.

"So, this part ties into the end of our reign?" Apollo, who had been silent for the whole meeting, asked.

The Three Sisters looked at Apollo with hatred. "We know who you really are, and you will suffer greatly in the end," the Middle Sister said.

The Sisters vanished without another word.

"That is horse manure!" Gaia cried. "My own son is trying to kill me, and after I saved him from his father!"

"We need to figure out what to do with Hera," Aries interrupted. "If she breaks free, which she is bound to do, she will go straight for the demigods. You know how she is about Zeus' children. Hercules will be at the top of her hit list, right after Aeolus' spawn… Xavior is it? She's not going to let that go." Aries laughter was bitter.

"I don't see what's funny." Khione, the minor goddess and Aeolus' daughter, proclaimed to the Council of Gods. "She will try to kill my half-brother."

"No, no, you get me wrong!" Aries said. "I would never laugh at her trying to kill your brother. I was laughing at how your brother was able to overpower her. It was rather impressive indeed."

Khione smiled at Aries. "Thank you," she said.

"Well, we have two options. Kill her and send her to Tartarus, or create a prison that can hold her."

"As much as I hate Hera," Demeter spoke up, "I think killing her would be a bit much. Yes, she has anger problems, but we all have our flaws."

"I vote to kill her. Someone bring the scythe sword." Aries raised his hand, voice firm.

"No," Gaia said shaking her head. "Demeter is right."

"So where to imprison her? Hephaestus, you are the God of Blacksmiths and Mechanisms; Terminus, you are the God of Boundaries and Landmarks; and Archimedes, you're the God of Invention. You three are tasked with the assignment of creating Hera's prison, I need it finished by tomorrow." Gaia spoke with such authority that they didn't dare question her. "As for everyone else, we have to prepare for battle against Zeus and Ouranos."

The gods gathered around the table and delved into a heavy discussion on how to defeat Zeus and Ouranos, which would be a difficult task. Zeus could destroy most of them without even trying, and Ouranos was by far much more powerful than Zeus.

"Before, we had to trick Ouranos into coming down to the Earth, and Kronos cut him to pieces while I held him down," said Gaia, "But we had to get him out of the sky, which I doubt we will be able to do again."

"Didn't The Fates say we're going to lose no matter what we do?" Hermes asked, with a look of despair.

"Sure did!" Dionysus shouted out, half drunk. He was the God of Wine, so he was always drinking to get drunk or drinking to get sober. "But they also said that if we don't defend ourselves, there won't be a second war. So we have to fight back!"

"Actually, Gaia, they said that you're the only one guaranteed not to make it. It sounds like you want us to risk our existence to save you…" Athena said walking into the room in the middle of the debate.

"Glad you could join us," Gaia said, scowling

"The pleasure is mine," Athena smiled at Gaia.

Gaia's return smile was bent with spite. "I was wondering where you had been, but I knew you wouldn't desert us," said Gaia.

"No, never that," Athena continued. "I did what I had to, and I will deal with the consequences later. And you're welcome," she said to Gaia. "You saved me, and I shall save you in return."

"How?" Gaia responded, her hopes rising. "Ouranos can't be killed when he is in his element. We would have to trick him into coming down from the sky."

"Not by us he can't," Athena corrected, her smile broadening and a twinkle gleaming in her eye.

"You didn't?" Gaia gasped, curiosity overwhelming her. "There is no way!"

"I did. I went to Jotunheim, the fourth realm—the realm of the giants—and recruited Abyblous, who was created to counter Ouranos, and Porphyrin, who was created to counter Zeus. They will have a week-long ceremony and then come to battle Zeus and Ouranos."

"What about Asgard? Are they coming?" Gaia asked, hope tinkling in her chest.

"No, they're having a problem with Loki and one of his sons, Fenrir. They have them both chained up, but they're not sure how long the chains will hold."

Gaia looked disappointed.

Athena went on. "And Thor is off in the eighth realm, trying to halt a battle between the dark elves and the elves of light—something going on there, too."

"Wow! I guess we're not the only ones having problems." Orion, the mighty hunter, finally spoke. He was normally quiet, but had seemed even more so at this meeting.

"Orion," Gaia said, looking at him very sternly. "What aren't you telling us? You have been acting strange since we began our meeting."

He sighed. "Well, six years ago, one of my cousins from the fourth realm saw Thor trying to fish Leviathan out of the devil's Sea in the Pacific Ocean. He dove right down to the bottom and cut the rope, to prevent the prophecy of Ragnorok from beginning."

"What's that?" Gaia asked.

"In the prophecy of Ragnarok. Thor and that great dragon that dwells at the bottom of the sea, guarding the ninth realm, fight to the death. Details of the battle were not written, but that war is said to disrupt all nine realms and utterly destroy Asgard."

"Okay…" Orcus, the God of Eternal Punishment, said as he stood up. "So, that was six years ago, and nothing has happened. I think we can safely say that we should focus on our war for right now, and they should help us because their prophecy thing isn't an immediate threat."

"Not so true, Orcas," Athena replied. "A prophecy can start in a blink of an eye. The prophecy about the war in Ragnarok could even be starting as we speak. We have to take into account all the events taking place. Our realm is being attacked right now. Their prophecy said that their war would affect all realms, including ours."

Their interest piqued; everyone gave her their full attention as she put their concerns into words.

"Also," Athena continued, "Thor is in the eighth realm… Why?"

"To try and stop the elves of light and the Elves of Darkness from battling each other," Orion answered.

"I feel like there's more to this prophecy. What else did it say?"

"I don't know any more about this one, but there is another—it says that King Odin of Asgard will be killed by a giant wolf." Orion's shoulders sagged as he answered Athena as best as he could.

"Okay. Well, the wolf would have to be the thirty-foot werewolf, Fenrir, Loki's son, wouldn't it? I can imagine Fenrir is going to be furious for being kept in chains. Since Loki is locked up as well, we can expect him to fight too. Loki is married to the giantess who is also Fenrir's mother. That means we can expect the dark elves and the giants to fight with Loki and the wolf."

"It is true," Orion said as he looked around the room at the gods. "The giants await instructions from Loki, and the dragon does as well."

NINETEEN

"Okay class, close your books," Mrs Norton called out as she closed her own. "What a great book!"

"Yeah, if we could ever finish it," a girl said, and she and the class busted out in laughter.

"We will in due time." Mrs Norton gave the class a pleasant smile, shuffling a stack of papers on her desk.

John was in his own world as the class and the teacher discussed what happened in the book, as they always did, before the bell rang. He was thinking about Ho Young and the powers that he had recently acquired.

What if Ho Young was the child of a god? John could barely contain himself at the idea. He was roused from his imaginings when the bell rang and dragged his focus back to reality.

Walking down the hall, he discovered that Marcus was thinking the same thing.

"Man, this is crazy," Marcus said, excited. "We're reading about people with superpowers, and Ho Young has superpowers. Do you think he's related to that Gemini guy?"

John was just about to agree when Ho Young came jogging up to them.

"Hey, what's up guys?" Ho Young said.

"How's it going, Ho Young?" Marcus responded.

"Oh wow, man, I can't complain. God has been too good to me."

"So, I'm guessing he got you a new shirt then, because the one you got on is not God being good to you." John said, trying not to laugh.

Marcus couldn't help himself, and had to grab his stomach because he was laughing so hard.

Ho Young's shirt had My Little Pony characters on the front, and holes under the left chest that looked as though bullets had passed right through it. If he raised his arms, it would fit him like a crop top.

"I don't know," Ho Young said, smiling and waving his finger. "I kind of like this shirt. It's real catchy, you know? Can't look away."

John looked at Marcus and Marcus looked back at John, and together, they both fell about laughing. It took them a few minutes to calm down enough for a serious discussion.

"Ho Young, we need to make a family tree for you," Marcus said, seemingly out of the blue.

"A family tree? Why?" Ho Young asked, still smiling.

"Well, we're reading this book about gods and demigods, and your powers are similar to this Gemini guy's powers. He's the *son of Aries*!"

"Whoa," John said to Marcus, giving him a befuddled look. "You don't actually believe that Gemini was a real person, do you? Dude, that was just a story."

"If it is just a story, how come Ho Young has powers then?" Marcus replied with an indignant drawl.

"Hmm, very good points on both sides." Ho Young said, scratching his chin with his pointer finger. "You know what? It could be that—or whoa, man! Wow, I just thought of something! What if I'm his clone?" He was jumping up and down in place, writhing with excited energy.

"Not answering that, Ho Young," John replied. "Give us one second to talk, if you don't mind. This is a graduated-on-time meeting, and well—I hate to say it—but you, my friend, don't meet the qualifications." John turned back to Marcus to finish talking as Ho Young stayed to the side, pondering about what a graduated-on-time meeting was.

"Look, all I know is that book says Thor and the nine realms are real. The Greek gods are real, and the Christian God is real," Marcus stated, waving his hands about unthreateningly, but very enthusiastically.

"Dude, those are three completely separate things—how can all three of them be real?"

"Well," Jasmine said, sneaking up on everyone, "It could be real in this sense… The Greek gods, as the book says, are angels, and when they were cast down to Earth the people just thought they were gods. Honestly, it's all guess work off the top of our heads. Why don't we do a study on it and see if we can tie them all together?"

"Do a study on it?" John was skeptical. The look on his face spoke volumes. His lips were curled, his eyes were pleading, and his eyebrows were raised in question. "Can we please not do any more studying?"

Jasmine rolled her eyes. "Oh no, we're studying this! I read that book too—*The War of the Gods*—and Ho Young's powers are similar to Gemini's" she said, not really giving John an option to argue.

The boys nodded in agreement.

"We're supposed to meet at my house tomorrow anyways, and we can just study this instead," she suggested.

"Um, what about homework? Marcus asked.

"Eh, missing one day of homework isn't going to kill anyone. That's not even one percent of your grade—and it's a Friday anyways. We can do the homework on Saturday."

"Yeah, you're starting to sound like John over here," Marcus said as he shook his head.

"Well, you know what they say, bro-ham. Great minds think alike." John tapped his temple, smiling.

"Yeah, whatever dude."

John and Jasmine laughed at Marcus' frustration.

*****

They all gathered by the cafeteria after school on Friday and walked together to Jasmine's house. John was glad Ho Young hadn't been busted yet. After the group had gotten into trouble, Ho Young was more careful and didn't practice around anyone.

"Something doesn't feel right." John stopped walking abruptly, scanning the area. He'd had butterflies in his stomach since they left school, and the hair on his arms was standing up. He felt like something terrible was going to happen.

"What do you mean?" Jasmine asked, frowning.

"I don't know how to explain it. In past experiences, at least for me, I feel the air thicken before something bad happens—and something bad always does."

The others stopped walking to look at him.

"Remember, Marcus? We were going to go eat about a year ago. I told you something didn't feel right, so we stayed in. That night, at the very same spot we were going to, thirty-three people were killed in a mass murder?"

"Holy crap, yeah, I remember that!"

"Wow," Jasmine said, "You don't think that could have been coincidence?"

"Maybe, but it's happened on way more than one occasion."

"We should hurry up and get to my house then," Jasmine teased, a playful smile playing on her lips. She obviously thought the night John was talking about was just a coincidence.

The four of them walked the eight blocks to Jasmine's house and as always, her dad was waiting in the living room for them. He was difficult to read: he could be mean sometimes, but he could also be really nice to them—it just depended on what kind of day he was having.

"Hello everyone," he said as they all walked in.

All four of them either said hello back out loud, waved, or in Ho Young's case, saluted.

"So, I hear you guys have formed a study group. That's great! Nothing like hitting the books. So, what are you studying?" Jasmine's dad asked, genuinely curious about their study group.

"Well, sir, we're studying why the aliens no longer abduct humans," John said jokingly as he watched Ho Young walk to the fireplace. Ho Young managed to climb halfway inside before he started howling.

"What the hell is he doing?" Jasmine's dad asked, getting up to rescue the young man.

"Well sir, looks to me like he is giving us our answer. Well, that was a quick study. See you guys tomorrow!" John was pleased when Jasmine's dad laughed at his joke before turning back to Ho Young.

"What in the devil's name were you doing, boy?" Jasmine's dad was staring at Ho Young, looking horrified.

"Oh no, never sir! Not in the devil's name! I do everything in the name of the Lord, my savior, Jesus Christ." Ho Young saluted as he answered.

"I see," Jasmine's dad said, giving him a weird look. "And—just clarify for my safety… why did you get in the fireplace and start howling?"

"Well sir," Ho Young began, "a lot of wolf spiders live in the fireplace, sir." Jasmine's dad started laughing hard, though he was trying to be serious. John laughed, too, almost falling to his knees in hysteria. Jasmine and Marcus both chuckled.

"So, your first time in my house, you thought the best first impression would be to go in my fireplace and howl at some spiders?" Jasmine's dad asked with a smirk.

"No sir," Ho Young saluted. "I wanted to communicate with the spiders and tell them that we come in peace." He nodded his head yes, over and over again as he always did.

"Hey, everyone, look at that. Do you see it?" He asked, pointing to the TV.

At first, everyone thought Ho Young was just being Ho Young, but soon John saw it too. Then, Jasmine and Marcus saw it. A very large thing was standing next to the president at a press conference on the news. The winged creature was bold red, and was half man and half horse.

"Is that a centaur?" Marcus asked as he rushed to kneel in front of the TV to get a closer look.

"I can assure you that number one, centaurs are not real, and two, there is no centaur anywhere on the screen," Jasmine's dad said, looking, confused, at Marcus.

"Actually dad, there is. I can see it too."

"I can as well," John said from behind Jasmine as he made his way around to get a closer look at the screen.

"What are you crazy kids going on about? No more TV for you, your imaginations are running away with you!" Jasmine's dad found the remote, and the picture on the screen flickered to black. "Time you bunch get to your studies, I think. A centaur? Jesus Christ, this new kid's possessed you all or something, because you guys are losing your minds."

"I don't know if we're losing our minds as much as you think, but whatever is going on, Ho Young is definitely to blame." Jasmine quickly muttered to her dad, rushing everyone upstairs.

As soon as they were out of earshot, John began issuing instructions. "Marcus, you and Ho Young research his family background, and Jasmine and I will research all we can on how all the religions and the mythology might be somehow connected."

"Sounds good to me!" Marcus replied, as he and Ho Young sat down to study.

"Okay, well my dad's name is Martin," Ho Young began immediately.

"Hold up." Marcus held his hand out. "Do you know all your family members off the top of your head?"

"No, I'm afraid. Too many names to remember…"

"Okay then," Marcus said. "Might be easier to start with Gemini and do a family line down from him to see if it leads to you. You know, from his time to this generation. Should be a lot quicker than going up from you to him, since you don't have all the information we'd need."

"This is some pretty cool stuff, man," Ho Young looked eager to begin, but John had to get started on his own task, and turned away from him.

"Alright, Jasmine," he said. "So… to prove anything about any of these religions, we're gonna need information on all of them."

"Yeah, I agree." Jasmine said, pulling out her laptop and arranging a notepad and pen in between them.

"Does your dad have a Bible?"

"I'll go get it." Jasmine nodded, getting up hastily.

When she returned, she sat closer to where John was set up on her bed, and he had to force himself to stay focused.

This is going to be a long night, he thought, peering over her shoulder at the laptop screen.

"Since God is the creator of all things, we need to start with the Bible," she said.

"I agree."

John's dad was a pastor. His mom and dad had divorced a few years prior, but John had been in church so much that he knew a lot of the Bible.

"Okay, so what to look for? Does the Bible mention any of the Greek god's names?" Jasmine asked.

"Well, I don't know, but maybe their names would be different?"

"What do you mean?" Jasmine asked, leaning so closely that she was almost on top of him, listening intently.

"Well, for instance, in English, the word 'see' means sight, but in Spanish, the same pronunciation means yes.

So… one word will mean one thing in one language but mean something completely different in another."

"I'm still not seeing your point… the Bible is written in English, isn't it?"

"Yes, this Bible is written in English, but the Old Testament was originally written in Hebrew, and the New Testament in Greek. So, maybe if we use the English name, Satan, we won't see it written in Greek, because it's not a Greek word."

Jasmine nodded thoughtfully. "That makes sense. It'll be simple. We just look up the Greek word for Satan, and we should be able to find a match." She sounded confident in her reasoning.

"Well, you have to get the right Greek dialect. Like, our language transferred from old English to modern English; Greek has done the same. There is ancient Greek and modern Greek. You couldn't just type 'in Greek,' because, most likely, it will automatically take you to modern Greek."

"Dang, John," Jasmine said, "You are really impressing me right now. Are you sure you don't study?"

"I never said I don't study. I said I don't do homework." John pointed both of his pointers at Jasmine in a cool, smooth kind of way.

"Okay, so let's look up the name 'Satan' in ancient Greek then," Jasmine said. She waited for John's answer before moving this time.

"Let's look up what his name was in Ancient Greece first. I think his name changes From the Old Testament to the New Testament."

"Oh! Okay," Jasmine said, and began typing. First, she typed in 'Satan' and all it gave was other names that Satan went by in Hebrew. The meaning of his name was *adversary*, and there were many variations.

Seeing the disappointment on Jasmine's face, John urged her to try again. "Hmm. Try using Lucifer, but type in 'what does Lucifer mean in Hebrew,' because that name was the name he used in the Old Testament. That is the name Satan went by in heaven."

"Got it!" Jasmine said, turning the screen towards John. On the screen it read that the name Lucifer' meant the morning star, the bringer of light, and Venus.

"Okay, good. That's more to work with," John said.

"Yeah, it is." Jasmine was smiling again. "Now I'm going to see if any of those definitions match any of the names we have for Greek gods."

Jasmine began typing again: 'what Greek god is known as the bringer of light.' The name, Phosphorus, popped right up, and they were shocked by what followed. His name also meant morning star, and he was also called Venus and Lucifer.

"Oh my God," Jasmine said. "We found him in Greek mythology! This is amazing!"

John was shocked that they had found Lucifer's name so fast, because for centuries, religious people overlooked it and had not been able to catch what probably could have easily shown a relationship between the two belief systems.

"Jasmine, do you know how big this is? What we just discovered… This could change all religions and history as we know it!" John grabbed her hands in excitement, but dropped them again as soon as he realized what he'd done.

"I know, oh my God!" Jasmine yelled silently again, her hands flying up to cover the bottom half of her face. "I can't believe it!"

"Me either," John said excitedly. They were silent for a moment, both astounded by their discovery.

"Should we tell Marcus and Ho Young?" Jasmine asked. They both looked over at the others, who were fussing at each other.

"Not just yet," John said. "We still need to see what Lucifer's role in Greek mythology was."

"Okay," Jasmine said, as she went back to typing, 'What was Phosphorus' role in Greek mythology?' A few sites came up. Jasmine clicked the first link that popped up which read, "Phosphorus was the personification of the morning star in Greek mythology, son of the Goddess Eos and the God, Astraeos. He had a half-brother from his mother, by Cephalus, whose name was Hesperus—the evening star."

"Wow, very interesting," John said. "Lucifer is the son of a Titan in Greek mythology." He paused for a minute, organizing the implications of what they'd learned. "So… we know for sure that Satan, who is listed in the Bible as

Lucifer the Angel, is also listed in Greek mythology as a Greek god," John said.

Jasmine's face lit up. "We've done it! We've connected Satan to Greek mythology. Now… who else should we look up?"

"Well," John said. "Rah is an Egyptian god."

"Okay, on it," she said. She typed on the computer: 'How do you say the Egyptian god Rah's name in Greek?'

They clicked on one of the sites. It had a lot of writing, so they scrolled down to where it dealt with the name, 'Rah.' It was just more mumbo jumbo; more rambling trying to explain why some Christians pray to an Egyptian god. It would've been easier if they'd just stuck to facts, definitions, and history—the embellishments were tiring.

Eventually, they discovered his full name was Amen-RAH, the God of Creation, the god that is invisible to all, the god who is eternal. As John and Jasmine flicked through different sites, they considered how interesting it was that Christians say Amen at the end of every prayer, and that Rah appeared to have all the same attributes as the Christian God.

"That is interesting, except… there's one problem… If I remember right, at one point in Moses' day, God said the gods in Egypt were fake. He said that Israel was the first nation since the olden days to call on him."

"Should we look that up?" Jasmine asked.

"Let's look up 'was Rah a god before or after Joseph was taken in by the pharaoh in Egypt and made a great ruler second in command under pharaoh.'"

Jasmine typed in those words, and they clicked on the first link they saw. They skipped six paragraphs down to where it finally spoke about the year Rah was made a god. The first bunch of paragraphs were just the author trying to debunk religions, saying they all stole their faith from Egypt.

After searching more sites, they finally found one describing when Rah became a god. It stated that the Bible's description of the Egyptian gods being fake was accurate, due to their Head God, Rah, beginning as a minor god. It took some time for him to be upgraded to the Head God. This was not done until after Joseph had interpreted the pharaoh's dream, and many of their gods were not added until different groups of people—with different religions—ventured through their lands. Most of their deities came after Greece conquered Persia and took over the rule over Egypt under General Ptolemy.

John and Jasmine checked out a few more official sites that confirmed the information.

"Okay," John said. "Egyptian deities are clearly not real, but borrowed gods from other nations, so… let's move on to the Norse mythology—about the nine realms."

"Sounds good to me," Jasmine replied.

They scrolled through many sites, but came across too many that made the religion sound fake. Some said the definition of this god was effectively 'the cooler one', but others said he was a downer. The further they read, the more fake it sounded, but the continued researching. After time, they came to realize that Norse mythology probably wasn't real, but it was very similar to Greek mythology.

"Jasmine," John said, after pondering for a bit. "What if the Norse religion… their mythology… is just their own version of Greek mythology?"

"What do you mean?" Jasmine asked as she looked up from the screen.

"What if the Norse gods are just the gods of Greece or possibly just like the Roman versions of the Greek gods? I'll bet the natives in Iceland passed the stories down from generation to generation, so the stories of the gods just kept changing until they became known as Norse gods."

"That's a thought." Jasmine sighed. She was tired of researching and she yawned as she closed the laptop. She stretched her arms as far as she could, hoping to shake off the weariness that overcame her.

"To me, it seems like it's either not real—like the Egyptian gods—or like you said, it is real, but it's the same as Greek mythology. It probably just got twisted into a different religion over the years."

John nodded. "Ho Young, Marcus, how is the family tree coming?" he called.

"It's coming pretty good," Marcus replied. "Except… there's no record of Gemini outside of the book we're reading in class. He's not even mentioned in all the information on Greek mythology we found.

"That's alright. Why don't you come and join us?" John said. "There's plenty of research to do still."

"I'm good bro, I'm just going to head home. It's already 10:30… It's already really late. I'll be lucky if I don't get grounded."

"It's 10:30?" Jasmine said in shock. "It can't be!"

"Wow," John said, checking the time on his phone. "The time really did fly… but I understand. If you have to go, you have to go—dude, is Ho Young asleep?" John looked over at their friends curled-up form.

"Yeah, he fell asleep about thirty-minutes in," Marcus replied. "He seemed real tired. Hopefully he doesn't live too far from here?"

"Yeah, I would sure hate to have to walk far if I were tired, and it's freezing cold out. You know what? I've never been to his house… or met his parents." John said. "He never talks about them."

"Oh my God, you guys don't know?" Jasmine whispered in case Ho Young woke up.

"Know what?" Marcus asked as his eyes narrowed in concern. Jasmine knew something that he didn't, and he wanted to find out what it was.

"Ho Young is homeless," Jasmine said, her face tightening with sadness. Her eyes were watery as she fought back tears. "His parents died when he was a child and he's been living on the streets ever since. He sleeps in the park over by the mall at night."

"You have to be kidding me. I never knew…" John felt dreadful for his friend. "You know," he continued. "My mom is never home. If Ho Young wanted to move into my house, she wouldn't care at all."

"That's nice of you, John, but he wouldn't. I already tried about a year ago.

"Really?" Marcus asked.

"I kept pushing the subject with him, and he ended up getting upset and walking away. You guys have to leave it alone—please. I shouldn't have said anything."

"Of course we will," John and Marcus agreed.

TWENTY

When they left Jasmine's house that night, John decided to follow Ho Young and find out exactly where he was staying. He followed from a distance for about thirty minutes before they reached the park where Ho Young had hidden his bedding and belongings behind a scraggly bush, about twenty feet away from a group of people sleeping on blankets—more homeless people. John bit his lip.

The skin on the back of his neck prickled and John turned to see a group of boys in red. Their faces were obscured by puffs of smoke, but the red durags on their heads or in their back pockets made him pause and look back at Ho Young. He wondered if he realized that a gang—which John assumed to be the Bloods due to their colors—were smoking weed and swisher blunts just a few hundred yards away across the field. A cop car passed on the side the gang was on, but they didn't seem nervous

He wondered if Ho Young was safe.

There were two dogs play-fighting and racing in the middle of the street, and it was clear that they too were homeless. The menacing light of the streetlamps cast a dim glow over the park. It looked like a warning: get out of the darkness, evil and death dwell here.

John considered Ho Young's position, and Jasmine's advice, as he walked home. There was nothing else for it—Ho Young would have to stay with him. He would have to talk to his mom first, but he knew she liked helping people and wouldn't mind. He would just have to find a way to confront Ho Young in private.

*****

"Hey, mom," he said, walking through the front door and setting his stuff down next to the living room couch. He knew she'd be up; she never slept for more than an hour at a time so she usually was.

"Hey," she replied. "I thought you must have been staying at Marcus' tonight?"

"No, we were studying at Jasmine's house."

"Studying—oh, I see," she said, grinning, and doing her best to give John a wink that wound up looking more like a nervous twitch.

"No mom, we were just studying." John hated talking to his mom about relationship stuff, and avoided it at all cost because she always found a way to make the conversations unbearably uncomfortable.

"You know," she began, fussing about in the kitchen. "I like that Jasmine girl. She's real nice and has a good head on her shoulders."

"Don't forget she has a nice body under her shoulders as well," John added, shrugging and flashing his mom a cheeky grin.

"Oh my goodness, I did not need to hear that," John's mom said, laughing softly. "But you really should ask her out on a date."

John groaned. "Mom, if I want to date her I will, but I don't want to talk about that right now. Actually, there's something else I need to talk to you about."

"Oh?" She handed him a steaming cup and settled herself on the couch beside him. "What is it?"

"Do you remember Ho Young?" he asked.

"Yes… I do." She eyed him suspiciously. She did not know what he had on his mind, but normally when he started asking questions like he was at the moment, there was an incentive behind it—he was going to paint a picture to encourage her to do something for one of his friends. At times, it was to buy them clothes if they didn't have any. Other times, it was as simple as her making meals for them.

"Well," he began. "Apparently he's homeless and sleeping in the park… and has been since he was a kid. His parents disappeared when he was little, but they left him a note saying to never give up and to succeed in life and all that other good stuff. I was going to see if he wanted to stay here, but I figured I'd better run it by you first."

Her smile faded and she regarded John seriously. "It is fine with me," she said. "As long as he can follow the rules and clean up behind himself."

"Okay, I'll ask him on Monday," John said, nodding. He was glad she understood. "And thank you!" He gave her a hug and pulled a face. "If one of the house rules is cleaning up behind yourself, you're grounded mom! The kitchen is always a hot mess."

"Anyway," John's mom said, ignoring his remark. "Are you going to your dad's church tomorrow?" she asked, as he was grabbing a frozen burrito from the freezer.

"No," He shook his head. "It's already 11:30 at night, and even if it wasn't, there's no way I'm getting up that early on any Saturday. I'll just go on Sunday. I don't even know why he's having church tomorrow to begin with."

"No problem," she said. "I could use some help around the house tomorrow anyway—moving furniture and deep cleaning the fridge and walls, and…"

John interrupted before she could finish, "I take that back," he said. "One day away from church is one step closer to walking on the wrong path!" He grinned. "I think I better go to church after all."

His mom started laughing, "You're always trying to get out of cleaning."

"Well, you know what they say mom. If kids were meant to clean, God would have made them the parents…"

"John, I have never heard that a day in my life!"

"Well, listen out for it because it's going to catch on!" He bid her goodnight and left her to think in the living room.

*****

His cell phone rang as he jogged up the stairs to his room and he looked at the screen before pressing the answer button. It was Jasmine.

"What's up?" John answered his phone with some concern—it was very late.

"John, come back over," Jasmine said. "I want to do some more studying."

"Tonight?" John didn't really feel like leaving his house again.

"Yeah, tonight… and bring a change of clothes," Jasmine started "I asked my dad and…"

"I'm there," John said, not even letting her finish the sentence as he ran a quick hand through his hair—sleep could wait.

"Okay, see you in a bit." Jasmine said. He could hear the smile in her voice.

John hung up and quickly grabbed some stuff to take to Jasmine's and spend the night: a towel, a pair of boxers, some pants, and a shirt. He also grabbed his toothbrush, an extra pair of socks, his deodorant, and his cologne.

He was careful to walk out the front door quietly. His mom was going to have a long day of cleaning the next day, so he didn't want to wake her. He knew he was going to go back and help. He always did, but he hated being there for the starting part of her big clean ups.

John closed the door gently so that it didn't make any creaking noises. As he walked, he looked up at the stars. They were beautiful, but they kept taking his mind back to their research. John and Jasmine had made a great discovery, but there was still so much that they had to learn.

"*Outside at your front door*." He sent a text Jasmine to let her know he'd arrived.

A notification beeped its way to life on John's phone, and he saw that she was on her way down, and she opened the door not even seconds later.

"What in the world are you wearing?" John asked, laughing to himself about her geographical pajama bottoms and wondering how she expected him to focus on studying when her short pajama top showed off her new belly button ring—and the smooth skin it sat on.

"Clothes…" Jasmine replied, eyeing him with a wry smile. "Come on in," she said, stepping aside so he could get past her.

She already had the laptop and books set up on the coffee table in front of the couch, so he sat, assuming she'd set them up there for the night. John was glad they were on the large, brown leather couch—it was heated, and much more comfortable than Jasmine's floor.

"You want any snacks?" Jasmine asked, as John rummaged through their notes.

He shook his head. "Nope, I'm good."

"Where should we start?" Jasmine asked.

"Let's start where we left off. The Norse religion is fake, the Egyptian religion seems to be just a mixture of a bunch of other religions and completely altered. So let's look to India," John said. He leaned back onto the couch and yawned.

They spent most of the night researching the variety of religions and noting what they had in common. Many of them led back to the Greek gods which in turn led back to the Christian God. They searched hard and wide to find a reason as to why the religions had become so far separated from each other when they'd once seemed so close together, but came up empty. It was nearing daylight when they both fell asleep on the couch, John with a book in his hands and Jasmine with the laptop on her lap.

*****

In the morning, John woke to the heavy footfalls of Jasmine's dad coming down the stairs. It was a good thing he was whistling, because Jasmine and John somehow wound up lying entwined around each other during the night and would have been in big trouble if he'd seen. John quickly rolled out from underneath Jasmine and onto the floor and pretended to be asleep. Jasmine's dad stopped at the entrance to the living room to examine them for a moment. Through barely open eyes, John saw him chuckle. “That’s what I’m talking about,” he said to himself as he walked away smiling.

John was going to pretend to be asleep longer, but his dad called his cell phone.

“You coming to church today?” his dad asked.

“I’m not sure, Pop,” John replied. “I was up all night working on a project at a friend’s house.”

“Okay,” John’s dad replied. His dad wasn’t very emotional, and as such, he saw everything in black and white—there were no gray areas. You either did something or you didn’t, and excuses didn’t exist.

“Okay, talk to you later Pop,” John said, hanging his phone up.

He heard Jasmine moving on the couch and adjusted himself on the floor so that he could look up at her, unable to contain his big smile. She was sitting up on the couch, stretching and yawning. He caught a quick sneak peek at her belly button and reached his hand out to poke it.

“Stop that,” Jasmine said, breaking into bright giggles.

“Sorry, I couldn’t help myself.”

“Looks like we got as much done last night as we’re going to be able to get done on that project,” Jasmine said with a big grin on her face, showing that she was pleased with her work.

“Yeah, we did, but it still leaves us no closer to the answers than we were before we began studying. If only we could find the book that the demigods found in the tale we’re reading in school.” John said, shooting Jasmine a confused grimace. He had no idea why she was happy that they had gotten as far as they could get, because it was literally the same place that they had started at.

"Yeah, that would help a lot," Jasmine said. "Of course, that's assuming the book is real."

John sighed. "Well, if Ho Young is real then maybe the book is too. That's what Marcus thinks."

"Good point," Jasmine responded. "So, do you want some bacon and eggs?" Jasmine asked John as she raised herself up and off the couch.

"Glad you offered. Yes, we would like some bacon and eggs," Jasmine's dad said as he came around the corner. "Make mine over easy."

"Mine too," John said, exchanging an amused glance with Jasmine's dad.

"Well, too bad," Jasmine said. "I'll make dad's over easy, but I'm going to make ours into omelets." She gave John a quick wink before heading back into the kitchen.

"No cheese in mine," John yelled to Jasmine as she disappeared into the kitchen.

"Oh my God," she yelled back. "I forgot you're lactose intolerant. It is going to be nasty without cheese, but okay, guess you'll have to deal with it."

They'd just finished breakfast when the weather report flashed up on the TV news.

"It looks like we have a heavy thunder and lightning storm coming in this afternoon, with expected showers throughout the rest of the week. Take care this evening folks, we're expecting up to twelve inches of rain tonight!" The weather reporter gestured enthusiastically at his charts.

John thought of Ho Young, who would get drenched and frozen if he had to sleep outside. It was due to snow any day now, too.

"Jasmine," he said, dropping his plate in the sink. "We have to figure something out. It sounds like it's just about going to flood for the next week, and Ho Young can't stay outside in it—no way."

The weather outside worked to emphasize his point. Thunder roared in the background as raindrops began to descend from the heavens, lightly hitting the roof in a relaxing melody. John looked out the window to see the sky. A lightning bolt slashed through the gray of storm clouds, briefly lighting the sky. John couldn't help but think that something was different about it. He was about to mention it to Jasmine when there was another giant lightning strike, followed by another, and then another. He was right—they were no ordinary lightning bolts. They were as thick as an ancient redwood tree's base, and they shot from the Earth into the sky, instead of following their usual path.

"We should go get Ho Young," John said, ignoring the look of confusion on Jasmine's dad's face. He had a bad feeling, and he wasn't just concerned for Ho Young in the rain. He could almost hear the words on the crackling air—speaking to him: "Go get Ho Young, no demigod is safe tonight."

Despite their strangeness, the words were crystal clear and he felt that they were extremely important.

Jasmine nodded, and she dashed upstairs to change while John changed in the bathroom downstairs. Jasmine's dad shouted after them as they hurried out the door, but they didn't have time to explain. "Later, Dad!" Jasmine called over her shoulder. "It's—it's—for the project! Important research stuff!"

Jasmine's dad tossed a couple of umbrellas to them, and they made it to the park without getting too wet. John led Jasmine to the spot where Ho Young had slept the previous night, and they found him curled in his makeshift bed, under a pile of covers and jackets, trying to keep warm. The covers were soaking wet, and John doubted that Ho Young had known the storm was coming. The clouds had probably formed while he was asleep, and he'd had no time to move when he'd awoken.

"Ho Young, come on!" John shouted over the rumbling bellow of thunder. "Come with us!" He looked up at the sky and shook his head in concern—it was too loud.

"Ho Young!" John yelled again.

Ho Young heard John this time and quickly sat up on his soaked bed. "Hey guys, what's up?" Ho Young asked. "Excuse the mess… I wasn't expecting any company..." Around Ho Young's bed were a few food wrappers and water bottles.

"Well, I would've knocked, but your door was wide open," John said, trying his hardest not to laugh at his own corny joke.

Ho Young grabbed his stomach with both arms as he laughed, paying little mind to the fact that John had found his residence. "That was a pretty good one, man," Ho Young said, as he began to clean up around his bed.

Jasmine's eyes widened and her mouth dropped open as she swatted John on the shoulder. "That was so rude!" she said. She frowned when the boys continued to chortle.

"It was a joke—calm down," John said. "I've known Ho Young for years, he likes jokes… and you saw it yourself—he laughed."

"We need to get him into a house," Jasmine reminded John in a whisper, flicking her gaze to Ho Young.

"I know and I'm going to work on it, trust me."

"Okay." She knew he was as worried as she was. "But no more jokes about Ho Young being homeless!"

"I can't promise that. Jokes are what I do—not to mention they might help relax the situation—get Ho Young to agree to move into a house."

Jasmine just looked at him without saying a word. She wanted to argue but John did have a good point.

"Besides," he said, interrupting Jasmine's thoughts. "If we're to be in a relationship, you have to accept me for my faults." John teased, poking her in the side.

"No, I don't." Jasmine scowled mockingly. "Because we aren't in a relationship, and there is no guarantee that we ever will be." The rain was pounding down on them and she had to wrestle with her umbrella to stop the wind from stealing it. She didn't mean to be so short with John, but the situation was testing her patience. She could see she had killed John's playful mood, but the damage was already done and her temper hadn't abated, so she continued.

"As a matter of fact," she said. "You're forgetting that Marcus likes me as well, and I haven't yet decided who I want to date. We're all friends right now, and I don't want to ruin it."

"That's cool," John said, turning away. As much as he liked to joke and have fun, Jasmine's words were too much. With every word, every syllable, and every letter, his heart cracked a little more, until it felt as though she'd broken it a thousand times.

"As a matter of fact," he snapped, after a moment. "Marcus can have you. I'm cool just being friends,"

"Oh—kay?" Jasmine replied, sounding a bit confused. "I mean, if that's what you want…"

Ho Young finally came out from his makeshift closet—the space between the bush he'd pulled his bedding from the night before and a few trees bordering the fence. He was dressed and ready to go. He even had a rain parka on to keep him dry.

It was silent as the three of them walked back to Jasmine's house, leaving the housing conversation for later. When they arrived, John pretended he left something at home and walked back.

*****

Walking in the rain was something he usually loved doing, but on this day, he didn't. John had so many negative thoughts crossing his mind. He thought of dropping out of school, because he didn't want to have to see Jasmine, but he knew his mom would never go for it. The rain continued to pour down as he walked into his house. He went straight to his room and laid down on his bed, not sure which sad love movie to watch.

*****

Jasmine's doorbell rang.

"How is everything going with the studies?" Marcus asked when Jasmine opened the door for him. He followed her up to her room.

"They're going good," she replied, gesturing for him to get comfortable. "John came over last night and we did a lot of studying. We figured out that most religions seem to stem from Greek mythology, and Greek mythology stems from the Bible."

Marcus gave her his full attention. "John came by here again last night after we left? Why?" It was obvious that he was feeling disgruntled and left out.

"Well… because I called him and asked him to, but only because it was John and I that were studying together—we were trying to find the connections in the religions, don't you remember?

"Oh, yeah that makes sense. I couldn't have come back anyways because it was past my curfew."

"John discovered that there is a strong chance that the Greek gods might actually be the angels from the Bible, like in the book we're reading at school." Jasmine explained.

"That's just a book though," Marcus said, not wanting Jasmine to know that he thought it was real too. He thought John might have told her so that they could play a prank on him—it wouldn't have been beneath John to do something like that. He leaned against the wall, arms crossed, trying to gauge her response.

"Well, I'm going to disagree." She replied, waving one of the articles from the night before in his face. "It may have seemed like a story in that book, but John proved it! He found evidence from Greek mythology and the Bible, so it looks like it's the same in real life."

"Really?" Marcus said, snatching the paper from her hands. "Show me."

Jasmine spent the next hour showing Marcus and Ho Young the research that she and John had come up with.

"Wow, that's some good stuff there." Marcus said. "Where is John, by the way?"

"He said he was going home to get some stuff, but that was a while ago." Ho Young looked up from what he was reading. He sounded a bit unsure.

"Oh, I see. Has anyone tried to call him?"

"No," Jasmine replied. "I just assumed he was coming back straight away."

"I'll call him then." Marcus grabbed his cell phone from his pocket.

The phone rang several times before it connected.

"If you've reached my voicemail, there's no need to leave a message if I didn't answer. I probably didn't answer because I don't like you," came Johns voice at the other end.

"Dang, man, that is a messed up voicemail," Marcus said aloud to himself. He was startled by John's laughter.

"Just kidding," he said. "What's up? How's it going?"

Marcus laughed, "Dang, man, you got me good. I really thought it was an answering machine."

"If you thought that was an answering machine, and then thought it wasn't, I'm not sorry to let you know that you're wrong again. Leave a message at the beep." John's voicemail message finished with more laughter.

"Wow—just wow… John's voicemails… He's always changing them, and they always get me." Marcus sat down on the bed next to Ho Young and Jasmine, just as her dad yelled up the stairs at them.

"That door better be open!" he said, and Marcus scrambled to make more of a gap between them.

"It is!" Jasmine shouted back, rolling her eyes at Marcus. "So, he didn't answer, huh?" she asked him.

"Nope," he replied. "He's probably asleep or busy doing something."

"No, he's mad at me, probably." Jasmine sighed and put her head in her hands. "He made a joke about us being in a relationship, and I told him that you liked me too, and that I haven't decided yet."

"Yeah?" Marcus asked, scooting back over beside her. He sat as close as he felt he could without her getting weirded-out.

"John replied that he was good, and that you and I should date. That was the end of it. We didn't speak the rest of the way here, except for him saying he'd be back because he had to go home and grab something."

"And what do you think about that?" Marcus asked, leaning in closer. He seemed to have forgotten all about Ho Young. This was his chance. Jasmine had clearly said that she was trying to decide between him and John, and with John having upset her, the odds were in his favor.

"What do I think about what?" she asked, not sure exactly what it was he was asking.

"About the two of us dating," he said, much louder than he had intended to. He didn't feel so great trying to get Jasmine to tell him that she liked him, mostly because he knew that John was in love with her. Still, he was interested too, and he wasn't about to let his friendship with John wreck his chances of dating the prettiest girl in school.

"Oh my God," she groaned. "Not you too! Well, like I said to John, I'm not going to decide right now. We're all great friends, and a decision like that will affect that."

Marcus backed away before he replied, worried that she was about to go off at him. "It's cool," he said.

She didn't say anything more.

TWENTY-ONE

Zeus appeared first on Mt Olympus. He looked at his hands and discovered that they were free from the dastardly chains. Hades appeared next, and then Poseidon. One by one, all the Greek gods began to appear around them; they had all been freed from their prisons in the pits of hell.

"What's happening?" Zeus asked, confused, as he looked around.

One of the lowliest of the gods was about to speak, but the words seemed to be stuck in his mouth. Instead he pointed towards Zeus' throne, on which a figure was sitting. All of them stepped back in a sudden wave of fear. On the throne sat none other than the Titan, Lucifer, himself. He was the general who had led their parents and ancestors in their war in heaven against The Creator. Most of them had never met Lucifer because he had been cast into the bottomless pit long before their time, but there were paintings of him next to those that depicted the war in heaven, so they all knew quite well what he looked like.

"Has your one thousand years expired already?" Zeus asked, trembling a bit. In his last battle against Ouranos, he was defeated easily.

Lucifer was far more powerful than Ouranos.

Lucifer stared at Zeus with a blazing look that stilled their entire audience.

"I must go to arrange for the death of Odin, Thor and all the guardians of Asgard," Lucifer began. "They betrayed me—and they betrayed the others in the war back home in heaven. Odin gave Michael the blueprint of our battle strategies, ensuring that Michael would know everything we were to do before we did it. I do not need those traitors meddling in this war and interfering again."

"Interfere in what?" Demeter asked, curious as to what Lucifer was referring to.

"We have been given time to prepare for battle. The Creator has decided to honor my request for one final battle."

"One final battle!" Zeus yelled in outrage. There should not be another battle for Lucifer. As he spoke, the sky shuddered with thunder, and lightning streaked in bright patterns across the sky.

Lucifer's laugh cut through them like a blade. "Your anger is cute, I suppose. Yes, Zeus," he said. "One final battle."

"But you and all those who followed you were destroyed the last time you led others into battle!" Gaia spoke up, watching her son warily from the corner of her eye. "And, we were destroyed again in the last battle we had with The Creator—while you were in the bottomless pit."

"True." Lucifer nodded and cocked his head, pretending to consider her wizened words. He barked out a mocking, twisted laugh. "Good times, huh?"

"You will send us all to our annihilation!"

"Silence," he bellowed, rising to his full height.

"So, tell us why we would want to stand against The Creator!" Aries yelled from the very back of Zeus' temple.

"Because he was just going to throw all of us in the Lake of Fire! I was able to convince him to give us a chance to defend ourselves. He will allow us to fight one last battle! If we lose…" He lowered his voice. "We will be cast in the lake anyway, but if we win, we regain control of Earth and all the realms that come with it."

There was silence for a moment.

"What's the catch?" Hades finally asked. "What I mean is, we know from the first two wars that we cannot beat Michael and his angels, so how exactly are we supposed to win this war?"

"That is a very good question Hades. You have much more intellect than your brothers." Lucifer said, flashing him a rare but dazzling smile.

Zeus began to speak, but Lucifer held his hand out to silence him.

"The catch is, Hades, that we will fight this war differently than the last time. The last time we fought this war head on, but the advantage went to The Creator. This time, we will have the advantage on our side."

"How so?" Hades asked.

"The Creator has agreed to battle us in a series of tournaments, instead of in direct combat, after much persuasion by none other than myself. There will be seven tournaments. We only have to win one of the tournaments to be free."

"Okay," said Hera, beginning to nod along, her interest piqued. "That's good to know, but what are these tournaments, and how do they favor us?"

Lucifer responded, "I only know about the first one for the time being. The Creator has chosen four champions of the humans and has un-bound their powers. In turn, we are allowed to pick four of our most ferocious beasts to battle them."

"Who did he pick, and what are their powers?" Hera asked, still a little skeptical.

"As of right now, only one is even aware of his power, so we don't have a lot to go on. We can be sure though, that The Creator will reveal all to the other three before the battle takes place. They are descendants of the demigods who fought the battle you lost while I was locked away! It is… possible… that they can be persuaded to join us."

"Are the battles in arenas? Are they going to be four on four? What are the rules?" Many of the gods were speaking, but Aphrodite's questions were the clearest.

"To answer your first question," Lucifer answered. "No, they will not be held in the arenas. As for the others—the platform is the entirety of planet Earth, and they will indeed be four on four. There is only one rule…" He paused and let his gaze meet the eyes of every single attendee. "We cannot interfere."

"Well, that does sound fair, and like it could definitely lean in our favor," Zeus said, massaging his chin with his pointer finger and thumb like he always did when he was pondering an idea.

"Yeah this might work." There was a collective nod and an uproar of tentative agreement from the gods.

"Now, to pick out our deadliest beasts, and then find the top four to send after them," Lucifer said as he slipped into deep thought.

"Most of our beasts were killed in the first war, so we don't have many options," Hades pointed out.

"I made a few special requests. I was allowed to get the soul of Fenrir and place him in a mortal body. He has all of his strength, and can only be killed by silver—I was lucky enough to find a fifteen-foot giant to place his soul in. With the change to his make-up, he can now change into a wolf whenever he feels like it."

"What other beast were you able to resurrect?" Zeus asked, now intrigued and feeling like they may actually beat The Creator this time.

"None, but I was able to find Chiron, the centaur, long ago. He has been controlling the human political system in secret, haunting the world's leaders, and keeping them in fear.

"We can use him to try and prevent these kids from joining The Creator's side, which will really ruin his plans! We will have to find two more beasts to challenge the champions, in case Chiron fails." Lucifer said, addressing everyone at once. All the fallen angels who had been praised by humans in their Greek mythology were present.

"You can help as well," Zeus said, mustering up the courage to speak. "Odin was killed in the last battle by Fenrir the werewolf, and Thor was killed by Leviathan. Asgard and its leaders are re-forming, so you have no need to go there."

Lucifer smiled and opened his arms to them. "Good news, then!" he said. "We'll reconvene tomorrow. For now, we need to be coming up with ideas for the last and final two beasts that will compete in the tournament."

There was a murmur of chatter as they separated.

TWENTY-TWO

As John walked down the halls of his school, he avoided Marcus and Jasmine. He wanted nothing to do with either of them. Ho Young said hi as he walked by, but John just kept walking without even giving Ho Young the time of day.

"Okay class," Mrs Norton said as John took his seat in her class. "We are going to read more of the book today, so open them up to the last page we finished reading."

*****

"We need to send someone to free Loki, which is nearly impossible to do, because Heimdall is always on the watch," Athena began. "The only god among us who has the power to do it is Hera, with her invisibility, but that just brings us back to square one."

"It's pointless," Aries said. "Nobody has ever been able to sneak into Asgard. We need to come up with another plan! I don't see why we're even talking about Thor or Odin. We need to be focused on Zeus and Ouranos!" He watched as Hermes paced angrily amongst the others.

"Wrong!" Athena cried, her expression vicious. "The Creator sent Ouranos to fight us. Asgard betrayed our ancestors in the first war. Thor and Odin sided with Michael and the angels against us, hoping to receive forgiveness from The Creator for their treasonous acts against him. He did not forgive them, but gave them a lighter punishment than our ancestors." She shook her head. "I doubt they plan to sit this one out expecting to receive full redemption from The Creator a second time. They want to be allowed to live again from whence they have been banished—their former home, a place called heaven—but they know that standing aside is not the way to do it. We need to defeat them first so that they're not around to sneak attack us while our attention is focused on Zeus and Ouranos."

"Very true," Dionysus agreed with Athena, twirling a crystal wineglass stem between his fingers.

"And!" Athena continued. "There has been one group that successfully snuck into Asgard. The giants. They discovered secret ways in, and they mapped them! Here is one right here, from our realm."

Athena laid out a map of the nine realms and showed the dragon at the bottom of the sea. "He guards a secret door," Athena began to explain the map to the other gods. "And that door leads to all the realms and is not in sight of any Asgardian."

"Okay, well why doesn't the dragon just use that door to sneak in undetected and kill Thor, then?"

"He can't," Athena answered quickly. "When The Creator placed the dragon as the guardian of the door, He made it so that the dragon could never enter—it is the same for all the doors and all their guardians. If they did decide to try, they would immediately disintegrate."

"How do we get the dragon to cooperate?" Gaia asked, liking the plan up to this point.

"The dragon wants to destroy Thor, and is waiting on his cue from Loki. We just tell him that Loki is being held prisoner and that we're going to go and free him. I am sure he will be more than willing to accommodate us."

"Oceanus?" Athena called his name and he appeared in a whisp of vapor.

"On it," he said, disappearing again to go and bargain with the dragon.

"Now, we have one more problem," Athena said, staring at Gaia. "Somebody broke our laws of secrecy, but it has been rectified."

"What do you mean?" Gaia asked, curious and gravely concerned at the accusation.

"This," Athena said as she threw the book The History of the Gods on the floor before all of them. "I stole it from the demigods while they were asleep. Our laws, if they had read this, would have forced us to kill them. That was a terrible gamble on your part, Gaia." Athena chided her.

"Hera had already promised it to them, so I just gave it to them to help with their journey." Gaia defended herself.

"Not yours or Hera's decision to make!" Aeolus yelled as strong winds passed through the room, obscuring some of his words.

"Anyway, the book is back in our hands and they didn't read it. No harm done." Gaia spoke with an unquestionable roughness in her voice. Her words clearly indicated that the topic was done and off the table. She wrung her hands, mortified that the others thought she had put the demigods in danger.

"No harm done? You just killed our whole purpose. You attempted to assist the demigods on their missions, and we all know that there are always consequences for breaking the rules," Athena reprimanded.

"Nice to hear." Gaia said as her eyes glowed red with anger at Athena's insubordination. "Can we get back to the mission at hand?"

Athena kept quiet because she knew she had reached her limit with Gaia, and Gaia was much more powerful than she was. If the other gods had shown signs that they would have backed her, she might have pressed further, but not one of them stepped in.

"Once Oceanus gets us access to the door leading into Asgard, Aries, you must go with Orion to free Loki and Fenrir."

"Wait a minute, why do I have to go?" Orion bellowed from the back of the group.

"Because if they see you, they will blame it on the giants, which will incite a war between them That will keep them distracted while our two giants destroy Zeus and Ouranos."

*****

Hercules paced back and forth while Jeffrey played with a stream of water, willing it into different shapes. Vanessa snuck up on Jeffrey in her invisible state, causing him to jump as she quickly and roughly grabbed his shoulders to scare him. The stream of water he had been playing with flew up in the air and came down on both of them, soaking their faces. They both burst out in laughter, delighted by the moment of unmarred enjoyment.

Xavior was relaxing on a cloud when Savannah screamed from where she was lying on the ground. Every demigod jumped to their feet, ready to defend themselves.

"What is it?" Xavior called down to them.

"The book is gone!" Savannah's things were sprawled all over the ground, but there was no book.

"Um, did you do this to your stuff or was it the thief?" Jeffrey asked as he walked up and saw the mess.

"I did! I had the book under my arm when I fell asleep, but when I woke up it was gone, so I dumped all my stuff out in frustration."

"Maybe the gods took it back. I do remember hearing that it's forbidden for anyone to read the contents of that book." Kikilliana suggested.

"But why would Gaia give it to us then?" Savannah asked as she raised her eyebrows and folded her arms in attitude. Savannah had an answer for just about everything, whether she was right or wrong, and hated when others tried to override her opinion.

"Because she only cares about herself." A tall woman spoke as she appeared out of thin air.

"Mom?" Savannah asked, as she recognized the mark of Athena on her mom's neck. Savannah's mouth hung open as she stared at her mother. She had never seen her before.

"Yes, it is me, Savannah. I took the book while you were sleeping to protect you. All of us are under attack, but Gaia is the only one that is prophesied to die. She is desperate to find a way to live, even if it costs one of you your life. She was hoping that you would be able to find an answer in our history and save her before the curse of the book killed you. Since you are my daughter, I couldn't let that happen."

Athena kissed her daughter on the forehead and disappeared into the air, leaving Savannah speechless and staring at the place where she had been.

"Good thing your mom showed up and took the book. That was pretty messed up of Gaia," Xavior said.

Savannah had tuned everyone out as she sat down. She finally got to meet her mom in person, and she got a kiss on her forehead. She had always wondered if her mom had loved her because she made no attempt to contact her. This was all the proof she needed. Savannah felt as though she was rippling with the new energy that overtook her.

The group prepared to sleep in the clouds as was now their custom. Gemini was the only one who didn't sleep—he'd become paranoid of danger and insisted on manning his post to ensure that they were all safe through the night. Somewhere near their camp was his evil half-brother, the minotaur. Gemini flipped out of his cloud, landing twenty feet below on the ground.

"Where are you?" he yelled ferociously. Fear surged through him as he heard sounds, but could not see a thing through the pure darkness.

Gemini never even saw his brother coming. All he knew was that he was suddenly consumed by a white-hot shock of pain and then he was landing with an almighty thud, thirty feet away from where he had been standing. His side had been punctured by the minotaur's ramming horn, and blood was pouring from his pierced skin like water from a fountain. He rushed to place both hands over his wound to try and stifle the bleeding, but the blood continued to leak from the wound in its promise of death.

He raised his left arm in the air and a fire leapt to life, burning in a circle around him. Droplets of blood splattered his face as they fell from his hand, but the fire would protect him from further attack by the minotaur. It rushed toward him again, but was caught in a lick of glowing flame, sending it falling backward. It writhed in place as it screamed into the night, and several of the other demigods were awoken in their clouds above.

Gemini was badly wounded, but at least now he had some light. He sat safely away from the flames, which blazed ten feet away from him in every direction.

"You are a coward attacking when I can't see you! No wonder you fear my dad," he cried, as he saw the creature rise in the shadows.

The minotaur jumped through the flames, wielding a large sword. "Well, you can see me now, and I don't know what lies your father told you, but it is the other way around. It is your father who fears me!"

The sight of his brother alone, caused Gemini's body to tremble. The minotaur was twelve feet tall, and looked to be about one thousand pounds of muscle with not one weak spot. It rushed forward again, wielding the sword. He was much too fast for Gemini, who didn't even bother raising his hands to defend himself—he knew he had no time; he knew death was coming.

Just as the minotaur was upon him, the glinting edge of the blade swinging down towards his neck, a flash of lightning sliced through the minotaur. It was lifted into the air, where it hung motionless and screaming in rage. When Gemini looked around, he was startled to find Hercules a mere three feet behind him, and Xavior flying just above them.

"Okay, drop him!" Hercules yelled, working in tandem with Xavior.

Xavior looked at the minotaur for a quick second, taking in how ferocious it was. He was the scariest thing Xavior had ever seen, and he was happy to drop it right beside Hercules, who smashed its head between his hands, killing it instantly. Hercules then picked up the dead minotaur by the legs and, spinning around a few times before releasing it, launched him into space.

"Hercules! Gemini is hurt. He needs help right now," Xavior yelled, his voice cracking upon seeing the wound. Hercules took one look at the size of the hole in Gemini's side and dropped down beside him.

"Man, he impaled you pretty good," he said lightly as the color continued to drain from Gemini's face.

"Yeah, he caught me in the dark. I couldn't see him."

"No worries. At some point, all of us get caught unprepared, and the best we can hope for is to live through it and learn from it. Just be glad you're still alive." Hercules looked to Xavior briefly, before offering Gemini a pointed look. "You're not alone, you know. We're here together to aid each other," he finished.

"Yeah, I will definitely remember that next time," Gemini replied quietly as they helped him to his feet and back to camp.

Savannah saw them first, and dove straight into her pack for healing ingredients. She started up a fire and set some honey to boil while she crushed two mint leaves into a fine powder. She grabbed a long-handled wooden spoon from her ouch and carefully applied the boiled honey to Gemini's wound. Gemini flinched away in pain, but the honey did its job and the bleeding stopped. When Savannah added the mint powder, the wound immediately hardened up, sealing closed even as they watched. Gemini looked dumbfounded.

"Wow, you're amazing," he said, as the pain melted away into nothing. Savannah smiled and thanked him for his words of kindness.

None of them were able to sleep after the ordeal, so Xavior decided to set the clouds to carry them on to their destination—it wasn't a good idea to waste time.

"It would be so nice if there was stuff like this that we could fly on without you having to be here," Gemini said as he looked at the retreating ground far below them. "No offense," he added, realizing that his statement could have come off as rude.

"No worries," Xavior replied. "I see your point. I'm sure everyone would love to fly, just as I would love to be able to create weapons out of nothing like you do."

"Wow." Gemini thought for a moment. "I never thought about it like that. I guess we all have a little of something, but want more."

"Yeah that is a true statement," Savannah said, offering her stamp of approval.

As they flew, the air became dense and clouds began to form, forcing Xavior to land earlier than he had planned.

"Everyone be on guard. It's probably Zeus or Ouranos forcing us down so another beast can attack us." Vanessa peered over the edge of her cloud, trying to spot what danger might await them. "This is getting annoying," she said as they landed. "The ocean is right there. I can see it in the distance. We only have five miles left to finish our journey. Let's just split up. The rest of us can stay here to fight off whatever beast they throw at us now, while Jeffrey and Hercules go and free Poseidon."

Jeffrey smiled at her, but shook his head. "That would be a great plan," he said. "But we have to go a lot further than the shoreline... I thought you guys knew that?"

"How much further are we talking about exactly?" Xavior asked as his shoulders dropped, and he gave an unwilling sigh. He didn't know how much more he could do, but he knew he was feeling weaker. He'd been exhausting his powers and he would be useless if he was needed for an encore performance.

"To the middle of the ocean." Jeffrey flashed an embarrassed grin.

"Are you kidding me right now?" Xavior asked, eyes wide and brows furrowed in horror—the thought of trying to fly them across the ocean was too much to even fathom. "I can't fly you guys that far."

"I know," Jeffrey said. "It gets worse though."

The group looked at him expectantly.

"Dad's castle is 27,841 thousand feet below the surface. How do the gods expect me to hold my breath for that long? Not to mention the ocean would crush my lungs by the time I swam eighty feet down—at the most."

"Oh, wow," Savannah said, desperation weighing heavily on her shoulders. "This is impossible. There is literally no way that this can be accomplished."

Gemini let out a mirthless chuckle. "Count on the gods to give us an impossible mission," he said.

"Well, actually, it's never impossible," Hercules said, still angry. He was remembering a lesson with Turally, when he was taught that no matter how impossible it may seem, there is a way to accomplish everything. "Just nearly impossible. I don't know how, but there is a way to accomplish this. They brought us all together because they believed that the seven of us could somehow figure out how to accomplish this."

"True, so what now? We need a boat and we have no money." Gemini said as he threw his arms up in the air, showing his complete loss of faith in the mission. He turned and walked a few feet away from the group. He was hot and flustered. He didn't want to talk to anyone. "Melakas," he said to himself, but out loud, for the gods to hear. He had used one of the oldest curse words in the Greek language.

"Who has no money?" Vanessa said, laughing as she pulled out a sack filled with gold coins and dumped it onto the ground in front of everyone.

All the demigods stared in amazement. There were at least a hundred gold coins on the ground in front of them.

"How did you get all of that gold?" Hercules asked as he stared at Vanessa in amazement.

"My mom… This sack always keeps one hundred gold coins in it. If I spend some, more will appear. I actually live with her, normally." Vanessa said very shyly, knowing that most of the demigods never had even met their parents."

"What! You live with her?" Jeffery yelled.

Vanessa nodded her head. "She didn't trust my dad to raise me, so she did."

Everyone became instantly jealous. They were shocked when Athena protected her daughter instead of protecting Gaia, and now they were finding out that Aphrodite was raising Vanessa. It was all quite unbelievable.

Zeus allowed Hera to torment Hercules and his mom, just because Hercules was the product of Zeus' infidelity. It made him a little bitter deep in his heart, and he assumed some of the others felt the same way.

"Let's just go buy the boat, so we can begin more of our never-ending journey," Hercules snapped. The group caught on to how he was feeling, and no one said a word about it—they understood. Zeus was notoriously the worst of the gods, and did not care for any of his children.

The seven of them walked in silence towards the shore. After purchasing the boat, Vanessa used more of the money to buy supplies. Much to the merchants' delight, they overpaid for everything as all they had to use as payment were the pure gold coins.

"Crap," Jeffrey sighed to himself as they boarded the boat they'd just bought.

"What is it?" Vanessa asked, looking at Jeffrey like he was crazy for his random outburst.

"I can sense sea monsters. It's part of the Poseidon curse, and there are maybe two hundred sea monsters between here and my dad's castle."

"I see," Vanessa replied, her eyes widening in worry. She sighed heavily and boarded the boat. "I guess that just means no breaks for us." She laughed to herself as she said it. A few of the demigods dropped in morale upon hearing about the monsters in between them and Poseidon's castle.

All seven of them were familiar with sailing, so they all manned different posts. It was good that Xavior was on board, as it meant there wouldn't be any need for rowing. He caused a great wind to push against the sails, and the ship began to move out to sea quickly. The crew watched the docks with a mixture of excitement and fear as they set sail. Many demigods had died on quests for the gods. So far, none of *them* had, but they all knew that could change in an instant. At sea, they were all vulnerable.

After they made it a good distance away from shore, the wind began to pick up. Xavior let the ship sail on its own as they rested below deck. Jeffrey could sense sea monsters, so they were dependent on him to give them a warning.

TWENTY-THREE

The school bell rang.

"Oh my," Mrs Norton said. "I must have lost track of time. Okay class, close your books and please bring them to the front of the room."

John, along with the rest of the class, took his book to the front of the room. Marcus reached the front desk at the same time, and he reached out to shake John's hand. John was hesitant because was still mad about what Jasmine had said but, deciding not to blame Marcus just because Jasmine had bad taste in guys, he shook.

"Dude, I have to show you something." Marcus said, almost bouncing from excitement.

"Uh, oh, last time I heard that Ho Young showed us his powers…"

Marcus smiled guiltily.

"You're kidding me. Dang, everybody but me. What are yours then?"

"Follow me. I want to show you," Marcus said, leading John out of the school and towards the football field.

"Dude, what are they?" John asked. "And… why do we need to go behind the bleachers for you to show me?" He eyed Marcus suspiciously.

"No, no. Watch this!"

Marcus bent and lifted the entire bleacher with only his left hand—it was made of heavy steel and seated about two hundred people.

John's mouth dropped open and he stared at his friend. "What the hell?" he said, gesturing wildly in his shock.

"Dude, I got strength." Marcus looked rather pleased with himself.

"Wait a minute. Ho Young has the same powers as that dude Gemini from the book, and you have the power of Hercules. Can you control lightning?"

Marcus raised one hand into the air and, with a click of his fingers, the ground shook with rumbling thunder.

"Hmm, how did you find out?"

"In a dream," he replied, a huge grin on his face. He was extremely excited about receiving his powers.

"Let me guess, there were a bunch of camels that looked like zebras," John said jokingly.

"Ha ha, no, there were no camels," Marcus laughed at John's reference to Ho Young's story.

"Oh and in my dream, you had powers, too. You could control the air… like Xavior."

John looked hopeful. He placed his hands out in front of him, facing the bleachers, and then raised them, as though to suspend the seating on a cushion of air. Nothing happened.

"Maybe that's too big for a first try? Maybe try something smaller."

He pointed his hands towards Marcus, who jumped back quickly. "No!" he said. "Not me. Try something else."

John laughed as he turned to a piece of trash on the ground and focused his attempts on moving the Hershey's candy bar wrapper.

After three tries, he gave up. "Nope, no powers," he said in disappointment. "But just to clear the air, don't think for a second that you can beat me in a fight now. I will still find a way to win."

"Got it," Marcus responded, laughing.

*****

After school, they walked to the park to play basketball with some of their friends. John, who was usually a star player, was clearly struggling with all the negative thoughts he'd accumulated over the last week. He knew it was showing and tried to mitigate his mood with a few sharp attempts at humor, but even they fell a little flat. When it became clear that the other team was going to win, he stormed off the court and across the park in an effort to bring his temper under control. He knew it was a better idea than letting his fists speak, but it was difficult to put into practice. Marcus was quick to follow after him, understanding that his friend was having a difficult time.

Marcus knew how he felt about Jasmine. John had loved her since he was eleven years old, but he had never told her. Marcus had teased him mercilessly, threatening to tell her for all of sixth grade. After that, John's parents divorced, and John had left town with his dad for a while, moving him away from Jasmine and to a different city, state, and school. He didn't move back into town until the middle of his seventh-grade year. Marcus remembered that every weekend, John had gone to the movies, hoping to see her, but he never did.

He dated a few times, but he always found a reason to break up with the girls, because no matter how lovely they were, they weren't Jasmine. He had tried to force himself to like people, searching high and low for someone to make him forget, but he never quite managed to fall out of love with Jasmine.

In ninth grade, John saw her again, but she was with someone else so he still didn't say anything, out of respect for her. John left again and didn't come back until the middle of their sophomore year. The next time he saw her, she was with someone else, but he mustered up the courage to tell her everything. It was too much—their friendship in sixth grade had been a long time ago, and she barely remembered him.

She distanced herself from him until they became friends again, letting go of bygones for their senior year. John hit on her, joking around a lot, but Jasmine couldn't make up her mind between Marcus and John. She liked both of them in different ways.

Marcus kept jogging while he recounted the memories. When he finally caught up, John was red in the face, and Marcus could tell that he was upset.

"Dude, just leave it alone," John said angrily as Marcus approached.

"I'm sorry," Marcus said. "I know how you feel about her. I'll back off."

"That isn't your decision to make," John told Marcus with a mixture of sadness and hate. "She has to choose me on her own. I have done everything in my power to prove to her that I wasn't lying when I told her that I fell in love with her a long time ago. I can't do any more without pushing her away again. I can't make her love me back, so I am done trying to, bro..."

John looked up, shook his head and cursed. "She isn't after you either, it looks like," he said, pointing back towards where Jasmine and another boy were snuggled up together on the bleachers.

"John," Marcus said in a low tone as he pulled away from him and walked away.

John walked without a thought to where he was going. His heart hurt. He blamed God for cursing him to fall in love with Jasmine and putting a wall between them so that they could never be together.

He walked and walked, allowing the solitude to clear his head. He walked until he reached the river front, where he curled up on a bench and fell asleep, exhausted from his emotional afternoon. When he awoke, it was to the chirruping of birds and the soft orange glow of sunrise. He must have slept there all night. Rubbing the sleep from his eyes, he glanced around. There were a few homeless camped out too, and a couple of early morning fisherman that were intent on trying their luck despite the signs reading *No Fishing, Unsanitary Water*.

John didn't want to get up, but he forced himself and walked to school in the same clothes he had slept in. He didn't bother to stop by his house to change or shower or brush his teeth, and his hair wasn't combed. His socks had been dampened by the dew, but he didn't care. He had nobody to impress.

"What's up bro?" Marcus said, when they met by the lockers in the hallway.

"Not much. How is it going?"

"Pretty good, not looking forward to going to biology," said Marcus making a disgusted face. "What about you? Are you alright?"

John could tell he was being sincere. "Yeah, I am good," he replied. "I was in my feelings a bit yesterday, I guess… Won't happen again. I can promise you that."

As they spoke, Jasmine walked by with the boy that she had been with at the basketball courts the day before.

John looked down at the ground, not wanting to see them together, and she walked by without so much as a passing look at them.

"Alright, I'm going to get to class," John said as he walked away. He had Human Health, and he hated it. Luckily for him, the time went quickly, and he was soon making his way back to the hall—unfortunately, at the same time as Jasmine.

She approached him this time and grabbed his arm, spinning him round to face her.

"Please don't grab me or put your hands on me," John said with a tone of anger and a dash of attitude.

"Okay," she said. "Here's the deal… no more playing cat and mouse. I have made my decision, and I have decided I'd like to be with Brandon."

"I can see that," John replied, flashing her a bright, sarcastic smile. He turned to grab a pen and paper out of his locker for the next class, and when he turned back, Jasmine was still there. Their gaze locked and he was once more awed by her beautiful hazel eyes.

"If you don't want to hang out anymore, I can't make you, but I am going to ask you to respect that I have a boyfriend and to not flirt with me anymore."

John looked at the ground. He didn't know how to respond. His heart was failing—its beating actually rapid; irregular. It rushed in his ears, drowning out everything else, and he could no longer hear what Jasmine was saying. John had no response for her, anyway.

"I'm sorry John, but that's how it is now, and I don't think you should come over anymore," she trailed off and looked away.

"Fine," John said, snapping back into reality. "Deuces," He held up two fingers as he walked off.

"Jasmine, that was messed up. John may not be all up in your face all of the time with it now, but you've known how he's felt about you for a long time," Marcus started but then he stopped. She looked sad. Her eyes were downcast, but Marcus could see that she didn't want to hurt John, she just wanted to do what she felt was best.

Inside, Jasmine was wondering about her decision, but she fought to quickly regain control of her emotions. What she did was the rational thing to do and second guessing herself wasn't going to get her anywhere. Besides, she really had no choice. She was now holding onto a secret that nobody knew but her.

"I understand how you feel," she started. "I know you and John are best friends." Jasmine sounded like she was near tears and her eyes had definitely become watery. "Look Marcus, I'll call you later. I don't want to talk about it now." She walked off with Brandon without glancing back.

That night, John went home and did his homework. He would do anything to get his mind off Jasmine. As he slept that night, he had a dream. Instead of a Greek god coming into his dream, Gabriel and Michael, the archangels, appeared. They showed John how to use his powers, and they were exactly what Marcus had predicted, only so much more. Not only could he control the movement of the air, but he watched his arm disappear before his very eyes as he did so. He could make himself invisible, too! The angels showed him how, with one batt of his eyelids, he could control the people around him. After all of that, he was stunned to find that he could fly, and super-fast.

Slowly, his dream began to shift, and through the fog he found Jasmine. He could see the two of them, thirty years down the track, happy together with four kids and a large house, filled with all the rooms they could possibly want. He wandered downstairs from the master bedroom—painted in stylish teal—and marveled at the four-car garage. It was all so perfect.

When he woke the next morning, he felt the sinking pull of disappointment in his gut. The dream about Jasmine and their happily ever after wasn't real… *but what about the other part*? he wondered.

He pictured grabbing the pen from his desk, just like he had practiced in his dream. When he yanked his hand back towards himself, it flew right at his face, with great force. With a face-splitting grin, he took to the air in his room, floating three feet above the floor

"Yes!" he shouted as he landed on the ground and focused on disappearing. He felt the ripple of magic as he became invisible right before his own eyes. His powers had definitely come in.

So now, he, Marcus, and Ho Young had powers. John was particularly excited because he could fly too, and the others couldn't. One part of the dream bothered him, though. The angels told John that Zeus and others, who had been passing themselves off as gods, would come to them for help. They were to say no, which confirmed John's belief that the Greek gods were indeed angels in disguise. He learned a lot in his dream. He had been wrong about the Norse deities, they were real, but Asgard had been destroyed in the first war. The Greek gods who fought another war against The Creator—and lost—were placed in chains in the deepest depths of hell. Now, their punishment was up and they were released from their prison. They were preparing for a final war to save themselves from the Lake of Fire.

The angels had also told him who he and the others were; that they were descendants of the demigods, Vanessa, Hercules, Gemini, Savannah, Xavior, Kikilliana, and Jeffrey. It was a lot to take in.

His head was reeling.

*****

"What's up?" John said to Marcus. They shook hands in greeting when they met at school.

"Not much, man. I literally just finished my homework before driving to school this morning."

"Yeah, I know what you mean. It was a little tricky, but I got mine done last night."

Marcus' jaw dropped, "You did homework?"

"Yeah, I was bored, but don't count on that happening again—once off for sure."

"Wow," Marcus said, laughing.

"Hey guys." Jasmine wore a sheepish smile as she ran up to them. As much as John wanted to ignore her, his love for her was much stronger than his hate for what she had done, and he managed to push his anger aside for a moment.

"Hey, what's up?" he replied. Jasmine's face lit up, as if they had never stopped being friends.

"Listen you guys. I had a dream a few nights ago. I haven't had a chance to talk to you guys alone… but, all of us have powers and are descendants of the demigods from that supposedly fiction book, *The War of the Gods*, that we're reading in Mrs Norton's class. I think we should all meet at my house tonight to discuss what I was told." She looked at John, "You come too," she said. "Because this is important, but don't get the wrong idea."

John nodded his head to show he understood.

John and Marcus walked to Mrs Norton's class, which they had first. John explained more from his dream—about how they were descendants of the demigods that they were reading about. He was so excited that he could barely even believe it was really happening.

"Okay, class, let's get to reading."

TWENTY-FOUR

Gaia cursed as she watched the demigods sail towards Poseidon's castle. "That has to be interfering!" she yelled watching hundreds of sea monsters closed in on the demigods' ship—presumably on order from the captain of Zeus' guard.

"They're doomed if we don't do something!" Aries yelled from behind Gaia.

"Orcas, is the only one that they'll listen to besides Zeus or Poseidon."

"It is not a problem," Athena said, appearing out of thin air beside them.

"What do you mean?" Gaia asked, confused and wondering what Athena knew that they didn't.

"I just left Poseidon's castle. I explained to the Cyclopes what happened to Poseidon, and they are now heading to intercept the sea monsters."

"Really?" Gaia asked, sighing in heavy relief.

"Yes. They will be fine."

*****

Jeffrey woke up first. He could feel the sea monsters heading toward the ship and he was afraid—there were too many of them, and he couldn't see how they would survive the looming encounter. He rubbed his face and shook the slumber away. "Everybody up," he yelled, stamping his feet between the others as they slept. "Here they come!"

The demigods all jumped up and ran up to the deck. Gemini reached it first, and ran to the front of the ship to look out with Jeffrey. The others quickly joined them. A little way away, the ocean had been blacked out with so many sea monsters that it was hard to see the water. They were all moving towards them.

Panic began to pass through the demigods. They didn't know what to do, but they had to figure something out. They had known about the monsters before they left the docks because Jeffrey had warned them, but seeing them so close up was a whole different feeling. Some of them were five times bigger than their boat.

"I have an idea!" Xavior shouted. "I can create a solid air bubble force field around the ship, and I'll be able to lift the ship out of the water! It will tire me doing both at once, but I'll hold it for as long as I can."

"And while Xavior is doing that, I can electrocute the water—" Hercules started, but Jeffrey cut in, eager to help.

"I can create a sinkhole underneath us, since we will be in the air, which will keep monsters from being able to attack us from the blind spot under the ship!" he blurted out.

"Okay, well let's get to it," Savannah said, feeling a bit useless. She was supposed to be the one to come up with the plans, being the daughter of Athena, and so far, the group had been devising them before she could think of a thing.

The ship lifted into the air as Xavior focused on making it hover above the ocean. He didn't break his focus when he closed his hands together, compressing the air around the ship into a tight force field. The air was too strong and the ship began to crack, so he dropped his hands quickly to his sides. The forcefield was a failure.

"Sorry guys, no force field," Xavior said, disproportionately disappointed in himself.

"It's fine," Gemini soothed. "At least now I can be productive and use my powers to attack the sea monsters!"

Within minutes the sea monsters were upon them, but none could get close enough to the ship to do much damage. A few of the larger ones attempted to jump out of the sea, but fell short of the boat.

Athena and the gods watched from above, impressed by the demigods' tactics.

"This is going to be a piece of cake," Hercules said, filling the sky with dark, menacing clouds. Thunder roared loudly as lightning struck the ocean, electrocuting monsters for miles. Monster bodies popped to the surface, where they floated—lifeless—wherever the electricity had reached.

"I thought this was going to be hard!" Hercules laughed as rain began to pour down from the clouds. The lightning was spectacular as it hit the water, sending shockwaves in all directions. Gold shimmered across the deep blue of the water, brilliant underneath the darkened sky.

Gemini was throwing spear after spear at the monsters that were not affected by the lightning bolts. The spears kept magically appearing in his hands, one after the other.

"Wow, this is way easier than I thought it would be," Xavior yelled, laughing, but speaking a moment too soon.

A large tentacle rose up out of the ocean and grasped onto the ship near the bow. With one tug, the tentacle ripped it off, wrenching it from the bulk with a blaring crunch. Xavior exhausted his powers to force the ship forward and higher in the sky, away from the tentacles, and then it began to fall. The demigods were suddenly in freefall, and though Xavior was able to regain control of the ship and land it on the water, he was unable to help the others. He passed out before he hit the surface.

Once the ship had landed, water began to rush into it and it began to sink. Jeffrey was the first to his feet, and rushed towards the gaping hole. He used his powers to force the water out of the boat.

"You guys better think of something!" Jeffrey yelled, as the others began to join him. "Because I can only do this for so long before I wind up like Xavior over there."

"Okay, just keep holding the water out, and we'll think of something!" Savannah yelled, frustrated and trying to think how to fix the problem.

"Well, I suggest you hurry, because, well, look..." Gemini yelled in a panic.

In the distance, tentacles were breaking the surface as a giant squid raced towards them at break-neck speed.

Savannah racked her brain, but she knew there was no way that they were going to save the ship.

"Is there a lifeboat?" Savannah asked in desperation.

"Yeah, actually, there is," Jeffrey said, still keeping his eyes on his task.

"Okay, let's ditch the ship and get out of here!" Savannah ordered the group.

The demigods all ran towards the lifeboat, and Hercules broke the chains holding it in place. He carried it to the edge of the ship, and was about to drop it down into the water when Savannah stopped him.

"Wait!" she cried, reaching out a hand to halt him. "If you drop it, it might crack or break." She turned to Jeffrey. "Do you think you can make the water rise up here to meet the boat?"

"Yeah, I can." Jeffrey said, waving his hand again. The water rose immediately.

"Everybody in the boat," Savannah ordered. "Hercules! Push the lifeboat in the water when it reaches deck level, and Jeffrey you might want to hurry it up! The squid is getting closer!" She looked over the side of the boat at the tentacles that were above the surface of the water, inching closer and closer. "And somebody grab Xavior!" Xavior was still unconscious and was almost forgotten.

Hercules pushed the lifeboat into the water the moment it reached deck level and jumped in with the rest of them just as Jeffrey lowered the water levels.

"Everyone, hold on!" Jeffrey shouted.

Everyone grabbed the side of the boat, then Jeffrey caused all the water behind them to whirl and push them forward. The boat jolted and picked up speed alarmingly fast. Vanessa was getting a little sick and Gemini had to close his eyes to keep from getting sick as well.

Shockingly, as fast as they were going, the giant squid was still catching up to them. Then, the boat stopped. Jeffrey was hunched over, his eyes only half open. Between creating the giant sinkhole to the bottom of the ocean beneath the ship and everything else he did, including controlling the water to make the boat go faster, Jeffrey had drained himself of his energy, and had nothing left that he could do.

"I'm sorry guys. I don't think I can even stay awake," he said, exhausted.

"Well, at least Xavior and Jeffrey get to die in their sleep," Hercules huffed to the others. The giant squid was nearly upon them.

Just as it was about to reach them, the squid disappeared beneath the water. The demigods were shaken and didn't bother to search for it beneath the surface. Instead, they chose to sit in the boat and wait for death to hit them. Most of them sat silently, refusing to say goodbyes, but Vanessa scooted over to Xavior and whispered to him. “I love you,” she said, as she laid down next to him.

It took over half an hour for them to realize they weren't under attack. Hercules, out of curiosity more than anything, jumped over the side of the boat to see if he could see the giant squid underwater. As he dove down, he opened his eyes to a sight that he did not expect to see.

There were at least a million Cyclopes attacking the squid underwater. Many of its tentacles were floating in the ocean, neither sinking down to the bottom, nor rising to the surface. Hercules swam back up to the boat.

“Did you see the giant squid?” Savannah asked as he climbed into the lifeboat.

“Yeah, I did,” he said. “It's being attacked by a ton Cyclopes. I don't know where they came from.”

“Cyclopes?” Savannah asked, a stunned look on her face. Savannah didn't like the sound of that, because Cyclopes ate humans.

“We need to get out of here before they turn on us,” Savannah said, grabbing an oar to row with.

Everyone followed suit and grabbed one of their own. Hercules grabbed two. They all began to row, but Hercules' massive swing launched the boat forward quite a bit each time. Still, they didn't get more than fifty feet before two Cyclopes were upon them. Hercules thought about striking the Cyclops closest to him, but the odds were against him. He was considering his options when the Cyclops eased itself back off the boat. It made a nodding gesture, as if to tell him not to be afraid. "Hey!" he called to the others. "I—I think they're trying to help us!"

*****

Four days went by, and Xavior and Jeffrey were still passed out. If it had not been for the Cyclopes bringing them food and water, they would have dehydrated. Jeffrey opened his eyes, very faintly at first. Savannah rushed to his side and hugged him, tears pouring down her cheeks.

"I thought you were going to die," she cried, clinging to him tightly.

"How long was I out for?" he asked, voice croaky from disuse.

"Too long." Hercules handed him some of the seaweed that the Cyclopes had brought them to eat.

"Four days." Vanessa said, from her post beside Xavior. She refused to leave his side, holding him tight as if he would fall out of the boat at any minute. Her voice was strained with worry and the fatigue was showing in the creases on her face.

"Oh, my," Jeffrey said, shuffling from Savannah's grip to get a closer look. "He still hasn't woken up yet?"

"No, and I'm starting to worry," Gemini said.

"He isn't dead though," Kikilliana said softly. "He will live, he's just in a deep sleep right now."

As the daughter of Hades, she would know if Xavior was near to death, which gave Vanessa some reassurance.

Still, she would not leave his side, relying on the others to bring her supplies as the Cyclopes offered them. They threw her pitying looks when they caught her pleading with him to come back, but Vanessa didn't notice.

*****

"I'm hungry." Xavior groaned as he grabbed his stomach in pain, three days after Jeffrey woke.

Hercules—working out in the front of the boat—was the only one awake to hear him. He had taken a break to investigate what looked to be a new army of Cyclopes battling the ones protecting them, and in the still of pre-dawn morning, he heard the rustle of clothes against timber and the low whine of Xavior's voice.

"Everyone wake up!" he yelled, "Xavior is awake!"

Vanessa was the first to bounce up from her slumber. She smothered Xavior in a long and tight hug, refusing to let go and crying hard.

"I'm okay, I'm okay," he murmured, wrapping his arms around Vanessa, returning her embrace.

"Dude, we are glad to have you back with us." Hercules said, patting Xavior on the back.

Savannah sighed and placed her hand to her mouth, watching Vanessa and Xavior hold on to each other with touching innocence.

Savannah glanced at Hercules for a split second but turned away quickly before he could see. She wondered what it would be like to date him. The sons of Zeus were known to be conceited and womanizing, but Hercules was nothing like that at all. He was calm, collected, kind, and humble. The only time Savannah had ever seen him mad was in the battle they fought with the Athenian demigods. She quickly rebuked her thoughts about Hercules. Hercules was not the one she had a crush on.

They celebrated Xavior's return to consciousness with hugs and laughter and an excited recounting of how Xavior had saved them all. Xavior was glad that he hadn't died. He struggled to wrap his head around the fact that he had been out for seven days—the incident must have nearly killed him. He would have to be more careful in the future.

"Okay, so we have a problem," Hercules said, deciding to get right to the issue instead of wasting anymore time. "Down below, there's a new group of Cyclopes—they're battling our Cyclopes—so there is no way that we can make it to the bottom of the ocean without engaging in a fight. They're hard enough to beat on land, let alone in the water where they're at their strongest."

"So, what can we do?" Jeffrey asked, feeling his previous excitement draining fast.

"Not much we can do," Gemini replied. "You said it's like thirty thousand feet down to the bottom of the ocean where your dad's castle sits…" He addressed the group. "Jeffrey's tunnel only went a thousand feet down before and he passed out… There's no way he can do thirty thousand feet without killing himself."

"I hate to agree, but Gemini is right," Jeffrey responded. "We have to find another way to do this."

"We need the gods to help us on this," Hercules said, gazing out at the ocean.

"I thought they couldn't help us on missions?" Vanessa asked.

"No, they cannot interfere on missions. They can, however, assist us if we ask."

"Okay, well everyone start praying to your godly parent, and we will see if any of them answer."

TWENTY-FIVE

"Okay, everyone, close your books and get to your next class. We will read more next time." Mrs Norton said. The class grumbled as they packed up and headed out for the rest of the day.

The day went by fast. After school, John walked with Jasmine and Brandon back to Jasmine's house. Brandon kissed Jasmine about twelve times before John summoned a wind to blow specifically against Brandon, knocking him down. Jasmine looked back and gave John a piercing look.

He shrugged his shoulders and lifted his hands as if to say, *What? It wasn't me…* with his body language, but she wasn't fooled. She stayed mad at him the entire walk from the school to her house. When they got inside, she sent Brandon upstairs and pulled John to the side to talk to him.

"I don't care how much you deny it, I know you used your powers to knock Brandon over and I'm not having it, so find a good reason to leave once we get upstairs. I want—I want you to leave, and never to talk to me again." She looked fierce. "Thank you," she added as she turned to go up the stairs.

Ignoring Jasmine's instructions, he turned as soon as she reached the fourth step, and walked back out the door without another word. He bumped into Marcus and Ho Young approaching from the other direction, but he kept walking without acknowledging them. He was tired and, once again, upset with Jasmine. She knew he was in love with her and just expected him to pretend he wasn't, which he was finding impossible. *Well*, he thought, *she said to never speak to her again, so that's exactly what I'll do.*

*****

"Hello everyone, spiders, and insects, and any clones that may be present." Ho Young saluted everyone as he and Marcus stepped into Jasmine's room.

"Um, what is he doing here?" Brandon asked.

Jasmine turned on Brandon with a scowl. As beautiful as she was, she was terrifying when angered.

"Quite obviously, he's my guest, so don't be rude, thank you." Jasmine said, turning away from Brandon.

"Hey, it was just a question," he responded. He was still confused as to why Jasmine had invited everyone over, especially John. He was even more surprised when John never came up. Something was going on, he knew, but he couldn't quite figure it out.

"So, I saw John leaving," Ho Young said.

"Obviously she knows he left, Ho Young," Marcus said, grimacing.

"Yeah, I guess so," he replied, "You know women, they're really smart."

Marcus snickered as he fought to hold back his laugh.

"No, really they are. Researchers researched it, and women are very smart… Smarter than men."

Marcus just shook his head. Ho Young could always be counted on to make any experience interesting.

"Thank you, Ho Young," Jasmine said, smiling.

Jasmine wanted badly to discuss their powers, but had to wait until Brandon left. He insisted on staying until seven that night, before he finally had to leave to do his homework. He gave Jasmine a big kiss on his way out, leaving her blushing from cheek to cheek.

"Okay, that was awkward," Marcus said.

"Would you like to join John?" Jasmine asked him with a quirk of her brow.

"I'm good," he replied.

*****

Instead of going home, John went to see one of his friends, Chris. Chris was a military man, and he always had a whole crew of people at his house, playing spades, dominoes, and a variety of drinking games. John liked playing spades with them, but this night he wasn't in the mood, so he just sat and watched the rest of them play.

"Why you ain't playing tonight little homie?" One of the military soldiers, who was already half drunk, gestured at him, and then at the table.

"Not in the mood tonight," he replied with his arms folded and his head tilted to one side. He knew his expression was giving him away, but at a party full of drunk soldiers, nobody was going to ask if he was okay.

"Nah, you just ain't trying to lose your money tonight." The soldier continued on, trying to be funny.

"Man, what are you even talking about," John said as he laughed. "You see these shoes I got on, and this gold chain, and this one-thousand-dollar watch? That isn't even ten percent of the money I've taken from you all times we've played. You can just call me child support because I've been taking all your money." Everyone around the table exploded in laughter. "Shoot, why get a full-time job when I can just retire off playing spades with you?"

"Dang you going to let him clown you like that," one soldier said as he jumped up and down laughing and pointing at the soldier John was giving cheek. John laughed a little at everyone's reaction to his joke. When people get high and drunk, they overreact to everything.

"Bruh, the little homie got you good." Another soldier joined in, between his laughing and coughing. "That kid right there is roasting them drawers right off you boy."

The group continued playing after they calmed down. They were slamming the cards down and heckling: 'Go ahead and throw that four of hearts down there, you know it's all you got!' People were tossing their cards into the pile on the table when they knew they had a winning hand. They were guzzling down beers inside, but they went outside to smoke. John didn't like beer, so he turned them down every time they were offered.

His cell phone rang while he was at the table. He pulled it out and saw Jasmine's name flicker up on the screen. He didn't want to answer, but curiosity got the best of him, and he sighed as he pressed the answer button.

"What's up?" he said coolly, while the guys around him erupted in fits of shouting about someone reneging on a play. "I thought you didn't want to talk to me anymore."

He was still upset, but he wanted to hear what she had to say. He walked outside so he could hear better. The music in Chris's basement was blaring a Tupac rap song very loudly.

"Yeah, well, unfortunately, I do like you as a friend and I don't want to fight with you anymore." Jasmine.

"I understand that," he said. "But if you cannot understand that I love you, and I cannot stomach being around you and that guy, maybe you are right. Maybe we need to just not talk anymore."

"I'm not going to beg for your friendship." Jasmine's voice cracked when she replied after a long pause. "If that's what you want, then you'll get your wish."

It took a long time for John to answer. “It is what I want,” he said, after carefully considering the matter. He thought about watching Jasmine with Brandon, and the thought of them kissing was too much for him to take. He hit the end call button on his cell phone before she could get another word in.

“You know what, stuff it” John suddenly said loudly, so anyone listening would be able to hear. “Toss me a beer.”

There was no hesitation. The soldiers all made their ‘trying to be tight’ jokes.

“Oh, he’s going for grown man today! Go on and drink that there, young blood,” a soldier crowed as he handed him a beer. He looked at the can. It was a Boor’s Light. He slowly brought it to his lip and took a sip. It tasted like dehydrated oatmeal. It was nasty, but he didn’t want anyone to think that he wasn’t up to the task of finishing off a single beer, so drank it little by little and sip by sip.

“Man, drink some more,” the soldiers were calling, trying to egg him on. He grimaced into his hand—he was doing his best, but it was disgusting. He took two big chugs as everyone watched him. Finally, he finished his beer and was ready to go. He told Chris and the crew that he would catch them next time and raised his hand in a half-hearted wave as he left.

When John got home, he eyed the old upright in the corner of the living room. He didn’t play often, but the echoing sound of the piano allowed him to release some of what he felt. He sat down in front of it and lifted the lid.

At first, he was just playing random chords, but when he struck a few that resonated soundly with his emotions, he settled in and closed his eyes. His fingers grazed the keys and a shiver tingled up his spine. He played and played until he felt his shoulders sag and his breath came in deep sighs. Exhausted, he made his way to his room and laid on his back, staring at the ceiling deep in thought. He didn't see how the four of them could work together. The angel specifically said the four of them had to stay together, but John wasn't going to work with Jasmine while she was dating Brandon. Slowly, he drifted off to sleep.

In his dream that night, he was running from all kinds of monsters. He fought a few of them using his powers, but at times his powers didn't work. He saw Jasmine with Brandon. They were getting married. John heard the cold cry of a werewolf howling at the moon. When he turned around to see it, he was confronted with a large giant in mid-transformation, with big humanlike bones and terrifying teeth. He woke with a start. His heart was pounding with fear and he was drenched in sweat. Even though he knew it wasn't real, he surveyed the room to make sure it was safe.

The next day of school was just a big blur of math and science. In Mrs Norton's class they read more of the book, The History of the Gods.

*****

Hephaestus answered the demigods cry for help and built them a boat that could travel to the furthest depths of the ocean. He named it a deep-sea ship. They used the ship to get to Poseidon's castle, where Hercules, Jeffrey, and Xavior swam out in special swimsuits given to them by Aphrodite. They freed Hades and Poseidon, but they were too late. The war above had already begun. As Hades and Poseidon rose from the depths, Gaia and the other gods above engaged in battle against Zeus and Ouranos.

*****

Just as John was falling into the story, eager to hear how the battle played out, the bell rang for lunchtime. He caught a glimpse of Jasmine walking with Brandon, and half expected her to ignore him, but she didn't. She watched him gently, with sad eyes as they walked by.

After school, Jasmine, Marcus, and Ho Young all met up and walked to Jasmine's house.

"In my dream last night, this alien gave me more lessons on my powers," Ho Young told the group once Jasmine had shut the door to her room.

"An alien?" she asked.

"Yeah, his name was, I think, Gabriel Angel," Ho Young replied.

"I think you mean Gabriel the Angel," Jasmine corrected him. "He gave me training lessons as well."

"I got them too," Marcus said. "And he said we've been given a mission."

"Yup, he said that to me too." Ho Young was bouncing on the balls of his feet, overcome with joy at the prospect of an adventure with his friends.

"Okay, so we all know that we have a mission," Jasmine began. "But how do we accomplish it while we're still in school?" She looked overwrought with anxiety.

"And without John," Marcus reminded her.

"Yeah, the angel guy said that to me too. He said that we needed John on this mission, and that his participation would determine whether we win or lose the tournament."

Jasmine wanted to shout at them to go get John, but she didn't. She had been told, prior to dating Brandon, that she would date one of the demigods and cause his death by Chiron the great centaur. She loved John nearly as much as he loved her, but she wasn't willing to get him killed over her feelings. She had to keep that a secret because if she ever told him, the centaur would kill him just as he had promised he would do.

"Well, if he comes, he comes," she said, against her own wishes. "But I for one, am not going to beg him."

Marcus nodded his head, his face twisted in sarcasm. He grabbed his phone to call John, but it went to voicemail. It seemed as though John was done with all of them, and it wasn't likely that he would answer any calls.

"He didn't answer," Marcus said, stuffing his phone into his pocket.

"Okay, well, there you have it then," Jasmine said, looking down at the ground.

"We need to discuss the first mission," Ho Young said, trying to get everyone back to the problem at hand.

"Yes, we do," Jasmine replied. "So, we have to go to Washington to find Leneechi Deshoven, the silversmith, so he can give us weapons to defend ourselves against a giant werewolf named Fenrir."

"I am not trying to fight any werewolf," Marcus said looking at his friends in horror. "That's crazy. Don't you get turned into a werewolf if he bites you?"

"I think so," Jasmine said, cringing as a shudder ran down her entire body.

"Werewolves are already as strong as can possibly be, and even stronger than most can be, but Fenrir is a giant werewolf. I don't think I'm going to fight." Marcus said, taking a step back.

"We don't have a choice. If we don't go to fight him there, he will come here to fight us, and if we hide, he will kill our families looking for us."

Marcus looked down at the ground. "So, if we go, we most likely die."

"Yeah, and if we don't go, we still die, as will our families and many others we love!"

"This sucks," Marcus replied angrily, leaning his head against the wall.

"I agree, but what choice do we have?"

*****

The next day Jasmine, wrote fake letters to the school from each of their parents, excusing them from school for a month for emergency reasons. She made sure each letter was different. Marcus' said he was visiting his dying grandpa, and Jasmine's letter said she was being flown to Washington for an emergency surgery.

"You know, we aren't going to get away with this," Marcus said, as Jasmine explained what she'd done.

"I know, but we need to just confuse everyone long enough for us to get to Washington. It's not like it matters anyways, seeing as how this may be a suicide mission."

"Speaking of that, what are you going to tell your dad?" Jasmine asked.

"I don't know," Marcus replied. "Truth is, nothing will work. They'll still call the cops and report us missing."

"Yeah, I think you're right," Jasmine replied. "We might not even make it to Washington before the cops pick us up as runaways."

"Yeah, they sure will," John said, as he waltzed in amidst their conversation.

"Wait, how did you get in?" Jasmine asked as she jumped up, blushing.

"Your dad let me in—I think he likes me," he said. "I got Marcus' text, and regardless of how I feel at the moment, I still love you Jasm—"

John stopped in mid-sentence as his eyes opened wide. He hadn't meant to say those words out loud. It was the first time he had ever spoken them to anyone other than Marcus. Jasmine knew that John loved her, but John had never actually said it.

Jasmine's eyes widened as well, and her cheeks flushed pink. She didn't smile or frown, so John had no idea what she was thinking. He scrubbed at his face with both hands, crimson in embarrassment.

"I imagine that you probably want me to go now," he said, walking to the door. "And—sorry. I… didn't mean to say that, it just came out."

"No, stay," Jasmine said. "We really need you here for this mission."

"For what mission?" Brandon's voice came from the other side of the door and John groaned.

"Oh my God," Jasmine sighed, putting her head in her hands. "Did my dad let you in too?"

"Yeah, he did," Brandon answered, not taking his eyes off John. "Again, what mission?" His frustration was evident in his voice.

"Brandon, now is a bad time. Could you possibly leave and just call me later?"

He looked taken aback. Without a word, he turned and walked out the door. Jasmine jumped up and ran out after him. She caught him just as he was leaving the house.

"What?" he asked, tremulous with anger. "What do you want?"

"I know you're upset, but I'm not able to tell you about what we have to do."

"Why, is it top secret or something?" he asked.

"Something like that," she snapped, frustrated by his lack of understanding.

"So classified that you can't tell your boyfriend, but you can tell that John guy. What is his deal anyways? Why is he even here?"

"Well, before John and I began to get into it, he was a big part of this project."

"What project?" he asked, cutting her off.

John watched from the window as Brandon and Jasmine argued outside. He didn't know Brandon very well, but he didn't like him and wanted to make sure that Jasmine was safe.

Marcus nudged him as he leaned against the windowsill, beside him. "I don't think Jasmine would like you eavesdropping very much," he said, worried his friend was only making his situation worse.

"Yeah, you're right." John sighed and retreated to the bed to sit down. He heard the door close downstairs and knew Jasmine was on her way back up. He hoped she'd given that loser a good telling off. As soon as he sat down, he slipped into a trance.

The angel, Gabriel, appeared before him.

"I don't have much time," Gabriel began. "I just came to inform you that you should not worry about Jasmine. Chiron cornered her and threatened to kill you if she got into a relationship with you. He wants to keep you two apart."

"Why does he care if Jasmine and I get together?" John asked, confused.

"He cares because you're the most powerful in the group, with Jasmine coming in second. My fallen brethren figure that if they can keep you guys fighting, you won't be able to function as a unit—especially you and Jasmine."

"So, we should be tighter?"

"Brandon is going to come up the stairs with Jasmine, and you must stop him from sleeping with her. He will try, and if he succeeds, Jasmine will fall for him. If you can prevent that from happening—without angering her, and without using your powers—you will have your chance to woo her.

"How do I do that?" he asked. Not using his powers was going to be hard enough, but not making Jasmine angry—stopping her from doing something that she wanted to do—was going to be dang near impossible.

"You will have to defeat Chiron before you leave from here, if you wish to win Jasmine's heart."

"I see," John said, the words catching in his throat at the weight of his task. "Am I powerful enough to kill whoever Chiron is?"

"He is the father of all centaurs, and the son of Kronos. He is powerful, but The Creator believes in you."

"Gotcha. I'll do my best then." John smirked wryly. "But how do I find him?"

"Oh, I have a feeling that he will show himself soon enough," Gabriel said, and disappeared.

As John came out of his trance, Jasmine walked through the door. He wanted to tell her what Gabriel had said, but he knew the timing wasn't right, especially since Brandon had walked in right behind her.

"Listen guys, can I get you to leave for a while? I need to spend some time with Brandon alone."

John's stomach tightened. He knew this was it, that Brandon and Jasmine were going to sleep together. He didn't know how, but he had to stop them.

"Yeah, sure no problem," Marcus said quickly, looking uncomfortable.

John wanted to yell at him and call him all kinds of names, but he restrained himself. He didn't want to make any mistakes. "Damnit," he muttered to himself. His hands shook. He wanted to give up on everything. It hurt so bad to think that Jasmine might actually go through with this. *I have to stop her*, he thought.

He was so overwhelmed by what he had to do that he walked out with Marcus and Ho Young. The further away they got from Jasmine, the larger the knot in John's stomach grew, and he came to a grinding halt before they had left her street.

"Look, guys," he said. "You guys do whatever. I'm going back to stop them." His face turned red, but not from embarrassment this time—all his feelings were swirling around inside, threatening to spill over.

"Stop them from doing what?" Marcus was getting sick of the secrecy, especially when it was within their own group. "Look, John, you have loved her for how long and haven't gotten her? Move on dude. All you're going to do is make it worse."

John looked at Marcus for a long second without saying a word. He sighed. “Look man, Gabriel came to me in a vision in the room, and he said if I could stop them from sleeping together without using my powers or making Jasmine mad, I could actually win her love, but if not, Brandon will win her, and our mission will fail.”

“What do you mean our mission will fail?”

“Well,” John replied. “Gabriel said that I’m the most powerful out of everyone, and Jasmine is the second most powerful. Chiron went to Jasmine and threatened to kill me if she fell in love with me. That’s why she’s with Brandon. She got with him to save my life. Gabriel also said that Chiron wanted to keep me and Jasmine apart, because if we loved each other our desire to save each other would bring our power to their strongest points.”

“Oh wow,” Ho Young said. “You better go stop them straight away then!”

“I agree.” Marcus concurred with Ho Young. “We’ll head to the school. I left my backpack in my locker, and I don’t want to fall behind on homework.”

John would have responded with a scathing comment except he had already turned invisible and was flying back to Jasmine’s house at full speed. He landed on her doorstep. What could he do? If he told her dad, she would get mad. He couldn’t use his powers, so he couldn’t do anything to mess up Brandon. If he barged in, she would definitely get mad, unless he could make up a good enough emergency excuse.

John paced back and forth on her front lawn as he did his best to come up with an idea. As he looked up through the sheer curtains on her window, he saw her silhouette stand and shimmy out of her shirt. Heat rushed through him. He was out of time. He felt like his heart was about to stop. He had to do something, but he didn't know what.

In desperation, he checked the front door. To his surprise, it was still unlocked, and he raced through and up the stairs, almost busting the bedroom door down in his panic-driven haste.

"Jasmine!" he yelled as he entered the room. "Don't do this. Please."

Jasmine was on the bed, divested of her clothes, and Brandon, in a similar state of undress, was looming above her, a startled look on his face.

"Dude what the hell? Get out of here, you psychopath! Man, this dude is crazy for reals."

John ignored Brandon and focused on Jasmine.

He caught her eye and held her gaze. "Jasmine, I love you with all my heart, and I have for a long time. Please don't do this with Brandon."

She didn't say a word. She just stared at him; at the tears pouring down his face as he spoke.

"I know about Chiron's threat," he pleaded. "And we're set to fight him soon. Gabriel told me—I have a shot at beating him, but not without your love."

"This dude is too thirsty. What's your name, John, right? Get your blocking ass out of here, bruh," Brandon said angrily, tugging his drawers back on.

Jasmine looked at Brandon with disgust, "No, how about you get out?" she said, grabbing for her quilt to cover up. She looked up at John, emotion pooling in the depth of her eyes. "John, I love you too! I just didn't want you to die. Chiron said he would kill you if I dated you!"

"Well, without your love it would feel like I was dead anyways." He looked at the ground, the walls, and everywhere but at Jasmine. A red glaze glowed on his golden-brown skin as his body temperature began to rise from nervousness. He didn't want to say something dumb that would ruin the moment or push Jasmine away.

"Deuces to you both!" Brandon hastily finished putting on his clothes, glaring at the both of them. "You're both nuts," he said, walking out of the room and flipping them off with the middle finger on both of his hands. He bit his lip in anger as he stormed off thuggishly.

Jasmine walked up to John and kissed him on the lips, and John kissed her back. The kiss was different than with others. They both had kissed people before, but this one somehow stole both of their souls right from their bodies, and locked their hearts together. They probably would have delayed the mission until morning and just stayed in bed cuddling all night, but the phone rang.

Ho Young was calling from Marcus' phone. "Help!" he shouted down the line, his voice strained in the beginnings of hysteria. "We're being attacked by an alien horse!"

John knew immediately that it was Chiron. He grabbed hold of Jasmine and, in the blink of an eye, they were both invisible, flying as fast as possible to the school, where Marcus and Ho Young were fighting Chiron.

As John landed, Marcus flew through the brick wall of the school, sending concrete and debris flying everywhere. John flew to catch him, which angered Chiron, who had clearly been enjoying the show. He looked past the centaur to see Ho Young lying on the ground, blood bubbling from his mouth. John looked back down at Jasmine, and anger filled him. He felt like he had the entire universe surging through him, and he directed it at Chiron, advancing on him with a powerful wind blast without warning. Chiron no longer had a smug look on his face as he staggered back through the wall he had been blasted through with the force of ten thousand pounds of compacted air.

Angered, the centaur pulled his bow and arrow out and tried to aim at John, but John had become invisible again and could not be seen. Instead, Chiron turned his arrow on Jasmine with lightning speed. Instinctively, John used the air to catch the arrow and turn it around, sending it back toward Chiron on the wind, ten times faster than it had flown at Jasmine.

The arrow pierced his stomach and he looked up in fear. The centaur's confidence was gone. John reappeared right in front of him, anger etched all over his face. With a single clench of his fist, the wind hardened like steel around both his hands, and he began to unload lightning fast, powerful punches.

Already bleeding from the mouth, Chiron fell back and split his head open, the pool of blood growing quickly.

John stepped back and caused a great wind to form in the shape of a giant hand, and with all his might, he punched Chiron with the strength of the Galaxy gathered together into a rock-solid fist of air. Chiron flew high into the sky until he was out of sight.

*****

Sirens sounded in the background as police cars raced towards the high school.

"John, we have to get them out of here!" Jasmine yelled from the ground.

"I know!" He flew over to Ho Young and picked him up, and then flew back to Marcus and Jasmine. He realized, after trying to fly with them all, that his arms weren't long enough to hold everyone. As he tried to take off, Marcus fell back to the ground. It was a good thing he fell at five feet and not two hundred feet.

"I can't keep a grip around everybody," he said to Jasmine, who was the only one conscious. "And we need to get Ho Young and Marcus to the hospital."

"Can't you call the clouds down to carry us, like Xavior did in the book?" Jasmine asked, thinking very quickly as the police sirens got closer.

"I don't know. I've never tried." Even as he spoke, the first police car pulled into the school parking lot. With a swish of his hands, the group was invisible.

He focused his mind on encouraging a large cloud down from the sky to aid them. It came slowly, and seemed to be nothing more than a falling mist to onlookers, including the police. It was nightfall, and it blended in well.

John leaned over and kissed Jasmine's cheek and whispered, "I sure hope this works."

"I do too," she said, smiling and blushing from ear to ear. John looked at her for a good minute. He couldn't believe that she had told him that she loved him. Hearing that he had a chance from an angel was one thing, but to hear it from her mouth buckled his knees.

Just as Jasmine was about to tell John to hurry, the clouds slowly lifted off the ground and began to move forward. John guided them to the hospital slowly, and low to the ground. He wasn't very comfortable flying them just yet. He landed them far away from people and cameras in the hospital parking lot, and sent Jasmine in to get help. He stayed by his friends, who were still unconscious. Marcus had a large handprint around his neck and bruises all over his body. Ho Young had a hoof mark on his forehead, and two on his chest. It would be very difficult to explain.

He watched the rise and fall of their chests, listening to the soft puffs of air as they kept breathing. They were alive. He just hoped they were both okay.

TWENTY-SIX

For three days, John and Jasmine slept at the hospital, keeping watch over Ho Young and Marcus in case the centaur came back. Ho Young regained consciousness on the second day, but Marcus was still in a coma. Jasmine's dad delivered their homework from school, and as much as he hated it, John did it—he didn't want to give the older man any reasons not to like him.

"Now I know how to get you to do your homework," Jasmine said, smiling.

"Homework is the least of our worries though," John responded. "Chiron is still out there, and Fenrir is probably almost here, since we weren't able to intercept him in a town far off somewhere." He gestured vaguely.

"Oh no, John! We're going to have to warn our parents," Jasmine said, with her hands covering both sides of her chin and a look of absolute anxiety on her face, as though she was just realizing the danger.

John groaned, but she had already grabbed her cell phone to call her dad, so he called his mom, too. Their phone calls were pointless. Jasmine's dad demanded that she come home, and John's mom thought he was joking around.

"We have to go!" Jasmine said, voice strained in panic. "Our parents are in danger and they won't listen!"

John agreed.

Ho Young came into the room just as they were preparing to leave. He came in singing a strange song that was at odds with his jaunty walk.

"Hey, are you guys leaving?" he asked as he noticed they had their belongings in their hands.

"Yeah, we have to let our parents and Marcus' parents in on our secret."

"Oh wow, a secret. I love secrets and I can keep them very well. Won't tell anybody. Can you guys tell me the secret, or is it classified?" he asked.

"Alright, I'll tell you," John said, motioning for him to come closer so he could whisper.

As he leaned in to hear the secret, John popped him on the back of his head. "Our powers, Ho Young, that secret." He laughed

"I had an idea you were going to do that," Ho Young said, laughing along with him. "Ouch!" Ho Young winced after a long pause, grabbing the back of his head.

"Man, I hit you like twenty seconds ago! Did you only just feel it?"

"No, I felt it then, but I got distracted, man!"

"Look," John's tone changed as he returned to seriousness. "Marcus is still out, and we have to warn all our parents that Fenrir is coming."

"Oh no," Ho Young said, sighing, as if this were new news to him.

"Listen," John said. "We need you to stay here and protect Marcus while we go get our parents."

"Okay, yeah, no problem." Ho Young said, nodding rapidly despite looking a little nervous.

John figured he probably was nervous because the last battle didn't go so well. "Listen," he said, hoping to be encouraging. "The only reason you got hurt in that last battle was because you tried to fist fight the centaur. Use your powers and avoid all physical contact with anything or anyone, got it?"

"Yeah, but in the last battle, I didn't even get a chance to use my powers. Marcus and I were just walking down the hall, and that horse guy broke through the wall. Marcus went flying, then that… thing… was on me before I even knew what was going on. I swung and he caught my arm, and that's the last thing I remember.

"I see," John said. "Well, stay away from the walls so he won't have that advantage again. Use your powers. Get creative—grenades, fireballs, lasers, and stuff. Knowing you, you would have tried to summon a foam bat." He laughed again.

"No, I would have summoned a ninja sword," Ho Young replied, nodding, as if that were any better.

"Oh…kay." John gave up and headed for the door. "Use the weapons I suggested if you want to live, my friend!" he yelled over his shoulder, waiting for Jasmine to join him.

"Be safe!" She turned around before rushing out to catch up to John.

"I'm scared," she confessed, grabbing his hand as they broke into a run.

His grip tightened on her fingers as they approached the bus stop. "I am too," he said. "But we have powers and are more than capable of defending ourselves."

"I know, but these are the first two beasts that we have to fight, which likely means they're the least dangerous of the four."

John paused. He hadn't even thought about that, but she was probably right. They wouldn't send out their toughest monsters in the first two fights.

He met her gaze in understanding. "Let's just—let's catch this bus and get to our parents." He stopped without warning and she would have tripped trying to avoid a collision had he not caught her by her arm and pulled her back to her feet.

"What happened?" she asked, scanning the area nervously. "Did you see something?"

"No, I just realized I don't have any bus money, do you have anything on you?"

"No, I am afraid I don't either."

"No problem, I guess we'll just have to fly." John pulled her into the alcove behind the bus stop and since no one was around, he waved his hand over them right where they were standing, rendering them invisible, and flew them to Jasmine's house.

As they flew, the gentle wind rippled through Jasmine's hair. She kept her eyes on John for the whole time they were in the air.

As John landed in front of Jasmine's house, he kept them invisible. He didn't want to give Jasmine's dad a heart attack, but it would be the quickest way to show him that they had powers and were telling the truth.

Jasmine's dad was sitting on the couch watching the news when they arrived—it was his favorite thing to do when he wasn't at work. From her invisible place beside the couch, Jasmine opened her mouth to speak, but clamped it shut again as soon as she saw the TV. The horrific scene was from the next town over. There were thirty dead bodies scattered on the ground, blood everywhere, and bits of flesh splayed between them. Some of the bodies had been dismembered and others had been torn to shreds.

John rushed to Jasmine's side as she gagged violently and vomited on the ground at her feet. He helped her to the bathroom, where they both heaved and she threw up again. Jasmine's dad called out to her from the living room.

"Jasmine, is that you?"

She retched again, and John heard her dad walking towards the bathroom.

"What the hell? Is this throw up?" her dad yelled, as one of his sock-covered feet squelched in a gooey puddle by the open door.

"Oh My Lord, that is nasty," her dad said, pulling his clean sock off to use it to keep the throw up from getting onto his hands. Holding his nose while looking away, he dragged the soiled sock off of his foot and headed for the outside trash can, purpose guiding his long strides.

"Jasmine!" he yelled as he re-entered the house.

"Yes?"

"What is the deal with all of this throw up on my living room floor? Are you sick? You aren't pregnant, are you?"

"No, dad! I'm definitely not pregnant." Her voice was weaker than she wanted, but she pushed on. "I threw up from seeing what was on the screen."

"What do you mean?" her dad asked.

"All those bodies…" she said faintly. It made her sick all over again to think about it.

"When were you even in the room with me?" Her dad looked confused.

"While you were watching that part of the news and it showed all the bodies all over that town. I told you the werewolf, Fenrir, was on his way here."

"That's pure nonsense Jasmine. They said that was done by a pack of wild wolves."

Jasmine and John had made their way into the living room, still fielding his questions.

"Come in here and talk to me," he demanded.

"I'm right here," Jasmine said, waving her hands in front of her dad. His face was screwed up in fright—he had heard her voice so clearly, but she was nowhere to be seen. "John! Anytime now…" She tried not to let her frustration overwhelm her.

"Oh, my bad," John said as they reappeared with a wave of his hand. You started throwing up, and my mind went somewhere else."

Jasmine's dad stumbled backward, away from them, until he tripped on the coffee table. He landed hard on the floor, and when he sat up he was in a daze and his eyes were unfocused.

"What the hell did I just see," he muttered to himself, rubbing his eyes. He swallowed hard, but he couldn't stop himself from crying out. "God, please help me! I need help!" He wasn't in his right mind.

Oh, what have I done? Jasmine thought, standing beside John and watching a myriad of feelings flicker of her dad's anxious face.

A piercing howl sounded in the distance and it tore right through them all. John wasn't afraid of anything, except for spiders, but that howl had him breaking out in chilling goosebumps, the hair on his arms standing on end.

Jasmine looked at John. "What can we do?"

"We need to get everyone together, now. Help your dad up," he said, a haunted darkness clouding his gaze.

As he called down three clouds from high in the ominous gray sky, just as he recalled Xavior doing in the book, Jasmine helped her dad to his feet. With a little encouragement, they got the shocked man onto a cloud of his own, and within moments, they were all invisible and making their way to John's mom's work to ensure her safety.

John's mom took their revelation much better than Jasmine's dad had, and after a quick demonstration, she believed in their powers. John could tell by the look on her face that she was struggling to believe her eyes, but there was no breakdown in sight, and they moved on quickly. With Marcus' parents out of town and Ho Young's parents dead, all that was left was to fetch Ho Young and Marcus from the hospital.

When they approached the large compound, John saw a grizzled pack of wolves circling and snarling and gnashing at each other on the freeway. Gabriel, the angel, chose that moment to appear on the cloud beside him.

"One-half is Fenrir and his wolves, which are all male," he said. "They only bite males, and those bitten will then become werewolves themselves. The other half are led by the Daughter of Apollo, a girl named Nichole. Her cousins are the daughters of Loki. They fight on your side. Zeus and the others thought they could beat the rules by considering a whole pack of wolves as a single beast, so The Creator, our Father, decided to even the odds for you."

John had a million and one questions for Gabriel, but the angel had disappeared before he could even begin. As they flew closer over the streets, he looked down to see a row of police cars just two streets over—they were surely heading for the wolves.

He thought that the wolves would attack the police, but before the police got any closer, they all dispersed—half in one direction and half in the other. By the time the police turned the corner, there were nothing but a few dead bodies. All of the dead were Fenrir's, so Apollo's daughter and her cousins were definitely better fighters than his converts. That was comforting news.

Landing in front of the hospital, John asked Jasmine to stay with their parents while he ran in to get their friends. He dashed in quickly through the large glass doors and was plunged into near darkness. The lights were all off, and the walls were gouged with long, deep claw marks; there were dozens of bodies in a pile of limbs and sinew at the door to the front waiting room.

The werewolves were already there.

With a startled cry, John ran back outside to warn Jasmine that not only was Fenrir there, but most of the bodies in the waiting room were male. It wouldn't be long at all before they started turning into more werewolves, and John didn't want Jasmine to wander into a death trap. He took to the air, so he could be in and out as fast as possible. Unlike Xavior, he didn't need a cloud to fly by himself; he only needed them to carry others. Marcus and Ho Young were on the third floor so, counting the levels, John broke through the first third floor window he could find.

He walked cautiously through the hallway. He had no idea where Fenrir was, and the uncertainty set adrenaline coursing through him until his legs felt like jelly and his muscles spasmed in their weakness.

"Marcus? Ho Young?" John yelled, though his voice wavered. He stumbled, and in no time, Fenrir was smashing through a wall, sending chunks of plaster flying. He was still in human form but immediately upon seeing John, his eyes turned red. In less than a second, Fenrir transformed from a fifteen-foot human giant into a full-sized werewolf. It was neither as slow nor as painful as TV made it out to be. He crouched before John, saliva dripping from his jaw and a deep, rumbling growl ripping from his throat.

John made to run—he didn't know why, but he was too weak to fight. It was too late though, and Fenrir charged. John was hardly able to jump out of the way. He tried to throw the raging wolf back with his powers, but Fenrir barely moved even a few inches. John's eyes went wide as he charged again. He was on top of him in no time and John was barely able to keep the long, filthy claws and snapping jaws from his neck. Like a dog with rabies, Fenrir kept on biting at the invisible shield.

John was on his back with his hands in front of him, holding up the weak force field, but Fenrir was inching closer and closer as John got weaker and weaker.

"Help!" John cried out. He knew Fenrir was going to kill him, and there was nothing that he could do to stop it. Why he screamed for help was beyond even his own comprehension. For all he knew, everyone was either dead or turning into a werewolf, and if he and his powers couldn't do anything, what could anyone else do?

He jerked back as hand reached up out of nowhere and grabbed Fenrir by his tail, slamming him through the floor. He landed in the basement on his back.

"We need to go! Now!" John yelled to Marcus. "Where's Ho Young?"

"He's hiding under the bed in that room!" Marcus pointed across the hall just as Fenrir's second splitting howl rent the air.

John looked down through the hole to check that he was still down, and what he saw sent another chill through his core. "Are you flipping serious right now?" he shouted angrily at the empty space where the wolf should be. "How is he not at least injured enough to give us a break?" John yelled, running back towards the room Marcus had pointed out. He was beyond flustered. Fenrir seemed invincible and impossible to beat. John's powers did nothing against him, and Marcus' didn't seem to be able to hurt him either.

"Ho Young, come on out from under that bed!" he called. "We're getting out of here." He stuck his hand out towards the window just as it bowed towards him, buckling and exploding outward in razor-sharp shards as Fenrir re-entered the third floor. His ragged growls were filled out by the snarling of others—he wasn't alone this time; he had brought along many of his converts.

John called the clouds to meet them at the windowsill and they arrived just as the first of the wolves entered.

"Ho Young, this is where you come in handy, man." John said in a panicked voice—rightfully so, because it was Ho Young he was talking to. "You can create weapons. Make something that can kill this werewolf and throw it at him!" John's voice rose to a yell as the wolves charged at him, and he stared down at Ho Young with pleading eyes.

Ho Young stepped towards the wolf and made a throwing motion with his hands. John and Marcus watched on impatiently, wanting to have faith in their friend, but unsure of his ability. Their impatience turned to shock rather quickly, as thirty speeding quarters flew at the werewolves from Ho Young's hand. While the quarters did no direct damage to them, they did stop them in their tracks. They were most likely confused as to why Ho Young, out of all of the weapons that he could have conjured, chose quarters.

"Really?" Marcus yelled in disbelief. "Out of all the weapons you could have created… Quarters— really bro?"

"Yeah, man," Ho Young yelled back. "Werewolves are allergic to silver!"

"Silver kills them, sure, but only if it pierces the skin, which I doubt quarters will do, man!" John made a face and dodged as the wolf charged forward again.

Marcus caught it by the neck and threw it back into the hall, which attracted the attention of every other werewolf on the third floor.

"Let's go," John yelled, as a werewolf slid past the door after losing his balance trying to get into the room.

The three of them jumped on the cloud waiting for them at the window. John hunted it along until it sped towards where he left Jasmine and their parents. As he drew closer, he brought more clouds down to form a giant one that could carry all of them.

Beneath them, the wolves were exiting the hospital to chase after them, with Fenrir in the lead. John looked back nervously, and the clouds began to lose altitude.

"John!" Jasmine yelled, almost falling through the cloud as she clambered over to the large one.

John quickly regained control and brought everyone back to the surface, where Marcus and Ho Young helped John's mom and Jasmine's dad move over. Instead of looking back again, John sped up and flew directly to a mall he knew well in the downtown area of Detroit, landing them on the rooftop.

"You guys stay here," he told the others. "I'm going to go and get us something to eat." John searched the roof and was relieved to find that it had electrical outlets.

"John," Jasmine said. "Please be safe." She kissed John on the lips, forgetting that her dad was right beside them in her rising worry.

He quirked his brow and shot an evil glare John's way. "Is there something I should know?" he asked.

"I can explain it later," Jasmine said. "I think there are far more pressing issues right now." He didn't respond, just nodded his head and groaned.

"I'll be safe." John said. "I'm just going to grab us a few things and I'll be right back."

Except he didn't move; he didn't want to leave Jasmine. "I can't promise much," he said. "Except that they have a good distance to travel, so we'll be safe for a few nights. So far, we're one and one against them."

"What do you mean we're one and one?" Jasmine glanced up at him, clearly confused in all the panic.

"Well, nobody won the one against Fenrir. He cheated anyway. It can only be him fighting, and not all his convert werewolves—that's what Gabriel said."

"Do you think The Creator will intercede and make it fair again?" she asked, her voice timid but hopeful.

"To be honest, I hope so. If not, I'm done, because the odds against us are impossible."

"Complaining never accomplished anything," Michael said as he appeared next to John. "Instead, you should be looking for answers."

"What answers?" John snapped. "My powers don't even work against Fenrir, and Marcus threw him through the entire hospital and he got up without a single scratch! We can't beat him."

"On the contrary, your powers work just fine. It is your fear of Fenrir that is crippling you. When you can overcome that fear, Fenrir will learn to fear you."

"Well, what about all of the extra wolves?" Jasmine asked, reaching for John's hand.

"We'll handle them, and when Fenrir gets here, he'll be alone unless Chiron shows up."

"Yeah?"

"They were allowed four beasts, and The Creator will penalize them one beast for cheating, so now you will only have to face Chiron, Fenrir, and one other." Michael struck an imposing figure, but his face was kind.

"What's the other beast?" John asked, forgetting all about his reverent politeness.

"Let me ask you a question," Michael said. "Would you rather trust yourself to save yourself and your families, or would you prefer to trust someone you don't know who is far less qualified?"

John stared off at nothing, silent for a long moment.

"Imagine those bodies you saw as you and your families because the demigods who were unqualified failed, and the wolves ravished the world, including you and your friend Jasmine here, and there was nothing you could do because you were powerless."

John looked at Jasmine and then at his mom, imagining what might happen to them in that scenario. It infuriated him and he stood taller, with his shoulders squarer and mouth set in determination

"I understand," he said. He looked fierce in his place on the edge of the roof. The wind was blowing hard and the flaps on the bottom of his letter jacket were swooped out behind him.

Michael continued. "It is best that you do not know the third and final beast. Just worry about defeating Chiron and Fenrir for now, and when the third beast comes, I will give you a warning and make sure you are ready. It will take Fenrir a few days to get here, but Chiron can get here in hours, so never get too relaxed. It is likely, though, that Chiron will wait for Fenrir to get here before he attacks you."

"Okay."

Michael considered them for a moment. "Actually, go ahead and relax—you might need it, and I will just tell you when Chiron gets here."

"You can't." A voice sounded from the clouds. "If you do, we get our fourth beast back for you cheating."

"Who was that?" John asked.

"Oh, it was Lucifer," Michael said, laughing. "Don't worry about him. He can't touch you."

"Okay," John said, looking at Jasmine. "We can do this," he said, more to reassure himself than anyone else.

"I believe we can too." Jasmine flashed him a glimmer of a smile.

"Now for the second thing," Michael started again, and John almost whined aloud. "The roof is not safe at all. That would give the edge to Chiron for a sneak attack."

"Yeah, I completely agree," Jasmine said, looking sheepishly at John.

"Well, we don't have any money on us," John said.

"This card will work on every machine that takes credit cards, and it never runs out, so buy what you need and pay for the hotel with it," Michael said, handing John a steely colored card.

"Thank you." John handed the card over to Jasmine straight away, unsure where to put it to keep it safe.

"Just one more thing," he asked, turning back to Michael. "Can you get our parents out of harm's way and keep them safe until we finish these beasts off?"

The angel smiled. "That I can do," he said, and without a word he was gone, as were John's mom and Jasmine's dad.

"Okay," John said to everyone. "You heard him. We have to get off the roof, so let's get to the ground and find a good hotel."

They climbed onto the cloud again, and John lowered them to the ground. Slowly, they walked through the streets, feeling less tense than they had since the whole saga had begun. Detroit was definitely a lively city and it reminded John a lot of Chicago. There were no big corporate stores like *Walmart* in the downtown area by the mall, so they had to travel to outskirt areas to find what they needed.

"Let's do a bit of shopping while we're here," John suggested. "Grab the stuff we're gonna need."

Ducking into the nearest *Walmart*, they stocked up on necessities like toothbrushes, combs, soap, shampoo, and swimming gear—they were all looking forward to a moment of normality with a swim in the hotel pool. They grabbed some food and snacks from the grocery store and grabbed a cab to the most expensive hotel in town. They were going to have as much fun as possible before Chiron and Fenrir arrived. Their parents were safe, and they had enough time to enjoy a short break from all the craziness.

When their cab pulled up to the hotel, they stepped out and stared in amazement. The hotel was huge and beautiful. The entrance had lights around every inch, and the walkway up to the door was made out of glow-in-the-dark lights, crisscrossing across each other in halos of red, green, and blue. The front door was fitted with stained-glass and surrounded in what looked to be a border of precious stones.

The four of them approached one of the sixteen check-in counters, intimidated by the vast space, but pleased there was no line. Jasmine filled out the rental agreement for the room. She had to fudge her age a bit to get past the room rules, but she thought she would probably pass for twenty-three without too much hassle. Worried about what would happen if they were caught, John was nervous about it, but Jasmine reassured him that the worst that could happen would be for them to be turned away.

They tensed collectively as the lady behind the counter asked for ID, but instead of insisting or turning them away, the receptionist handed Jasmine five keys—one each and one for the elevator.

"What happened back there?" Marcus asked, once they were in the elevator alone.

"My ID changed," Jasmine said. "When she handed it back to me, it showed that I was twenty-three." She pulled it out to show them, but it now said she was seventeen, just as it should do.

"That's weird. I swear it said I was twenty-three."

John squeezed her hand. "We believe you. Michael or Gabriel probably changed it so we could get the room, and then changed it back." He leaned in and kissed her.

"Um, what the heck?" Marcus said, jealousy bubbling up as Jasmine kissed John back.

"Oh yeah, we're dating," John said, with an exuberant smile. He couldn't help being proud.

Marcus wanted to be upset, but he was too happy for John. He had only been interested because she was beautiful, and John actually had feelings for her. It was probably the way it should be. "Congratulations, bro," he said, offering his friend a real grin in return.

"Man, I need one of those too," Ho Young said.

"One of what?" Jasmine asked, laughing to herself. She already knew the answer but wanted to hear Ho Young explain it.

"A girlfriend, I've never had one. You know, I hear they're very expensive though," he said, as if you could just walk into a store and buy a girlfriend.

John and Marcus joined Jasmine in laughing.

"Yes, Ho Young, girlfriends can be expensive, unless you meet them at the ninety-nine-cent store!" John joked.

Marcus and Jasmine started laughing again. Ho Young began to laugh with them when he realized what had set them off.

It took a while, but the elevator eventually stopped as they finally reached the top floor. They were in the *Double-Oh-Seven* suite—room number eleven hundred and nine, located at the end of the hall. Jasmine stuck her key in the swipe lock and the door popped open. What greeted them was fantastical—there were chocolate water fountains with strawberries and bananas and cotton candy machines; the floor was made out of blue marble, and like outside, when the lights were off, the blues, reds and greens all glowed in the dark. In each of the rooms, there was a seventy-inch TV, and the living room was equipped with a one-hundred-inch theater screen.

There was a bar, but none of them drank so that remained untouched. The long couch in the living room was flanked by three oversized armchairs, and the kitchen was equipped with everything they could possibly need. The bathroom even had a miniature sauna right by the massive hot tub bath.

"This is really nice," Jasmine said, eyes bright with child-like wonder. "I've never stayed in a suite this nice, and I've traveled a lot with my dad."

"I haven't either." Ho Young said. John considered making a joke, but there was nothing humorous about Ho Young's homelessness. John could only imagine what it could be like to sleep outside with no heaters, showers, refrigerators… without any standard living necessities.

"Let's pick the rooms," Jasmine said, her enthusiasm cutting through the tension building around them.

"No need," Ho Young responded quickly. "You and John take the master bedroom, and Marcus and I will take the other two rooms."

"Um, thanks Ho Young," Marcus said nodding. "Very noble of you to give away the room that has the waterbed."

"Oh, water beds aren't that great," Ho Young said in a serious manner as he prepared to lecture Marcus. "My bed used to get wet all the time, but all it did was make me itch. I actually feel sorry for people who waste their money on waterbeds."

"Really, you don't say?" Marcus said, giving him a wry look, as if he had just noticed that he didn't think quite like the rest of them.

"Oh, but I do," Ho Young replied.

Everyone burst into raucous laughter. They all adored Ho Young—he was everyone's favorite. Even though John roasted him all the time, if someone ever tried to hurt him, he would be the first to give them the beating of their life.

Ho Young looked around for second. "Man, I did it again. I said something dumb, didn't I?"

"No, not at all," John said. "Not at all. We're laughing because Marcus was about to argue over the waterbed, even after you told him that it'll make him itch. As a matter of fact, I don't feel comfortable sleeping on that waterbed, you?" he asked, pointing to Jasmine.

"I really don't either," Jasmine replied with a smirk.

"I already had my mind set on that room right there." Marcus said, catching on and walking towards the room closest to him.

"Well, I guess you get the waterbed then," John said to Ho Young, grabbing Jasmine's hand and walking into the other room, leaving the master open.

"Ah man." Ho Young sighed, but went to check out his room.

Jasmine found herself being genuinely impressed with how John tricked Ho Young into taking the best room. His attitude in life might have been a bit rough, but he was definitely maturing, because the old John would have seized the opportunity to milk the joke for all it was worth, but instead he'd been kind.

"Oh wow!" Everyone heard the joyful whoop and the gentle slosh as Ho Young tested out the bed. "This mattress is awesome! Ah, I mean--noooo! This is the worst! I can't stop itching."

John and Jasmine, making themselves comfortable in their room, chuckled at the sound. It was rather beautiful.

"Tomorrow, we start training." John rolled over to face her, his expression becoming serious. "We all need to maximize our powers. Michael said that we're far more powerful than we know, and that if we can just focus on our powers, they will grow."

"I agree," Jasmine said with a half-smile as she reached up to cover her yawn. "And it's also about time you started doing your homework," she finished, as she closed her eyes to go to sleep.

TWENTY-SEVEN

"Zeus, you idiot!" Poseidon yelled. "You cost us a beast with your cheating!"

"Quiet," Zeus snapped back. "These champions are no champions at all. They struggled with only one beast. If we have all three of our beasts attack at the same time, they'll all be killed and we will have won this tournament easily."

"Yes," Hades replied drolly, rolling his eyes. "I see Zeus still thinks he reigns supreme, but we have not forgotten the last war and you are no king of ours," Furious blue flames erupted around his body and his facial expression hardened until it resembled a thunder storm in monsoon season. He was almost incandescent with aggression.

Zeus stood up from his seat which stood at the head of the throne on Olympus, preening as his appearance shifted to accommodate the electricity fueling his pride. Lightning bolts flared all over his body and his muscles rippled beneath the charge of his skin.

"No!" Poseidon yelled. "We need not to be at odds with each other if we are to win this war and our freedom to avoid the Lake of Fire." He spoke with such passion that, eventually, Zeus sat back in his throne, with Hades sitting across from him. Both their chests heaved with the unfinished effort of their burgeoning battle, but with a collective sigh, all three settled amongst the others to face their challenge.

"Until these trials are over, there will be peace between us! After that, we will finish what we started so long ago." Zeus spoke the warning to Hades in a tone that left no question of its authenticity.

"Agreed," Hades growled. He wanted revenge on Zeus more than anything for imprisoning him and Poseidon. He was going to get it if it was the last thing he did.

Hera *tsked* from her place at the table. "Now, can we please discuss the matter at hand? We need to discuss it while you're all getting along. What beast are we going to use for the finale?" she asked.

"That's already been decided." Zeus stood up to make his point seem more official. "I know a beast has to be cut out, but we all made the fourth beast the fourth beast because it was the most dangerous."

“But it wasn’t unanimous!” Hades said, leaning forward and giving away his enthusiasm. I thought we could use the drakon,”

“And here we go again, every time you pick a monster, it is that same stupid drakon! Tell me dear brother, how many times has it lost to a demigod? I’ll save you the trouble of counting; the answer is every time. The drakon is out,” Zeus said, turning away from Hades, unwilling to waste more time talking about the blasted creature.

“Well then, what beast could we use that has never lost before?” Poseidon asked the council of his brethren.

“He has lost before…” Aphrodite said. “But only once, and he killed his adversary as well. Why not bring back Leviathan, who once guarded the realms? He is the great dragon who killed Thor so long ago.”

“Great idea!” Poseidon yelled, grabbing Aphrodite’s hand and raising it. He was glad there had finally been a reasonable suggestion. “I can’t see why we cannot all agree to that. What say ye?” Poseidon asked, looking squarely at his brothers.

“I like it.” Hades nodded solemnly.

“I cannot argue. I cannot think of a more ferocious beast than Leviathan,” Zeus said, smiling at the idea.

“Okay, let us put it to a vote!” Poseidon shouted.

“All in favor of the Leviathan, raise your hands!” he yelled, ensuring everyone could hear.

They all raised their hands in agreement.

“It is settled then,” Zeus said as he sat back on his throne. “Leviathan it is.”

Hades and Poseidon sat on their throne room seats next to Zeus. The Big Three were working together again as had not been seen since they destroyed Kronos. All the gods rejoiced and called for a celebration and a great feast, and within no time they were drinking and eating and dancing, celebrating their now assured victory.

*****

Hera alone did not join in. She stayed to herself off to the side. She knew from the book she had once tried to give to the demigods that The Creator knew how to toy with them and make them think that they had a chance to win—like he had done with their ancestors. She knew that The Creator knew all things, and that these new demigods were just getting started. The Creator knew they were going to use the Leviathan long before they did, and it did not bode well.

"You seem deep in thought, my queen," Athena said as she sat next to Hera.

"I am. I cannot celebrate. You know as well as I do that The Creator knows all that was and is to come. He knew from the day that he created us that we would rebel and that, in this challenge, we would use Leviathan. Zeus and the others are happy because the demigods have survived thus far on luck."

"Perhaps, just maybe, this time is different. It is our only hope." Athena said gently, attempting to cheer her ruler.

"Tell me, Athena, have not all other victories by demigods been won entirely with luck? Why should this time be any different?"

"Hey, I'm supposed to be the wise one here." Athena chuckled and took Hera's hand, holding her gaze steady. "Yes, what you say is true, but these knuckleheads didn't listen in the last two wars that destroyed us. Why would they listen now? I do agree, though, that we should not be so cocksure" she finished.

*****

"Send word to The Creator that our final beast will be Leviathan," Zeus said to Hermes, as he downed an entire bottle of rich red wine.

"Okay," Hermes said, nodding his head. He was far too drunk to deliver any message, and instead he passed out on the steps of Olympus. In the morning, he sobered himself up and flew to Michael to deliver their message via him to The Creator.

"We have chosen Leviathan for our final beast," Hermes said with a sly grin as he delivered the news.

"Great! What perfect timing! Leviathan is due to be released from his prison in two weeks!"

Hermes frowned. "Why does he have to wait two weeks to be released?"

"Because that is when his sentence is through," Michael replied.

Hermes looked at Michael for a long, hard second before nodding his assent and taking the news back to the others.

"They didn't care," Hermes said immediately as he landed back on Olympus.

"Of course they didn't. The Creator knew from the day he created us that this was going to happen; that clearly comes with knowing all things!" Hera grumbled into her almost-empty goblet.

"How can we be sure?" Hades asked.

"He knows what we're going to do before we even do it. We are going to lose again, and I guarantee you, we haven't seen the full extent of these demigods' powers yet."

"Nonsense! He just claims to know all things. If he really knows everything, then why did he allow Lucifer to stay all that time, plotting against him?" Zeus argued.

"He was toying with him."

"That hurts." Lucifer materialized beside Hera, wearing a condescending smile and a mock look of pain. Hera stepped back in horror. She had not been expecting him to hear her. He raised his finger and she lifted into the air.

"You know, you talk too much," he said, and with a crunching and twisting motion of his hand, he crushed her voice box, silencing her for good.

Tears poured down Hera's face as she looked at Zeus mournfully. He rose quickly into his full size, glistening with anger. Lucifer was forced to drop Hera and focus on the god bearing down on him. He managed to knock down the first three lightning bolts that came his way, and caught and javelined the fourth one back to its owner, but it was easily pushed aside. Still ten feet from Zeus, Lucifer thrust his palm forward and with the power streaming from his hand, smashed him against the ground. Making a grabbing motion with his hands, he slammed Zeus down, over and over, until the ground split further with a shattering rumble, and blood was pouring from Zeus' mouth.

"You can't kill an angel except to take the breath of life out of him," Lucifer muttered to himself. Then, without warning, he began to suck the breath itself from Zeus. Zeus paled as the life was being drawn from him, and Hades stepped in, unable to watch his brother's death. He grew to full size and blasted Lucifer into the wall, turning back towards Zeus to return the air stolen from him. Lucifer stood up to attack, but before he was able to strike again, he was blasted by jets of acid water from Poseidon's triton.

"We may not be able to take you one on one, but you can't beat us all," Poseidon said.

Lucifer was outraged, but on seeing all the angels united against him, he knew that, together, they would indeed be too much for him.

"Fine," he said. "I suppose I'll just go and tell The Creator that we forfeit the challenges."

"That is not for you to decide!" Zeus shouted, his voice hoarse as he struggled to regain his breath.

"Oh, but isn't it?" The Creator's bargain is with me, you fool. You are just the pawns of our deal. If I forfeit this tournament, the bargain is off, and it is straight to the Lake of Fire for us all."

"You wouldn't!" Zeus buzzed with building irritation, lightning beginning to appear once more. He snarled as he took another glance at the broken goddess who was once the love of his life.

"Try me and see," Lucifer said, smiling.

Zeus pondered the matter heavily. Lucifer, from what he had read in the scrolls, was unpredictable. Zeus wasn't willing to chance their one hope at freedom, so he unwillingly conceded, knowing that if he did not, Lucifer would call it all off just to get the better of them.

Hera, with her voice gone, disappeared from the throne of Olympus. She was happy that her ex-husband had stood up for her—nearly lost his life defending her—but she was ashamed, because the best thing about her was her voice. When she spoke, people listened, and now she would never be able to speak again.

"All of you!" Lucifer commanded the room. "Either bow to me or prepare for the Lake of Fire," he said, a powerful smirk on his face. All of them did as he asked, including The Big Three: Poseidon, Zeus, and Hades.

Lucifer laughed as he sat on Zeus' seat on the throne. "I better not ever catch you in this seat again," he roared at Zeus, hand raised in warning.

All the gods knew that Lucifer was power hungry; many of them felt that power may have been his driving purpose in the first war against The Creator. They looked in disapproval at him, but he was in control and there was nothing they could do except obey him if they wanted to avoid the Lake of Fire.

TWENTY-EIGHT

Each night, Michael and other angels visited them in their dreams. John, Jasmine, Marcus and Ho Young were being trained to understand their powers; trained to use them. John had far more power than he had known, and he learned quickly to teleport himself and the others to anywhere he could clearly imagine. Within days, he had finessed his skills to the point where he could control other people without even having to bat his eyes.

Jasmine learned that she could not only control just water, but all liquid, and her command of her power increased incredibly. She lifted the entire Atlantic Ocean, and put it back down without harming any of the ships on it. She also learned that she could focus on someone and know what they were going to do even before they did. Up until then, she'd had no idea that was possible.

Marcus was already at full strength, but he went through training in combat and acrobatics. He also learned to channel electricity through his body instead of having to only depend on lightning bolts from the sky.

The Creator considered the beasts as weapons, so Ho Young could not only create weapons, but could also turn into any monster or beast that he chose. He was taught specifically what weapons to use against each beast, because he used the wrong ones in practice. Michael grew frustrated with him, and assigned a more patient angel to his training, and Ho Young began to flourish.

After a week of relative safety in the hotel, Michael suggested they return to their hometowns.

John was eager to fight with Fenrir now that his powers were stronger and they were more evenly matched. "We should head back. I believe Michael is right. Fenrir and Chiron are going to wait for Leviathan's sentence to end before attacking, so we need to get back to school and finish hearing what happened in that book. At night, we can hunt Chiron and Fenrir."

Jasmine's laugh was tinkling and joyful despite the situation, "It's funny, isn't it?"

"What do you mean?" Marcus asked, thinking she was losing her mind.

"The beasts started out hunting us and now we're hunting them."

John laughed, too. "I never even thought of that, but that sure is right. Okay." He scanned the room." Are you guys ready?"

"Yeah, I sure am… And thank you guys for letting me sleep on that waterbed," Ho Young said.

"Aww, you're welcome," Jasmine replied.

"You know, I really had fun here," Marcus said as the elevator descended. "We should come back here if the credit card still works when this mission is over."

"Sounds like a plan," John said. He was thinking the same thing.

After turning in their hotel key, John teleported them back to the southside of Chicago. They hadn't known about his new ability, and they delighted in its handiness when they arrived at their destination.

"Whoa!" Ho Young yelled. "That was *tight*."

"It *was* pretty awesome," Jasmine agreed, pressing a quick kiss to John's cheek.

Marcus grinned. "Now have a fast way to travel places," he said. "That's gonna be a big help! Now—if you don't mind, we all need to get home to rest for school tomorrow. They'd barely started off home before a shout from John stopped everyone in their tracks.

"Wait!" he yelled. "Our parents are still gone… and Ho Young! There's no way in hell that I'm letting you sleep outside with Chiron and Fenrir on the loose. You're coming with us." He finished with a pat on the back for Ho Young.

"Um, what do you mean with us? My parents get home tomorrow, and I need to be there."

"Well, that's too bad, because until this is over, we have to stick together."

"Only on the condition that you use your teleportation power to get us into the Chicago Bulls game." Marcus crossed his arms and flashed his friend a cheeky smirk. He knew he would agree.

"It's a deal, my friend!" John said. "I didn't even think about that." John spent a moment enjoying the realization that he could now go anywhere he liked—completely free.

John gave Marcus some dap as they discussed how they would teleport into the bathroom four minutes before the doors to the stadium opened for fans, so that they wouldn't be seen.

"No, we will not be using our powers to steal." Jasmine reprimanded both with a stern look.

"Well, good thing it isn't stealing then," John said, turning his head back just enough so that he could see Jasmine and give her his best Leo eyes—a sideways look that was at once stern and sarcastic. He hated it when she insisted on taking the fun out of everything.

"I'm serious! We've been trusted by God to carry out this mission, and I want to do it right."

"Well, actually, we were technically born into these powers just because we're descendants of demigods—trust really isn't a factor," John retorted.

"True, but the powers skipped our parents and all the generations before them, so they could have skipped us too. God has been sending angels to teach us how to use them. If God hadn't sent Gabriel to tell us we had powers in the first place, who would have showed us how to get started? We might never have even known about them."

John opened his mouth to speak, but Jasmine cut him off. She wasn't finished.

"No." She held out a hand to quiet him. "God didn't have to use us because we're not the only descendants of those demigods. There are three-hundred-and-sixty-eight descendants alive today. All of them live in small towns and all hang out in groups of four like we do."

"Wow," Marcus said. "And how exactly do you know all of this?"

"You forget, my powers enable me to focus on something and know its past and its immediate future—and read minds," Jasmine said, giving John the Leo eyes back, but with more attitude and her arms folded.

"Good luck winning an argument with her," Marcus said, laughing at his own joke.

John scoffed. "No problem," he said, creating an invisible magnetic field around his head, blocking Jasmine's access to his mind.

"Wow," she said with a chuckle. "Any reason you don't want me to read your mind?"

"Yup, it's called privacy," John replied, smiling sarcastically. "Nobody wants someone knowing their every thought, especially if you're trying to make a point that they disagree with.

"I guess that's fair." Jasmine sighed. Just as she was getting ready to launch into a tirade about the basketball game, a vision came to her and she froze on the spot.

"Whoa, something is wrong with her!" Marcus yelled, jumping back and pointing at her unfocused eyes. He was genuinely scared; his heart was pumping at an incredible speed. It looked like she had been possessed by a demon.

"No, she's okay. She's getting a vision like that Savannah girl did in the book; remember how Jeffrey and the others reacted with Savannah when she did it?"

Marcus relaxed a little at that, and after a short moment, Jasmine was back to normal and filling them in. "The school has filed a missing persons' report for us with the police. They were unable to contact our parents." As she spoke, she looked at the ground and shook her head in disappointment. She was sure that her notes to the school excusing them should have worked, so why didn't they?

"It's most likely Chiron's doing, since he's the one who keeps control of the government officials for Lucifer," John suggested.

"Yeah, it was him." Jasmine nodded, eyes closed and deep in thought. "And he's watching us," she said, pointing discreetly to the sky above them. "Good thing you stopped us from separating because he was planning on killing Ho Young in the park tonight after he fell asleep."

"Whoa! Kill me? Oh no, I want to live!" Ho Young shouted, hopping around in a circle and looking skyward.

"Hold on. Michael!" John yelled.

In less than a second, Michael was standing next to them, clad in full body armor.

"Is everything okay?" John asked, eyeing him with irritated suspicion.

"Oh, yes. I was just doing a bit of training. What is it you need from me? Why did you call me?"

"Well, we need our parents here, but we need them off limits from attacks. The schools put out a missing persons' report on them—and us."

"I know, and we sent your parents home yesterday. The beasts can't get within several miles of your families."

"Okay. Good," Jasmine said.

"The only catch is…" Michael said and then paused.

"Is…?" John said, gesturing to Michael to continue.

"Well, they can break the protective enchantments if you are there with them, so it's best that you stay away from your parents for the time being, until the battles are over."

"Okay." They agreed, unhappy but determined to keep their parents from danger.

"Also, it would be a good plan to attack Fenrir and Chiron before the next beast arrives. The next one will be hard enough to beat by himself. He once killed Thor, a very powerful second-generation angel."

"What does it mean to be a second-generation angel?" Ho Young asked.

"Well," Michael said. "I'm an original angel, meaning I was of the first that The Creator made. The rest were born just like you humans are born, but differently. So for instance, Thor is a second-generation angel because he was of the first angels born to the first-generation. Zeus is a third-generation angel. He was born to a second-generation angel named Kronos. Do you get it now?"

"I do," Ho Young said, with both of his arms in front of him hanging down with his hands cupped together as he balanced back and forth on his tippy toes.

Michael looked at John. "You can handle Chiron by yourself. The rest of you need to go after Fenrir."

John looked at Jasmine for a split second, before saying, "no."

He wasn't about to risk her for any cause.

"I figured you would say that. Well, good luck to you then," Michael said, disappearing into the air like usual.

"I'm sorry, but I'm not risking any of your lives," John said, looking at everyone. We have to stick together."

"Agreed." Marcus, Ho Young, and Jasmine all bumped fists together as if it sealed their agreement.

They had to decide where they were going to stay, because they couldn't stay with their parents until the challenge was over.

"Let's just stay at Jasmine's house, and all of our parents can stay at Marcus's."

"I like that idea," Jasmine said.

"I like it too," Ho Young agreed.

"Um, I think we need to ask my parent's first," Marcus said, thinking of how his parents would react to the news of sharing their home with others.

"No problem,"

"Gabriel!" John yelled into the sky, "I need your help real fast."

Instead of Gabriel appearing as Michael had, a letter dropped from the claws of a pigeon that was flying overhead. Ho Young opened grabbed it and opened it.

"What does it say?" John asked. Ho Young was reading it to himself rather than out loud.

"It says that Marcus's parents have been informed and that you guys' parents are already there."

"Well, there you go," John said. "I guess it is off to Jasmine's house then. We have school in the morning, so we need to set the alarm for 9:45."

"Um, how about no… While you're at my house, we go to school on time."

"Okay, mom," John said with a joking smirk.

*****

The next morning, the four demigods headed to school. The morning seemed to trickle by, until they met at lunch.

"You guys have Mrs Norton's class next, right?" Jasmine asked, taking a large bite out of her burrito.

"I don't." Ho Young responded through a mouthful of his school milk.

"You do now," Jasmine said. "John can turn us invisible, and we all can take the class at the same time.

"Yeah, I think that would be a good idea," John said.

When the bell rang, the four of them headed to Mrs Norton's class. "I'm glad you two are back," she said as they walked in. Jasmine and Ho Young snuck past without anyone noticing. John nodded his head at Jasmine to show his appreciation for her idea.

He pulled up two extra chairs and sat one next to Marcus for Ho Young, and one next to himself for Jasmine, taking care to place them in such a way that they were barely noticeable.

"Okay, let's do a quick review for the students who have been absent from class. We didn't get much read last week, since the school was closed while they fixed up all the storm damage."

"Storm?" John said, more to himself than anyone else.

"Yeah," Jasmine whispered. "God had an angel send a storm after we left, to make it look like the storm did the damage to the school."

"I can see how that would work… except the police were already here when we were leaving… They must have seen the damage then…"

"God must have modified their memories." She was more guessing than actually knowing, because she didn't feel like going into a trance to find out the factual answer.

Mrs Norton continued, interrupting their musings. "We did, however, get to read last Friday, so I'll do a quick overview to catch a few of you up."

"Wait, if they only had school one day, how did they know we were missing?" Marcus asked under his breath.

"Because when they tried to reach our parents, they couldn't get ahold of them, and Chiron sent letters to the school claiming our families had been abducted. So, they sent someone from the school over to check, and after seeing none of us were home, they contacted our neighbors who said they hadn't seen us all week. Acting on Chiron's letters, they feared the worst…"

"Not cool," Ho Young said, a little too loudly. "Chiron is very dishonest."

Everyone in the class heard Ho Young and looked right at Marcus and John.

"Can I help you?" John said, staring back at everyone.

"I just heard Ho Young," a student said, and a few others chimed in to agree.

"I know. I was imitating his voice," John said in his best Ho Young voice.

"Oh, dang, you sound just like him," one of his classmates said.

"Ho Young, you have to be quiet," Marcus whispered, annoyed. The class continued to stare.

"Sorry," Ho Young whispered back.

"That's enough, class," Mrs Norton called, regaining their attention.

"Last Friday, the demigods freed Hades and Poseidon. Poseidon, along with his Cyclopes, battle Sheba, a god from India. Poseidon was able to push them away from his castle, and the demigods returned to land thinking that they were going to be able to part ways. Before they left, however, they received a warning from a stranger named Gabriel, saying that it wasn't over yet. He warned that the Greek gods would be distracted and wouldn't want to waste their time rescuing demigods from Arachne, who was still after them. Now, open your books and let's begin reading from where we left off."

"That is pretty messed up," Marcus mumbled.

"Agreed," John said.

TWENTY-NINE

"This is bad. Do you guys think we can trust that Gabriel guy?" Vanessa questioned.

"I don't think we have a choice," Hercules responded. His eyes were focused on the ground, gaze sharp with anger, as if the ground had just insulted his mom or something. He was beyond upset that, though the mission was over and they succeeded against all odds, the gods left them to fend for themselves. Disappointment showed all over his face. "Damn the gods to Tartarus!" Hercules yelled as loud as he could.

The other demigods stood motionless in shock, wondering if the gods were going to come down and kill Hercules, and possibly them as well. After some time, they began to relax, and Vanessa slapped Hercules for putting them all in danger. He took a step towards her, causing Xavior to rise into the air. For an eleven-year-old, Xavior was quite intimidating. Hercules didn't see him, but walked right past Vanessa without even looking at her.

"This does suck," Gemini seconded Vanessa's statement. "But I want to know who that guy named Gabriel is as well. And how does he know who we are?"

"I don't know. I tried to read his past, but I couldn't. My powers didn't work against him," Savannah answered.

"Maybe he's a god…" Jeffrey said, jumping in on the conversation—he suspected that would be the only reason that Savannah couldn't read him.

"Maybe, but either way we need to stick together, especially if Arachne is really still after us."

"I hate spiders," Hercules said, making a disgusted sound. He had managed to calm down a little bit and decided to rejoin the group.

They decided to rest, and Vanessa bought them a room at the local inn for the night with some of the money Aphrodite had given her. Exhausted from their mission, they fell asleep quickly and slept for the rest of the day and all through the night.

They awoke in the morning to the sound of terrified screams and the cracking of buildings. One of the two giants that raged in fierce battle above the town was certainly Zeus, and he was being thrown around like a rag doll.

"Interesting isn't it?" Gabriel said as he appeared in the middle of the group.

"Are you a god?" Savannah asked.

"No, but neither are your parents. We are all angels, and there is only one god, and we call him our Father, or The Creator, because he created us."

"How come we've never heard of you?" Gemini asked, with a suspicious narrowing of his eyes.

"That story is far too long for now, but all you need to know is that Michael and I fought on the side of The Creator, so we reside in heaven—and plan to stay there. They, on the other hand," he said, pointing upwards, "have another fate coming. They will be cast into prisons and will await sentencing to the Lake of Fire. Before that, though, one final battle will be fought, which is why you demigods must stick together and survive. You play a large role in a war which takes place many generations from now."

"Are we immortal now?" Hercules asked. The other demigod's eyes went wide with excitement, hoping that Gabriel was going to say yes.

"I have said all that I may say, except that Arachne is nearly here. Unless you are ready to die, I think you should find better ways to watch the fight between Zeus and Porphyrion." With those words, Gabriel disappeared.

*****

Savannah noticed them first. A few Tarantulas had gathered on a few of the roofs and were unquestionably focusing their attention on the demigods.

"Time to go," Xavior said, calling a large cloud down to transport them out of danger.

They jumped on quickly and took off just in time, as one of the Tarantulas had jumped at Kikilliana—just barely missing her. As they rose in the air, they could see Arachne approaching in the far distance.

"Take us as high as you can Xavior!" Savannah yelled, her heart beating so fast she felt it might explode.

"I am fine with that plan," Xavior yelled back at Savannah, and the cloud rose further. He had to keep zigzagging and diving through the sky to avoid them becoming casualties in the battle between Zeus and the giant, and a few times, they nearly flew right off the edge of the cloud. Xavior's quick wit in having the clouds clamp onto them around their waists kept them just steady enough to continue onwards.

They watched on as Zeus threw lightning bolts left and right at the giant to no effect. Eventually, Zeus dropped to his knees so that the giant could kill him and end the battle, but Ouranos appeared with a roaring clap, and interfered. He blasted the giant off his feet, causing a small tidal wave to hit the shore. The townspeople would have been killed, but Jeffrey and Xavior worked together to keep the water from making it past the shoreline.

"I have an idea! We can use the ocean to drown Arachne and her spiders."

"Good idea," Savannah said, without hesitation. "Let's do it."

Jeffrey channeled the water past the town and guided it towards Arachne. To everyone's surprise, Arachne wasn't slowed down, not even a little, when the water hit her.

She was determined to get them, and they gaped in fear as she braced herself for impact as the water hit her. She did not hesitate to swim through the fast current, and was still making her way easily towards them.

She quickly reached the surface of Jeffrey's wave and sprinted across the surface of the water, straight for them. Jeffrey dropped his hands and allowed the water to fall from beneath her, hoping that it would make it harder for her to get to them.

A baby spider landed on the cloud as the demigods were discussing a plan. Xavior blew it off, but then another landed. He blew that off too, with a mighty gust of power, but more appeared.

"Umm, you might want to just go at top power on that wind stuff," Kikilliana said, looking over the cloud at thousands of baby spiders flying towards them.

Xavior drew up a mighty windstorm that picked up all the small spiders that were in the air and on the ground. It carried them far away across the ocean. Arachne, somehow, didn't get picked up. Xavior stared in disbelief; his shoulders hunched, wanting to retreat.

He tried to speed the cloud away before she could recover, but before they got even two feet further away from her, Arachne webbed the bottom of the cloud, and began to pull them towards her.

Savannah screamed frantically as they drew nearer and nearer to the great spider queen. She tried to read her mind and summon any future moves that she would make, but for some reason, her powers didn't work on her.

Hercules struck her with a few lightning bolts, and each time they hit, she stopped pulling for just a second, but then she'd continue as if nothing happened.

"I have an idea," Jeffrey said. "I'll cause the ocean to rise and land on her, and while it is pouring dow—"

Xavior suddenly dropped their altitude to avoid the giant's axe, which had swooshed right past Jeffrey's head, and the word was lost in the swoop. The good thing was that the axe missed decapitating Jeffrey by inches. The bad thing was that they were now much closer to Arachne. Jeffrey had no time to thank Xavior for his quick thinking: he had to finish his sentence in order to save them.

"Hercules, focus!" he said. "While I'm dumping the ocean on her, keep hitting her with lightning bolts; we might just be able to electrocute her."

"Okay," Hercules said, standing strong at the edge of the cloud. "I'm ready."

"Okay, here it goes." Jeffrey raised his arms and the ocean rose again, above Arachne's head, thirty feet in the air. He let go, and it fell on Arachne in waves. As it did, Hercules began sending his lightning bolts, striking the water to electrocute the mother of all spiders.

At first it seemed like not much damage was being done, but soon smoke began to rise from Arachne, and not only was she not pulling, but the web holding the cloud began to shake violently. Arachne was being electrocuted.

Gemini formed ninja stars in his hand, made out of mint oil and acid, and began throwing them at parts of

Arachne's body, as the water slowly receded back to its home on the ocean floor.

She began to fall, lost amid a large cloud of smoke as she hit the ground and died. Arachne had been beaten before, but never had she been killed. The demigods jumped for joy and shouted, but were quickly reminded of the battle still roaring overhead.

Zeus and Ouranos continued to attack the giant, pushing him back. The giant fell while trying to avoid Zeus' sword, which was forged from the electrical current itself. Just as they thought it was finished, another giant leapt from the sky knocking both Zeus and Ouranos down. It was the giant created to destroy Ouranos. Ouranos looked up with fear etched all over his face and the giant grabbed him out of the ocean and tossed him to land.

Gaia appeared and began to wrap around Ouranos. She had him in her clutches for a second time, and was going to kill him, but Ouranos wasn't going without taking Gaia with him this time. Focusing on the sky, he yelled at the top of his lungs, causing dark clouds to form.

"Forty days the Father has already permitted for it to rain, for forty nights' water from heaven shall come down, and though I die again right now, Father has already declared that by this storm's end, Gaia shall die as well!"

Those were Ouranos' last words before he disappeared under the Earth.

Rain immediately began to pour down over the entire planet. Zeus, knowing he would not be able to defeat the two giants, fled. The demigods were going to go home and help their villages, but Gabriel appeared to them again and forbade it, saying that anyone caught in this great storm would die, and that they must live.

"Why can't we help our families?" Savannah asked Gabriel, with tears pouring down her face, as she thought about her mom and dad. "If this storm is going to kill anyone caught in it, can I please save my parents?"

"I am afraid that your request must be denied. The Father has made up his mind. Humans have sinned against him, by worshiping their false gods and turning on their creator to worship his creations, the angels whom he cast out of heaven."

"Please?" Savannah begged. She had fallen to her knees and was tugging at Gabriel's robes, sobbing.

"Just be happy that the Father has decided to spare you seven, and one more."

"One more? What do you mean?" Gemini asked.

"Ah, here she comes now."

A beautiful woman emerged from the forest just beyond the village. Gemini fell in love the moment he saw her. She had light brown skin and her hair was a bright neon blue. Gemini wanted to marry her.

"Really?" Savannah asked, as she wiped her tears and stood to her feet. She was looking at Gemini with disgust. "I did not need to see that, ew."

Gemini's impure thoughts had flooded her mind.

"I'm sorry that you can't stop being nosy. Quit reading people's minds without them asking you to!" Gemini growled angrily.

"Trust me, it was not on purpose." Savannah turned away. "Sometimes my powers are more of a curse than anything," she added as she walked off, with her nose scrunched up and her eyes narrowed.

"Okay, that's enough," Jeffrey said, as he jumped between Savannah and Gemini to stop them from getting into an argument. "Let's just focus on greeting the new girl and figure out how we can save our families."

"If you disobey the Father and don't get in the submarine ship that was made for you, you will all die. He is trying to save you, but you have to get in the ship."

"I think we better listen to him," Hercules finally said. "He's done nothing but be truthful with us this whole time."

"I agree," Vanessa said. Gabriel had been completely honest with them.

Kikilliana spoke up for the first time in a while. She had been so silent the group had almost forgotten that she was there.

"You guys can't see him, but I can. Death is sweeping through the nations right now. I asked him how many he is taking, and he said everyone except us, that girl walking towards us, and a man named Noah and his family. There are two boats, ours and Noah's, and Death will take hold of anyone not on a ship." Her expression was grave as she addressed them all.

"If we stay and try to save our families instead of getting in the ship, Death will be forced to kill us as well. Gabriel is right; we will die if we don't get in the boat. My dad said we need to get on the ship right now and stop stalling. He has to help Death kill everyone on the Earth and not in a ship right now. He said he doesn't want to take our lives; especially mine, but he will if has no choice…

"My dad, he says all of the gods are going to be rounded up and placed in hell for what has happened in a place called Asgard.

"Gaia, along with the other gods, set Fenrir, the great werewolf, free and arranged for a great war to take place upon Asgard. Fenrir received help from the giants and the dragon, Leviathan."

No one responded, dumbstruck with shock.

"And Fenrir, Leviathan, the giants and the dark elves joined together and launched the attack on Asgard. Almost everybody on both sides died."

"What about your dad?" Gemini asked. He'd missed most of her explanation because his attention had been stolen by the girl walking towards them.

"Since Poseidon and my dad were not a part of that attack, The Creator, as my dad calls him, is not going to imprison them, as long as they leave us humans alone. It is our job, and Noah's families' job, to re-populate the Earth."

"What will they do?" Gemini asked.

"My dad's job will be the same as it is now—to harbor the dead. Poseidon's job will be the keeper of the souls in the sea. Hades and Poseidon will no longer act as gods from this point on. If they want to remain free, they will play out their roles as angels under the Father, or they will be imprisoned with the rest. Hades must stay in hell, and Poseidon must stay at sea."

"First things first," Hercules started. "What is Asgard? And how come I have never heard of it?"

Gabriel decided to answer that instead of allowing Kikilliana, who would only have her dad's side of the story, to give them half a tale. "Asgard was another realm connected to Earth, where more of the angels that were cast out of heaven lived. Asgard has an entrance to Earth in the north, the giants have an entrance in Canaan, the dark elves have an entrance on an island to the east, and the dwarfs have an entrance to the west. All the realms have a special, united entrance which is located at the bottom of the sea and was guarded by Leviathan until today."

Savannah began to speak but Gabriel was too fast.

"The good elves have no entrance," Gabriel said, understanding that Savannah, as the daughter of Athena, was going to ask that very question.

"Why?"

"They closed their realm off a long time ago to keep it safe from attack. However, the dark elves, or bad elves, which ever you prefer, somehow forged another doorway to the realm of the Light elves, or good elves, and they were in battle until Thor and his warriors came and aided them in defeating the dark elves."

"What do elves have to do with the gods… or I guess, Angels?" Hercules asked.

"With Thor being distracted, the fallen angels of Greece, which you know as the Greek gods, freed Fenrir and summoned Leviathan to attack Asgard. Fenrir died in that battle with Oden. They ended up killing each other.

Only Leviathan and the giants survived, and they did not leave. Instead, they hid themselves, waiting for Thor's return. By the time Thor and his soldiers got back, it was too late.

"As they reached the throne of Asgard, Thor and his men were ambushed and killed. They were able to kill Leviathan and the giants as well, leaving not even one survivor on either side. I imagine that with Leviathan no longer guarding the master doorway to the realms, the Father will close all doorways between the realms to keep Earth safe from the Ice Giants. They did not fight in this war, but have a strong taste for human flesh." Gabriel paused for a moment. "That's enough now. You are running out of time," he said. "Get in the ship. Even in the short time that we have been speaking, as you can see, the water has risen to your ankles. I trust that Xavior can get you to your ship, and that Jeffrey here will be able to get the water out of your boat."

The demigods hadn't even noticed that the water had risen so high; maybe because of all of the rain that was pouring down on them so hard and non-stop, or maybe because of how intently they were listening to Gabriel's story. They could hear him so clearly that his voice seemed to drown out every raindrop, and any other sound.

Xavior flew the seven of them, and the new girl, to the ship on a cloud. They hovered above it while Jeffrey summoned every drop of water and returned it to the ocean, and then they got in and quickly closed the hatch.

The inside was freezing cold but, fortunately, there was a wood stove and plenty of firewood. The boat was thirty feet long, twenty feet wide, and two stories high.

"Gemini, before we do anything, can you use your powers to start a fire in the stove, please," Vanessa asked, shivering. The fact that her clothes were soaked didn't help much either.

"I can help a little as well," Jeffrey said. He made a motion with his hands and focused his mind on everyone on the ship. Immediately, all the water soaking everyone's clothes began to disappear.

"Wow, thank you," Savannah said, giving him a hug and a kiss on the cheek, making him blush.

"Um, you're welcome," he replied, reaching out to give her a hug.

"Okay, you guys can take that to the bottom of the ship," Hercules joked. "We do not need to see what comes next." He grinned at Kikilliana as he spoke. Kikilliana smiled back.

"Actually, before anyone does anything, we have a new crew member," Gemini said, pointing to the new girl. He took a moment to introduce everyone, before pausing expectantly.

"My name is Sadie," the girl responded, sounding like she felt a little bit out of place.

"Do you have any powers?" Gemini asked Sadie.

"No, I'm just a regular, plain human. I was out walking when I saw the battle between Zeus and that giant, and then I saw you guys battling that giant spider. Curiosity got the best of me I guess, and while I was trying to get a closer view, a strange man told me to keep walking in the same direction I already was. He said to talk with someone named Gemini, which I know now is you."

"Gabriel told you that?" Gemini asked.

"I don't know his name, but he said that us meeting, or not meeting, would affect the future."

"Hmm, I wonder why he didn't say anything to me?" Gemini wondered aloud.

"Because he didn't need to. He knew you would fall for her on sight," Savannah said with a teasing smile.

"She can read minds and people's futures," Hercules said, laughing at Gemini who blushed with embarrassment.

"Yeah, I sure can." Savannah said, giggling.

"Tell us about your journey," Vanessa asked, refocusing their attention on Sadie, trying to save Gemini any further embarrassment.

"What do you want to know?" Sadie asked, smiling a bit for the first time, more at Gemini than anyone else.

"For one, where do you come from?"

"I come from the south. My people are hunters and growers of food."

"How old are you?" Savannah asked, even though she already knew the answer.

"I'm twenty-two."

"Oh, wow, that's close to my age," Gemini said, feeling less embarrassed.

Sadie smiled at him, her eyes twinkling like the stars.

Above the ship, Michael and his angels gathered together in battle formation.

"You," Michael said, pointing to three angels. "Zeus is there in those caves to the west. Go and capture him. And Poseidon, you are to kill almost all of the monsters in the sea, leaving just two of each." Poseidon looked taken back, but he knew not to question Michael if he wanted to stay free from hell. Michael and his angels stood in battle formation as the fallen angels, still posing as Greek gods, began to appear, geared up for battle.

"Do not kill them. Our mission is to capture them, is that understood?" Michael yelled across his battlefront. "Attack!" he yelled, suddenly and without hesitation.

The rain was pouring down hard as the angels, good and bad, clashed in the sky. Within fifteen seconds, Michael, had captured three of the opposing angels, and tossed them into the sea as was the plan for all of them. They battled for a week straight before taking their first rest. Michael and his angels were capturing their brethren, the fallen angels, with ease. The only reason it was taking so long to capture all of them was because the fallen angels began to run and hide, so Michael and his angels had to find them.

The demigods stayed in the boat the entire forty days and forty nights until it stopped raining. Then, they waited for a full six months before any dry land appeared. Occasionally, Xavior would go flying off with Vanessa, and Jeffrey would go swimming with Savanna. The ocean was different. Jeffrey no longer felt the presence of sea monsters, and it was very peaceful.

When, at last, they were on dry land, they set out to find a good spot to start a village. They built their peacetime houses in pairs: Savannah and Jeffrey, Xavior and Vanessa, Kikilliana and Hercules, and Gemini and Sadie. In contrast to the time they spent in battle, the days were long and pleasant and free. In time, they all had children, who had their own children, too. The little village that was once just eight was soon as thriving and as beautiful as the towns that came before it.

THIRTY

"Okay, class that is the end of the book, *The War of the Gods*! So, tell me, what did you think? I mean, wouldn't that be cool if this wasn't just fiction, but real?"

"I liked it," said Paris, an Italian girl in the class who sat towards the front. She was pretty, but she was a bit high maintenance and thought she was better than everybody, so not many of the kids in the class liked her.

"I liked it too," Jacob, another kid in the class, said.

Pretty soon the whole class was in discussion, talking about what they liked about the book.

"It would be so cool if we had powers like that," Jay said, imagining what it would be like to have the strength of Hercules or the command of others, like Vanessa.

"Yeah, Vanessa's powers are awesome. I like how she can make everybody disappear and can control people with her eyes." Rowan said, clasping her hands together.

"Heck no," Eugene said. "Kikilliana's powers are the best. Shoot, what she did in the battle against the Athenian demigods was dope."

"Yeah, I agree," Marcus said, smiling broadly with a bright twinkle in his eye.

"This guy," John whispered to Jasmine, rolling his eyes. Jasmine giggled as quietly as she could.

"Let's not forget, either," Mary replied to Eugene, "that Hercules destroyed that metal guy."

"Yeah, that is true," John said. "But without Xavior? They would have all died multiple times without him—with Arachne, twice, and the minotaur would have easily been able to sneak up on them if Xavior didn't have them in the air! And that's not to mention the giant squid..."

Marcus looked at John and mouthed, "Really?"

He laughed and offered his friend an exaggerated shrug. "Don't be mad, I'm just pointing out the facts."

"Yeah, okay, but let's not forget Hercules did go on to do much more than Xavior in history, making him the most famous demigod." Marcus retorted.

"Obviously Vanessa and Xavior were busy being happy and minding their business after that. I mean, Hercules did get divorced and remarried about what— three times. Not because he was a bad person, but maybe, the fact that he was always away on a mission and never at home could have had something to do with it."

Jasmine wanted to intervene, but she wasn't supposed to be there and an invisible person speaking in class would probably really freak everyone out.

"Well, I'm glad you young men are taking an interest in this subject so strongly, especially you John," Mrs Norton said, shocked at John's participation, as he never participated in class.

"It was a good book," he replied coolly

"I am glad you liked it," Mrs Norton said, smiling. "Class, I have an assignment for you. Write a one-page report or longer, at home, about who your favorite demigod was, which demigod you thought was most influential to the outcome of this mission, and why—"

Mrs Norton never got her sentence out, because Chiron was flying just barely off the ground outside the classroom. John forgot he was keeping Ho Young and Jasmine invisible, and rushed to the window to stand between the centaur and the class. Everyone who had seen it were backing away, as Chiron inched closer to the window as if he were about to break in and attack.

John didn't know if he was imagining it, or if Chiron actually looked bigger, but there was definitely a new glow in his eyes that was cutting to the soul. In the distance, there was a howl that was just as chilling as Chiron's glare.

"Listen everyone, please don't say anything about what you are about to see. We don't need the government interfering while we're carrying out our mission."

"What?" Jason, a boy in the class, asked from the back of the room, as he slowly shuffled his way along the wall towards the classroom door.

"Woah, he's a lot bigger than last time!" Ho Young yelled, which was noticed by more than a few of the students, and by Mrs Norton.

"Ho Young, I can hear you, but why can't I see you?" Mrs Norton asked, her fear evident in her shaky voice.

"John, you have to make us visible! This is no time to hide our power. We have to help our classmates!" Jasmine yelled frantically.

"Okay then, here goes nothing," John said out loud, as he returned Jasmine and Ho Young to their normal state with a flourish of his hand.

"Whoa!" a few of John's classmates yelled, as Jasmine and Ho Young suddenly appeared in front of them. John looked back at the window and Chiron was gone. He shook his head, realizing that they'd fallen into Chiron's trap—he had just been trying to expose them.

"You guys have some explaining to do!" Mrs Norton demanded, still rigid with fear, leaning against the front wall.

"Listen," John said. "Chiron, that beast you just saw, only did what he did to expose us. We need you guys not to tell anyone, *please*."

"That's a big secret for everyone to hold… even me," Mrs Norton said, still trying to get a grasp on everything.

"Can you guys just explain a little about what just happened? How did you two just pop up in the middle of us like that?" a girl named Joanna asked.

"Well, it's complicated to explain…" Jasmine started.

"We still have twenty minutes left in class, so you better start sooner rather than later if it is a long story!" Mrs Norton said, more composed but no less insistent than she was a moment earlier.

"We're the descendants of the demigods in the book you just read. Ho Young is the descendant of Gemini and Sadie, John is the descendant of Xavior and Vanessa, Marcus is the descendant of Hercules and Kikilliana, and I'm the descendant of Savannah and Jeffrey." Jasmine's quick explanation was met with disbelief.

"Bruh, are you serious right now? Eugene asked. "This is a lot for me to handle," he muttered.

"You have to keep it a secret," Jasmine pleaded, looking to the others for support.

"I can't make any promises, but I'll do my best."

"Thank you," Jasmine said, before she continued explaining everything to the class.

"We have powers like they did, and we have been given an impossible task. Right now, the fallen angels are facing judgement and, instead of just throwing them in the Lake of Fire like I wish he did, God is allowing them seven tournaments to defeat him—to defeat us. For the first, they were tasked with choosing four of their most fearsome monsters to fight against four champions chosen by God—who happen to be us."

"Amazing," the teacher whispered to herself in awe.

"We've already fought against Chiron, who you just saw in the window. That's why Marcus and Ho Young were in the hospital. He ambushed them. John and I got there just in time to stop him from killing them."

"Can you show us your powers?" A boy named Tremaine interrupted.

"Yeah, we can," John said, smiling. He was worried that they'd been exposed, but it was still exciting to finally be able to share their new lives. As it turned out, the class was much more receptive than he and the others had expected. He flew a few feet above the ground and turned invisible for a just a second before reappearing and gesturing to Ho Young. Ho Young began creating weapons and turning into different beasts, while Marcus caused lightning to strike through a window into the classroom,

"Sorry," he said, mostly out of embarrassment.

"Wow." Mrs Norton watched them, face alight in wonder. "We're sitting here reading about your ancestors and talking about how cool it would be to have their powers, and you do." She paused to think. "What gets me is that the book is listed as fiction, but clearly it's true... So, God is real, and the Greek gods are really just angels posing as gods?" she asked.

"That is correct," Jasmine replied, smiling encouragingly. "And, we have to destroy Chiron and Fenrir before Leviathan is released... but, I'm sorry to tell you guys like this," Jasmine said to John, Ho Young, and Marcus, more than to the class. "I don't know if you noticed, but Chiron is not only bigger than before, but he's been given extra powers, as has Fenrir. They're stronger and even more deadly than before. And… and we need to get out of this classroom, because Fenrir is on his way here. And you know the rules— if we're not here, Fenrir cannot attack them," she made a sweeping motion towards the other students. "But if we are, they're fair game."

"We have to go, Mrs Norton, and now," Jasmine said, fully opening the window.

Mrs Norton nodded, gesturing for them to hurry. "Will I see you back in class tomorrow?" she asked John and Marcus as John was climbing out the window.

"No," John replied. "Until this battle is over, we have to stay away from everyone so nobody gets hurt, but assuming we win—and are still alive—we'll be back as soon as it's all over. If you could cover for us with our teachers, that would be great. Maybe tell them that you've talked to our parents and we're all very sick or something? You could say you came and saw us to confirm that we're actually sick so that no one will suspect anything."

"Yeah, if you could, that would help us out a great deal," Marcus said.

"Okay, I will," Mrs Norton said, still filled with amazement. She was in disbelief that her students had powers at all, much less just like those in the book she had read with many classes over the years. "Class," she addressed the rest. "If any teachers or students ask you about, John, Jasmine, Marcus, or Ho Young, say you saw them at their houses, and they are really sick, please. I have a feeling this is bigger than a few unexplained absences."

The students agreed and John and the others were soon gone from sight. John kept them invisible until they were completely away from the school. He didn't like that Chiron looked much bigger, and agreed with Jasmine. It was safe to assume that, since their powers had been increased, the beasts had too.

"We need to get Chiron over the ocean," John said, giving voice to an idea he'd been developing before they left the classroom. "I just need to knock him down into the water and Jasmine can drown him, and Fenrir won't be able to interfere."

"That's actually a really good idea," Jasmine said. "But how do we get him out to the ocean?"

"That I don't yet know yet, but whatever plan we come up with, we need to come up with it fast, because we only have four days until Leviathan is released, and we can't handle them all together." Another idea popped into his head. "Actually, Jasmine, can you focus on Chiron and see if you can see everywhere he will be for the next two days?"

"Yeah, I can," Jasmine said, and disappeared into her mind, searching for the centaur.

Twenty minutes later, she came out of the trance and rushed to tell the group what she saw. "Chiron is definitely following us right now, so it shouldn't be too hard to get him out to sea," she began. "He's had his powers increased, so it isn't going to be easy to beat him now, John." She looked worried, but crossed her arms in an attempt to hide it.

"Don't worry. We were picked for a reason: because we can win, and The Creator, who knows all things, clearly believes we can."

Everyone stared at John for a minute, not grasping what he was saying.

"In the words of the great villain, *Scar*," John said, shaking his head in mock disappointment. "I am surrounded by idiots." He mimicked Scar's voice dead on.

"Aw, man, I'm not an idiot, am I?" Ho Young asked, though he was still smiling.

John didn't even look up properly. He just flashed a 'do you really want me to answer that?' look at Ho Young, trying not to laugh. "Think about it everyone… God knows all things, and the same god that knows everything that is going to happen believes that we are going to win these battles… Do you get it now?"

"Wow, I never thought of it like that," Marcus said, feeling emboldened by the enlightenment.

"I didn't either," Jasmine said, feeling at once more comfortable and less nervous about their mission.

"I did say I was surrounded by idiots," John reminded everyone as he laughed out loud again.

"Ha ha ha." Jasmine's laugh was fake, but her grin was real.

"Well, we need to get a boat and lure him out to sea once we get there," John continued.

"Can't you just fly us over the sea like you're doing now—on the cloud?" Marcus asked.

"No, I can't, because once I start battling Chiron, I won't be able to focus on holding you guys up and you'll fall into the ocean."

"Oh yeah, that does makes sense," Ho Young agreed.

The four of them continued to travel towards the Pacific Ocean, off the coast of Washington. They were just going to go to a lake in Chicago at first, but Jasmine very wisely suggested that the group go to Ocean Shores, Washington, since they had to go there anyway to pick up the weapons they were told to get at the start of the tournament. John kept a steady pace, but he didn't push it, as he feared that traveling such a great distance would exhaust his powers. Each night, the four would rest and sleep in a hotel, paid for with their new credit card.

Chiron kept his distance and never attacked. The group knew that he and Fenrir had been ordered to wait for Leviathan before attacking, but if the centaur refused to bring the fight to them, they would take it to him. Catching Fenrir and Chiron by themselves was their best hope of winning against the first two beasts without any more injuries. They needed to be fresh and at one hundred percent for their fight with Leviathan, who had never really lost to a demigod—or group of demigods—before.

When they finally reached Ocean Shores, they landed right next to Starbucks. It was 4:00 in the morning, so fortunately for them nobody was outside. As soon as they landed, John made them visible and led them out of the inner city and towards the piers.

The city had an eerie feeling to it, and Jasmine wasn't sure if that was because of the mission they were on, or because it was near pitch black outside. Ho Young created bright flashlights for everyone in the group, but none of them mentioned how strange it was that none of the lamps or streetlights were working. The darkness began to disappear, replaced by the morning light that preceded the sunrise, but they knew they'd not be able to see its beautiful colors in the gray light that filtered in through the gloomy clouds and blowing wind.

"Okay, stay here," John said to everyone as they reached the docks, switching his flashlight off. It was already bright enough to go without. "I'm going to go from boat to boat and find an empty one for us to borrow—just in case that oversized goat tries anything. I better keep you guys invisible, I think. Keep an eye out for him. If he figures out what we're doing, he's likely to try to kill at least a few of us before retreating…"

*****

It all happened so fast.

Jasmine was talking to Marcus about how proud she was of John, and how she was glad they were finally dating, when an arrow pierced Ho Young right in the heart. Marcus turned, but before he could work out what had happened, and find Chiron, arrows had pierced his and Jasmine's hearts as well. All three were killed instantly.

*****

John was jumping from one ship to the other, and was nearly hit by an arrow but, feeling it coming, he jumped out of the way just in time.

"Ha!" he cried in adrenaline fueled elation. "You missed, you idiot! You shouldn't have come by yourself!" John yelled at Chiron, unaware that anything had happened.

"Jasmine, hit him with the water, now!" John smiled as he called out to Jasmine, but the water didn't come. "Jasmine, do it now!" he yelled again, but once again, he got no answer.

John turned and saw Jasmine lying dead on the ground, alongside Marcus and Ho Young. His chest felt like it might split with agony, and rage pulsed through his veins. He took to the skies, flying as fast as he could at Chiron, blinded by anger. The centaur fled over the cities, heading back towards Chicago. John followed him over a random wooded forest until he suddenly dropped out of the sky and waited for John on the ground.

John landed not more than ten feet away from Chiron, his anger spurred on by blind hatred and highlighted in the fresh tears on his face.

"You coward!" he managed to shout. Chiron notched an arrow into his quiver and prepared to fire. Just as John went to move out of the way, he found himself frozen.

He looked down at his arms and legs and they were white with a tangle of spider webs.

He tried to fly again, but instead of going forwards he flew backwards, hitting the ground hard. He tried to get up, but just as he moved the web started pulling him over the rough and rocky ground at an extremely fast rate. He looked behind him and almost screamed when he saw the humongous black widow that had him webbed and was pulling him in for dinner.

"Jasmine!" John yelled, as he neared Arachne, "Jasmine! Jasmine!" John continued to yell even as his voice broke against sobs and a new flood of tears blurred his vision.

Jasmine opened her eyes to John shaking her.

THIRTY-ONE

"You're alive!" Jasmine yelled, engulfing John in a bear hug. She was crying too hard to get any words out, and everyone was stumbling over each other to find out what was wrong.

Finally, she was able to speak. "One of Chiron's new powers is that he can see us when we're invisible." She gripped John's shoulders tightly. "When you go checking the ships, he's going to sneak attack us from the sky, killing us with his arrows. You see what he does and you chase him! And… and he tricks you—you chase him into a forest, and he leads you to Arachne—when she gets you…" she trailed off, once again overcome with emotion.

"Arachne?" John gulped as his eyes widened. He was petrified of spiders.

"Yes, Arachne."

"Wow, you 've never done that before," Marcus said, looking torn. He was excited by the new power, but horrified by what she'd said. "You came out of your trance as if it were real. You were yelling all kinds of curse words while you were… off somewhere."

"I must have been repeating what John was yelling, because he was cussing up a storm."

"Now that we know what his plans are, there's no point in waiting to get out to sea. We fight him here and now." John said boldly, taking the leadership position in the group. "Marcus," he said, focusing on his friend. "Even though you can't see him, can you focus a lightning storm to hit him hard?"

"Yup," Marcus replied, and got straight down to preparing himself. He did not need to see him; if he focused hard enough, the lightning would find Chiron itself.

*****

High above the clouds, beyond the sight of the demigods, Chiron watched them with a smile. "They have no idea that I'm here," he said to himself. "I don't need Fenrir to kill them. This will be all too easy." He watched Marcus summon up a storm, but assumed they were going to use the wind from the storm to push their boat—once they had secured one. He was far too arrogant to submit to the possibility that the storm was meant for him.

Chiron grabbed his bow and readied to shoot Marcus right through his big, steady heart, but just as he was notching the arrow, a mass of lightning rained down upon him, surging through his body. He screamed in agony, the sound vibrating through the tensed muscles of his neck. The arrow left the bow in an upward direction as his arms flailed when he was struck.

*****

John took to the sky and focused on discovering where Chiron was by following the lightning bolts. They streamed upwards instead of down, indicating that the centaur was higher up than they were. Following them closely, he was on Chiron before he even knew what was happening, and using all the strength he possessed to pull him down into the ocean water. Chiron resisted despite the intensity of the lightning assault—he was definitely the stronger entity.

As his hooved feet touched the water, Marcus' lightning doubled in size. At the same time, Jasmine sent the water to grab him in a great fist and hold him firmly beneath the surface.

He was dead in no time at all.

"One beast down, and now to the other," Jasmine said with a dark look on her face. Chiron was her first kill, and her face contorted as she tried to come to grips with what she'd done. Beside her, Marcus looked much the same. Even though Chiron was bad and was trying to kill them, they both felt weird— like they were in a dream. Killing did not come naturally to them and it felt awful.

"I just… I just…" Jasmine said as she watched the body rise to the surface of the water. As it surfaced, it changed from centaur to human, and the new image almost brought her to her knees.

"It's okay." John comforted her. "We all took part in it, and… it's either them or us, now—you know that. We had no choice; you had no choice."

Though he thought his words would be comforting enough for Jasmine, she double over and vomited until there was nothing left but bile. When she collapsed into a heap beside him, John helped her up and walked her to the ocean to help her clean up.

"You guys go over into town and get her another shirt?" he asked, shooting Marcus a pointed look. Her shirt was drenched in throw up, and there wasn't much they could do to fix it. While the others were off shopping, John rendered them both invisible so that he could help her get her shirt off and get cleaned up in the water. Once she was clean, he took off his shirt and gave it to her, so that she would be dressed when the guys came back.

Marcus and Ho Young, though they were supposed to only be shopping for a shirt for Jasmine, couldn't help but stop in a few other stores and buy a few items for themselves, Ho Young bought himself a glasses-with-mustache disguise, while Marcus bought himself a new pair of sneakers.

When they returned, John stared at them, confused. "Ho Young? Why?" he asked, wondering why on Earth a twenty-year-old would buy disguise glasses.

"I figured I could sneak up on the werewolf guy, you know… Just start walking by him, minding my own business, and then, bam!"

"Bam is right," John said to Ho Young. "If you think any human walking past a werewolf won't be brutally attacked by it, then you, my friend, have another thing coming. That 'bam' will be him biting into your neck and turning you into a werewolf yourself."

"I didn't think about that," Ho Young said, handing John the bag. Marcus gave the credit card back to Jasmine.

"If werewolves didn't attack humans, I think you would have fooled him, so it was a great idea." Jasmine said to Ho Young as she placed a hand on his shoulder and gave him a warming smile.

"Yeah, I thought so," Ho Young said as he offered her a slightly frightening grin in return. His face turned red hot and his eyes went far too wide. John turned around so that he wouldn't see him laughing.

"Are you alright?" he asked, with his back still turned.

"Yeah I think so," Ho Young replied. "I feel a little warm, but I think I'm okay. Should I get medical help?"

"I think I speak for the universe when I say yes, but not because of why you think… I asked if you're okay because your face is beet red… and your expression looks a bit like a crazy version of the joker," John started laughing again. Jasmine smacked him on the arm, trying not to laugh herself, but she had to give in. She couldn't help herself. Marcus had to walk away a few feet from the group because he was laughing so hard. He was laughing so hard that it made Ho Young start, too, and for a moment, they all forgot about the recent battle with Chiron.

Marcus soaked up the peace that was Ocean Shores for a few minutes, watching a man on the dock with his dog, feeding the ducks.

"Well, let's get a hotel room and then go find the silversmith that Michael said had weapons for us," John said, addressing the group as soon as they had composed themselves. "While Ho Young here can produce all kinds of the wrong weapons, the rest of us need to have silver weapons for ourselves, so that we can actually kill Fenrir this time—we don't need a repeat of last time."

They walked into town and made a beeline for the first multi-story hotel they saw. After securing the room, they googled 'silversmiths' in Ocean Shores, Washington, and found three—J & S Silversmiths, Al's Silver Shop, and Silver, Copper, and Gold Services.

"Did Michael mention which silversmith in particular we're supposed to go to?" Marcus asked Jasmine.

"No," she replied. "He just said to come here and go to a silversmith to get weapons, but that also was at the beginning of this tournament. There's a chance that whichever silversmith it was that had the weapons may not still have them."

"Let's just try Al's Silver Shop first," John said as he scrolled down the list.

*****

The shop was in a building that looked like an airplane hangar. The front of the store was an old pawn shop. It had extremely dirty white tiles on the floor, with a bunch of bins to search through. There were rows and rows of clothes for customers to choose from. John was eyeballing a few Christmas sweaters that he thought were nice. For such a dirty shop, they had quite a few customers—it was still early in the morning, but there were quite a few people around. They could see why the store was packed instantly. The pawn shop was a shopper's heaven.

Besides the large variety of clothes, they also had every electronic device you could think of, and the whole middle section was designated to toys and games. Before following the arrows out the back to the silver shop, they spent some time walking around, looking at all the cool instruments that they had in the back, in between the pawn shop and the silver shop.

After a half hour of window shopping, they finally made it into the silver shop. If they thought the pawn shop was something to see, it was nothing compared to the silver shop. It was beautiful. The floor was covered in a stunning silver tile, and silver chandeliers hung from the ceiling. There were rows and rows of shelves with silverware, silver dishes, silver cooking items, silver trophies, silver tools and all sorts of odds and ends.

They waited patiently for the clerk to return from helping a customer, eyeing off the carefully crafted pieces surrounding them.

"Hello," the clerk said. "My name is Sterling. How can I assist you today?" He stepped behind the counter. He was tidy in his work uniform, reasonably tall, and just a little overweight. His hair was a reddish brown. There was nothing outwardly remarkable about him at all, but once he looked up, he froze.

"Is everything okay?" John asked, seeing the expression on his face.

"You're the four," the man said, still staring at them with a mixture of fear and excitement.

"Excuse me?" Jasmine said, feeling a bit nervous and wondering if maybe they had been caught on camera during one of the battles, and it had been posted on the world news.

"A man came to me in a dream three weeks ago," he answered. "He said four champions with special powers would be in to visit me today, and he showed me a vision of you four. He told me his name was Michael, and that I was to make weapons for your battle with somebody named… Fenrir, I think he said."

Jasmine smiled. "He knew we were going to come in here today?"

"Um, I'll say it again. The Creator knows all thing's, Jasmine, which includes things we plan to do."

"Amen to that. He knows all things, including the exact number of hair strands you have on your head," Sterling said, referring to the Bible scripture.

"I see you're a Christian," John said, a friendly smile crossing his face.

"Actually, the whole town just about is," Sterling replied. He continued to look at them as if they were the starting lineup for an NBA team. He was almost squirming in his pure excitement, eyes gleaming like a child at Christmas who received the best present ever.

"Nice."

"Did Michael tell you to make specific weapons for us, or to just make whatever weapons we requested of you when we came in?" Marcus questioned.

"Oh no, he told me specifically which weapons I was to make, and he said that you would all be trained to use them for your battle tomorrow with that Fenrir guy."

"Guess that means another training session tonight," Jasmine said, making an exhausted face.

The man bent down and grabbed one item at a time from under the counter.

"Okay," he said. "So, I have a bow and arrow for a Jonathan…" He looked between the four demigods trying to determine which one was John.

John reached out to take the weapon. Both the bow and the arrows were made of pure silver, and the bow was a little heavy. Fortunately for John, the arrows were not so heavy, and he was able to wield them comfortably.

"And I have this silver, double sided spear for a Marcus…" Sterling said, waiting for Marcus to identify himself so that he could hand it over.

"Thank you," Marcus said, taking the spear.

"You're welcome," Sterling replied with a warm, friendly smile.

"And last but not least, I have this silver outfit for a Jasmine. See here, these blades stick out around the shoulders? Here too, at the waist? And down the sides of the legs? They're all silver," he said, taking great pride in his work. "There's a silver knife in each shoe, too—all you have to do is stomp the heel of your foot on the ground with a decent amount of pressure, and the knives will come out."

Jasmine took the outfit and traced her fingers over the intricately spun fabric.

"And that's all I have," the man said as he pointed under the counter.

"Hey," Ho Young said, looking offended. "But what about me?"

"Ho Young," John said as he motioned for Ho Young to lean in closer, giving the impression that a secret was coming. As always, Ho Young leaned in.

"Every time," Jasmine said, laughing. "Ho Young, when are you going to learn not to lean in with John? I don't know how you still fall for that."

Marcus busted out laughing, as Ho Young jumped back, watching John with curiosity.

"Ho Young," John said. "You have powers that can create all the silver weapons that you could want. You don't need anything from here."

"Oh yeah," he said, scratching his chin and laughing to himself, which the man behind the counter seemed to find quite funny.

"I have to get back to work, but it is an honor to meet you guys. Take this Fenrir down for the world."

"Oh, Fenrir is the least of our problems," John unintentionally said out loud.

"What do you mean?" Sterling asked, a worried look casting a shadow across his face.

"Well, after Fenrir, we have to fight Leviathan, the dragon that killed Thor."

"Wait, what? Are you saying Thor was real?"

"Yup," John said with confidence, as they were entering into a subject that he knew very well. "You see, many of the non-Christian religions worship angels that were either cast out of heaven, or who have visited Earth. And you know how we humans were back in the day—anything that showed even a hint of power was worshiped as a God."

"Wow," Sterling said, "That's crazy, Thor is real… What about Zeus and Hades, and Poseidon? Wow!"

"Yes, wow," John said. "I'm sure I'll share your enthusiasm after we finish beating them in this challenge. The four of us against their greatest beast—what could possibly go wrong?" he finished sarcastically, which everyone caught onto.

"Understandable," Sterling said. "And good luck to you four. I hope you'll come and visit my shop again, once the battles are over."

"Oh, we most definitely will," said Jasmine, giving her word to the kind silversmith.

"Guess I'll see you soon enough, then," Sterling said, and with that, they were out the door and headed back to relax at the hotel, for what might be the last time.

"Well, that was a bit of good news," John said as they walked together down the uncrowded footpath.

"What do you mean?" Jasmine asked.

"Well, he said the battle with Fenrir isn't 'til tomorrow, so that means we have today to ourselves and can relax a bit," John said, smiling and sending her a quick wink.

"Dude, you're so right, I didn't even think about that. What do you want to do then?" Ho Young asked the group.

"Well, we are tourists, and Ocean Shores is known for its beaches."

"Good point," John said. "Let's go and buy some beach clothes and head to the beach!"

THIRTY-TWO

After a great day on the beach, John gathered the group together to discuss the thing they had been avoiding. "I know today has been fun, but it's getting to about that time—we need to get back to the hotel and start planning for tomorrow."

"Yeah, I know," Jasmine said. "I've been focusing on Fenrir, and he's killed seventy-three people in the last twenty-four hours. He needs to be stopped."

"Well, where is he?" John asked, wanting to know how long their journey would be the next morning.

"He's just one town over for now, but he plans to devour people in Chicago tomorrow."

"Devour?" John asked, confused at her specific and colorful choice of words.

"Yeah, he plans to eat all the women and bite all the men… He wants to build a werewolf army."

John sighed. "Wow, that isn't good. There's really no point though, because only Fenrir can fight. The other werewolves can't do anything except attack the town and convert more people."

It didn't take them long to return to the hotel, and sleep came easily that night—they had exhausted themselves in a flurry of joy and anxiety at the beach. As Jasmine slept, Michael appeared to her.

"Fenrir will struggle to attack you," he told her. "Your silver body armor will perplex him, but he can be brilliant when the need arises, so he will find a way. You need to keep moving—make yourself an even more difficult target… use the spikes on your armor to attack only when it is safe."

After Michael finished lecturing Jasmine, he showed her how to do even more with her powers. First, he taught her to do real time predictions, which would help her work out what her target's immediate intent was. As he began to teach her about the power she had to damage from the inside, using the liquids that were saliva and blood, she felt the dreamscape shift and wondered if it had become a nightmare. Turning someone's own bodily fluids on them was a frightening prospect, but she rested more easily knowing she had such a strong defense.

Michael visited Ho Young's dream next, urging him to use his power to its full extent and become a dragon for the fight with Fenrir. Fenrir was petrified of fire, and a dragon's roaring blaze would be a most effective deterrent.

"Oh, kind of like Sher-Khan the tiger, right?" Ho Young asked in his sleep, leaving Michael with a bewildered look on his face.

"Um, yeah sure, just like Sher-Khan the tiger."

"You know that Mogli was lucky that lightning struck, otherwise that tiger would have ripped him to shreds."

Michael, who never had much patience for Ho Young's winding tangents, sighed and agreed. "So, you are to turn into what?" he asked, confirming that Ho Young understood his instruction.

"A dragon." Ho Young smiled serenely, picturing the shimmering scales and sleek outline of a massive dragon.

"Very good," Michael said and disappeared to venture into John's dreams.

"Last time Fenrir got the best of you because you feared him, so we must practice the scenario until your fear is well controlled."

Throughout John's dream, Michael took the form of the great werewolf, launching training attack on training attack at the already-tired young demigod. John fought valiantly, but his powers grew weaker each time Michael defeated him.

By the end of John's training session, he was useless. His powers wouldn't even lift a feather off the ground. When he woke from his dream, he felt the choking pressure of a weight on his chest and fingers tightening around his throat. The shadows around him grew into towering silhouettes of centaurs and wolves and spiders, and the walls seemed to get closer and closer—he had no way to escape. Breathing heavily, he focused on the lamp beside his bed, and slowly the panic attack abated, but Michael feared that if he didn't get a handle on his fear, he would surely to die in the battle.

"Marcus, you are doing very well with your weapon," Michael said, shaking off his nerve-wracking experience with John and moving onto his final charge. "You and the staff seem to have been made for each other." Marcus' dream was short as his command of his weapon was already great, and Michael felt that little interference was necessary.

Michael left them feeling wary—Marcus and Jasmine might be their only hope if John couldn't get his act together. He hoped to see Ho Young blossom into a warrior in the coming days, but he feared that he was just as likely to transform into Puff the Magic Dragon as he was to become a fierce, fire-breathing monster.

*****

The next morning, Michael appeared in the flesh to deliver a further blow to their mission. Upon Lucifer's whining, The Creator had disallowed Jasmine's armor, on the grounds that it would give her an unfair advantage since Fenrir didn't actually have any powers. The news caused Jasmine's previously fighting spirit to plummet, and she fought to hold back her tears of frustration.

"Well, what am I supposed to use now?"

"I don't have anything for you." The angel bowed his head. "I would suggest for you to use your powers as best as you can to evade Fenrir, and stay close to Marcus."

"Um, don't you mean John?" Jasmine asked, eyeing Michael, confused.

"No, I mean Marcus. John lost his powers in his training session overnight. His fear of Fenrir is blocking him from being able to use his power almost at all."

"Oh, no," Jasmine said, holding her hands to her face as she dashed to John and wrapped him tightly in a reassuring embrace. "I'm so sorry," she said softly. "I think I know why he has trouble with Fenrir, and I think he does too." She turned away from John to address Michael and the others once more. "When John was six, he was attacked by a pack of wolves. He was able to get up a small tree trunk, but one of the wolves grabbed onto his ankle. He struggled for a while and was able to get all of the way into the base of the tree."

"That could be why," Michael replied, watching John shift uncomfortably from foot to foot.

"The wolves stayed for hours trying to get into the tree," Jasmine continued, despite the quieting look John was giving her—it was too important a matter to be concerned with keeping his confidence; his life depended on it. "They were determined to make a meal out of him. That experience must somehow be unconsciously messing with his mind every time he thinks of, or sees, Fenrir."

"I see… but if he doesn't find a way to get over it before Fenrir gets to Ocean Shores, he'll be in grave danger."

"Wait, here? I thought we were going home to fight. Jasmine saw him going into our hometown," Marcus said, trying to figure out what was going on—everyone's powers seemed to be off kilter.

"That was his plan yesterday, but Zeus spoke with him an hour ago, and told him that to change his path of destiny, he must come here instead. Zeus knows how to manipulate people's futures; to trick seers such as yourself. Fenrir is on his way, and his pack of werewolves are following, even though they cannot help him in battle."

"He plans to use them to distract us by attacking civilians," Jasmine said, frowning as she focused on Fenrir's mind. "What a coward."

"Wait—I don't think he can do that. I'll be right back." When Michael said right back, he meant it literally and was back within three seconds.

"Okay," he said, leveling them all with a serious look. "The Creator says there are no rules preventing him from using the converted werewolves to attack civilians—only the four of you, and your parents, are safe from the pack."

Fear twisted John's face, and for a moment he thought his feelings might be enough to muster up his power, but he wound up on the ground instead. The darkness was smothering, and he was yelling for help as another panic attack hit him hard. For a second, he felt sure he was being stabbed and he clutched at the pain in his chest. Michael and the others tried first to be soothing and then to yell at him, reminding him to breathe.

Jasmine balled herself up on the floor beside him, whispering softly. "It's okay," she said gently, over and over until John overcame the panic.

The group rallied immediately, keen to start focusing on the upcoming events.

"Okay, you guys better come up with a plan, because they're on their way," Michael warned.

"How can we fight Fenrir and protect the people from the werewolves? I just don't see how it's possible."

"I know," Ho Young said. Everyone looked at him waiting for him to say something quirky and nonsensical. "I can fly high in the sky and meet the werewolves, long before they get here, I can turn into a dragon and burn them into ash with silver fire."

Even Michael stopped and looked at him in amazement. "Wow, there might be hope for you yet," he said, smiling as he patted Ho Young on the back before he vanished as quickly as he had appeared.

"I guess I better get to it. Good luck to you guys with Fenrir." Ho Young said, as he leapt out of the hotel window and dissolved into a small dragon before anyone had the chance to discuss his plan with him.

Their fear grew as, at first, they thought he had decided to keep the body of the tiny, four-foot dragon, but as he rose into the sky, his wingspan stretched to sixty-feet and he became a striking full grown beast.

"Well, I guess that leaves us here in the hotel waiting for Fenrir," Jasmine said. John felt his pulse hop and groaned as quietly as he could, hoping Jasmine didn't hear.

Marcus had just stepped up to take the first watch—much to John's irritation, when Jasmine cried out. "Oh no! There's someone else with Fenrir! He's a butcher… but also a monster! He butchers humans for a living and cuts up their bodies to feed to Hades' three-headed dog…"

"But that isn't possible," John said, panicked. "Fenrir has to fight us alone, right?"

"Not necessarily," Jasmine began. "Zeus and the other fallen angels can't ask any other beast for assistance, but if one happens to see us fighting, there's no rule against him jumping in of his own accord…" She shuddered. "It seems this butcher is an old friend of Fenrir's."

"Well, that really sucks," John said. "So, it's three on two now, and the butcher is a bit of an unknown."

"No," Jasmine insisted. "It's two on two. You aren't fighting; not without your powers. No—I won't let you."

John wanted to argue, but the worry on her face made him stop. He turned away; his piercing glare was directed toward the ground instead. He was beyond upset, but not because Jasmine didn't want him to fight. He understood, but the idea tore him up inside because he couldn't stand the thought of anything happening to her; he didn't want her to have to take on more of the fight in his stead.

"I can't let you go out there. Not unless I'm there to protect you," he said, more calmly than he felt.

A howl pierced the air from right outside of the hotel and John clutched his chest tightly as he began having trouble breathing.

"He's coming!" Jasmine yelled as she jumped away from the door. A fat, burly looking giant whose head was just brushing the ten-foot ceiling walked into the room smiling, with two glinting chopping blades twisting in his meaty hands.

"Well, what do ya know?" he said with a cruel snicker. "Fenrir'll be disappointed that I found the lot of ya first. He was sure ya'd be on the top floor, but here ya are, only on the third floor. An' I don' so much feel like waitin' for him..."

"John—duck!!" Jasmine yelled. John did as she said, and a blade flew right by where his head had been. He swore.

"What have we here then? Another demigod who can predict the future I see. That didn' help that Savannah girl against me when I caught her in her home while her husband was away. To know the future is sometimes to realize too early that there's no way out."

The butcher charged at Jasmine with alarming speed. She didn't move in time and a blade slashed against her cheek. Luckily, its touch was light, but it left a cut nonetheless. John jumped to his feet, snapping to legs off the wooden chair he'd been sitting on and engaging the butcher in a reckless fight.

The butcher tried to swing under John's arm, but he managed to kick the butcher's forearm, stopping him in mid-swing. John tried a three-hundred-and-sixty-degree turn, letting the chair legs add to the force, but the butcher was too fast. John yelped when the butcher not only blocked the chair leg, but also struck one of his middle ribs with the razor edge of his blade. Pain shot through his body and his hand came away wet with thick, red blood when he instinctively grappled at the wound.

No!" Jasmine screamed.

"Not to worry miss, I'll be getting to ya shortly," the butcher said as he bellowed a laugh. A second howl rang out from several floors above them.

"Fenrir must be on the top floor," Marcus yelled. "We need to hurry, before he comes down."

Marcus began to attack the butcher with his staff. Though the butcher was a small giant, he was still big compared to Marcus. He was also strong and lightning fast, but for a time, Marcus managed to out match him for strength and speed. He did all kinds of flips and twirls and maneuvers with his silver staff, and in any other battle it would have been impressive. Unfortunately, this time, the butcher was doing the same, and blocked each and every one of Marcus' deadly swipes.

As they battled, John heard Fenrir in the hall on their floor and knew he could most likely hear the battle taking place. John had to act fast. He hit the butcher in the back of the head with a tall lamp he found beside him, trying to draw his focus away from Marcus.

"Come on!" he yelled to the others. "We have to jump right now."

The three of them launched themselves at the open window, and threw themselves out, clutching at each other's elbows. Fenrir was right behind them, and would have grabbed them easily, but somehow John's powers kicked in and he was flying them quickly away from the hotel. Fenrir hit the hard concrete with a sickening thump and he howled in anger. The demigods were on their way to safety and out of his reach. They could see Ho Young in the distance, having an easy time flying over the heads of the werewolves that had been following Fenrir. It almost looked as though he was enjoying shooting silver flames at them.

John had gotten them a good distance from the hotel when his powers left him again, and the three of them fell onto some grass. Luckily, John had been flying low to the ground to reduce Fenrir's opportunities to spot them.

"Okay," John said getting up as the howling continued somewhere in the distance. "We need to run. Now." The four demigods took off in a sprint. They had no idea where they were going, but they knew they had to get somewhere and prepare for round two.

"Look you guys. Over there!" A marbled-red, four door Cadillac was sitting in front of the hotel right beside them. There was no one around, but it was running—almost as if it had been left just for them. John glanced around and gestured for the others to get in. As he backed out of the car park, he saw a hotel worker run out, yelling at them. The worker pulled out his phone, most likely to call the cops.

"Cops will be after us soon, we have to ditch the car somewhere." Jasmine said, gripping the door handle as John hit the brakes. The three of them got out and began to run on foot. They had no idea where they were going. "Look," John said. "There's a Greyhound bus station."

But it was too late.

Just as they were getting ready to run towards the bus station, a loud rumbling sounded from the sky above them, and when they looked up, they were met with an array of military jets and choppers flying steadfastly towards an enormous dragon.

"Crap," John said, as the determination on Jasmine's face became a pleading desperation. "Don't worry Jazz," he said. "We'll save him."

They headed back to where they left the car, staying off the main road. When they reached the hotel, they were relieved to find that Fenrir was long gone, but the danger was not over. The butcher was in the kitchen, and John was certain that he'd seen them as they made their way towards the elevator in a panic.

"What do we do?" Jasmine asked.

"We fight," John said. "You guys go help Ho Young. I got this fruit cake." He ran a hand over the tender cut on his ribs, anger rising quickly. "I have my arrows… Marcus, can you leave me your staff?"

Jasmine didn't like the plan at all, but Ho Young needed help lest he ended up captured or worse. "John, please just come with us! You cannot beat this butcher guy without your powers!" she pleaded, clutching at his arm.

"Oh, I can win," John said as his eyes flared, still fuming that the butcher had managed to cut Jasmine.

"Okay," she said, diverting her eyes as she kissed him on the cheek. The three walked into the hallway.

*****

"Running again I see," said the butcher as John approached him, fury in his steps.

"Oh no, they have more important issues to deal with. I'm staying to waste my time with you," John said, a feral grin splitting his face as they engaged in battle.

John's arrows were still in the hotel room, but he had Marcus's staff in his hands. The hulking butcher was quick and the slices and slashes came lightning fast, but empowered by anger, John was not afraid and his powers were at full strength. He was a full step ahead of the butcher, and within moments, the lumbering man was covered in gashes from the spear end of the staff.

*****

Jasmine and Marcus didn't have to drive far. Ho Young was flying boldly towards the town to escape the missiles streaming towards him from the aggressive military crafts. They were in luck, as Fenrir and the werewolves were nowhere in sight, having fled at the sight of the military. A jet fired a missile directly at Ho Young, but Jasmine focused on its liquid components, and it burst into a fragmented explosion long before it reached its target. A spray of bullets was released from one of the jets, Marcus pulled over and picked up a boulder. He launched it at the jet and it struck right in the center, splitting the massive body in two.

Marcus and Jasmine jumped back into the car and followed Ho Young back to the Ocean Shores downtown area. He was heading back toward the hotel.

When they next looked skyward, John was flying high above the hotel, using the wind to carry the butcher. They stared on in open-mouthed horror as the oncoming jets got closer and closer to Ho Young, but John diverted the danger: with a look of deep focus, he summoned a mighty surge of power and used the wind to throw the butcher into the jet on Ho Young's tail, and it spiraled to the ground on impact.

Both the butcher and the pilots were killed.

John landed on Ho Young's back and in a flash they were gone—he'd made them invisible.

As Jasmine drove, the car began to slow down until it wasn't moving at all. The door opened and Marcus jumped, staring at the opening in fear until Ho Young—back in his human form—appeared from thin air. Marcus clapped him on the back and Jasmine backed off the gas, allowing the car to come to a stop. John appeared at once, climbing into the car.

"Okay, we need to find Fenrir," he said, with a confidence he hadn't had earlier in the day.

"You got your powers back!" Jasmine said, with tears in her eyes. She had been worried about him from the moment the elevator door had closed, and was struck by intense relief at the sight of him.

"I sure do." He smiled back at her. "Now let's go kill all these damn werewolves!"

"Okay, let's go," Marcus said, mouth curling into a buoyant smirk. "Do you have my staff?"

"No, I was kind of focused on saving Ho Young, so it slipped my mind. My bad."

"It's all good," Marcus said.

"No, here, take this," John said, handing Marcus his bow and arrows. "I don't need it now that my powers are back. Take it."

"Are you sure?" Marcus asked, even as he was grabbing at the weapon with an excited look.

John nodded, chuckling. They needed to find Fenrir. "Jasmine, can you find Fenrir for us?" he asked.

"I think I can." Jasmine stopped driving to focus on the wolf. As she was in her trance, her face twisted into an expression of abject horror and her foot slammed down on the gas pedal. It was a good thing that the car was in park, because they could have wound up in a terrible wreck. Marcus pulled Jasmine's leg off the gas and she jolted forward, hitting her left cheek on the steering wheel as she came back to real life.

"You guys, Fenrir and his werewolves are in a Seattle mall, attacking people."

John swore, trying to keep control of his fear. "Everybody out," he ordered the group. They were going to have to teleport, as it would take nearly two hours for them to drive the distance from Ocean Shores to Seattle. "How the hell did they get there that fast?" He turned to Jasmine.

"I don't know," she said, shaking her head. "When I looked back into his past, I didn't see much. He and the wolves were just running along the road, and then they looked up and found themselves at the mall."

"Remind me to talk to Michael about that later, because that's pure crap."

They huddled together and John teleported them to Seattle in less than an instant. They landed in what looked like the set of a horror movie, among limbs and chunks of flesh and bone strewn about the floor—the wolves were eating people without mercy everywhere they looked.

One lunged at them, but with a wave of his hand, John sent it flying through the glass ceiling. This did not go unnoticed by the other werewolves and John's stomach began to clench. Where was Fenrir?

The werewolves began to attack the demigods in waves. Jasmine caused all the fountains to explode so water poured onto the floors, and the wolves began to slip and slide all over the place. John lifted their group into the air as Marcus shot a bolt of lightning down to strike the now flooded floor, sending a shock of electricity through the wolves. They got up quickly and continued walking through the water which was now waist deep.

"Do it again," Ho Young said to Marcus.

As the second round of lightning left Marcus' fingers, Ho Young shot a stream of liquid silver into the bolts, and they mixed together perfectly. Striking the werewolves individually, Marcus and Ho Young managed to kill them all before John landed the group on the top level.

Once they landed, Jasmine caused the flooding waters on the lower levels to recede. The four demigods were immensely proud of their teamwork.

"He's here—on this floor," Jasmine said as she focused on Fenrir's thoughts. The top floor was dark, either the lightning strikes or the flooding—or possibly both—caused the power in the mall to go out and the reserve lights were dim.

Before anyone knew what happened, Fenrir had sped across the floor and slammed Marcus into the far wall, hurting him badly, and was gone again. Despite being hurt, Marcus got up and ran back to his companions. *Better to be hurt than dead*, he thought.

John looked around frantically. "Ho Young!" he yelled. "Create some brighter lights so we can see!"

As he spoke, Fenrir struck again, and as before, Marcus had no chance. The beast was on him before he could move a muscle. John saw him fall to the ground, four gashes striping across his sweater, pouring blood.

"Flood the mall," John said, and without warning, teleported everyone outside. "Stay here with them. I'm going back in."

"But…" Before Jasmine could finish her sentence, Fenrir was on her and she was running for her life.

Abandoning his plan for the mall, John teleported himself so that he was between Jasmine and the werewolf, appearing only feet from Fenrir. The wolf leapt at John without losing his stride, and with a wave of his hand, John threw him off, slamming him against the wall.

Using his power over air, he attempted to bring the full weight of gravity down on Fenrir, but Fenrir was strong and fought his way up through the squashing force. Jasmine focused her mind and powers on all the liquids flowing through Fenrir's body as Michael had showed her how to do, and his blood cells began to explode. He fell to the ground in pain and howled in such a high pitch that it broke her concentration. Fenrir realized immediately, and before Jasmine could move, he caught her and threw her into the path of a nearby car. Jasmine hit the car hard with her back, and fell unconscious.

John teleported right in front of Fenrir and punched him in his nose as hard as he could. He went to swing again, but Fenrir caught his arm and threw him hard against the brick building closest to them. John sat up, dazed as blood poured down the side of his face. Everything was a blur. He could just make out some kind of dark form getting rapidly closer to him, but he couldn't see or think clearly.

Fenrir leapt in the air to kill John but found himself in the talons of a giant dragon. Ho Young lifted Fenrir high into the air and tossed him just high enough to cook him with silver flame. As Fenrir fell to the ground he began turning into his human form, an indication that he was dead, just like Chiron before him.

By the time Ho Young landed, John and Jasmine had gotten to their feet and were addressing each other's wounds. Trying to turn into his human form on landing, Ho Young twisted his knee and let out a gasp of pain.

"Only you, Ho Young, can fight in a battle, not get touched, and wind up in the hospital for injuries you received leaving the fight," John said, but smiled so that Ho Young would know that he was joking.

Ho Young nodded in embarrassment.

"Let's find Marcus so I can give him a telling off for missing the entire battle," John said, his amusement turning into anger quickly.

Jasmine and Ho Young didn't respond. Instead, they both looked at the ground. Tears poured from Jasmine's eyes and John immediately knew something had happened to his best friend; he could tell by their reactions.

"Where's Marcus?" he asked them, swirling with a mixture of hatred and fear and sadness—his annoyance vanished. "Please tell me?"

"He's dead," Ho Young quietly said. Even though John inwardly already knew that was most likely what had happened, hearing it out loud brought him to his knees. A panic attack was starting, and he needed to regain control before it turned into a medical emergency.

Ho Young and Jasmine rushed to his side and tried to calm him down as he began to shake, murmuring Marcus' name over and over.

"Breathe. Please, John, breathe."

He did his best to focus on breathing, but it was hard and it didn't seem to be helping any. John could feel his left arm going numb. He looked up to heaven, "God, please help me, I don't want to die." Slowly, he began to calm down and regain control over his body. Once he was breathing better, Jasmine let him go, turned away from him, and began to sob.

"I thought I was going to lose you too," she said through her tears.

"No, you will never lose me. I will always find a way to live for you." John was looking down at the ground as he realized how close he had really gotten to death.

THIRTY-THREE

A day later, after he'd been given space to adjust to Marcus' death, John had questions. "What happened?" he asked. "How did Fenrir get Marcus? And where were you at, Ho Young? Why didn't you save him?" His voice twisted in anguish, and an angry flush spread over his cheeks. Ho Young, more concerned for his friend than correcting him, stepped up to take responsibility but Jasmine shook her head.

"It *was* my fault," she said bitterly. She was terrified that John would hate her when he found out what happened.

Unable to accept what she was saying, John intervened. "No, it wasn't anyone's fault. Michael warned us that Fenrir is a genius."

"No," Jasmine said firmly "It was my fault. I was focused on your thoughts to make sure you were okay when I should have been focusing on Fenrir and where he was. I was worried about you because all you could see was darkness. You wouldn't have seen Fenrir coming if he attacked… So I—I sent Ho Young to go and help you. He hadn't even been gone for thirty seconds when Fenrir jumped through the window of the first floor in the mall. We didn't even see him. I ducked out of instinct when I heard the glass break, but he slashed Marcus's neck with his claws before he could move. All I saw was blood gushing from—there was so much blood, John."

Jasmine could barely finish for her sentence. "Fenrir had tripped after attacking Marcus. I screamed and started running before Fenrir could get back up and get me. I screamed your name as he chased me."

John tried to fight it but a few tears began to roll down his face. His best friend was dead, and they had no idea where the body was. When they had gone to retrieve it, it was nowhere to be found.

Gabriel appeared in their midst, "As much as I hate to be the bearer of more bad news," he said. "You have two days to mourn your friend before Leviathan is released, and he will come straight for you."

"Can we get a pause in the challenge? From The Creator? Can't he stop it… Our friend just died."

"I wish I could do that for you, but I can't. He must be released as was promised, and he will come straight for you."

John stood up angrily, gesturing wildly at the others. "Fine," he said. "You guys stay here. I'll go fight him." He couldn't bear the thought of losing one of them, too.

"No, your power is over the air, which is made up of oxygen. Oxygen increases fire, and fire is what Leviathan breathes. He also has other powers. He can transform into people, objects, or animals… So, once he is released, please do not relax—not even for a second. Don't even trust the chair that you sit in." Gabriel's warning was grave.

John sat down. Everything seemed hopeless. Marcus was dead, and in two days, they probably would be as well.

"Stay encouraged, my children. Like Fenrir, the dragon has been around since the beginning of creation and is very wise and cunning. He won't just use brute strength. He will trap you, separate you, toy with your lives until you have given up hope—then he will go for the kill."

"Way to keep us encouraged," John said sarcastically.

"Knowledge that enables you to be ready for such an opponent is the best encouragement you can receive. Now you can plan and be somewhat ready. When anything is out of the ordinary from this point on, you should assume the worst, and do not be caught alone—not even for a second."

"Well, that is going to be kind of hard with us having different classes at school," Jasmine said, suddenly remembering their other responsibilities.

"Here," Gabriel said, handing them all new schedules. "You are all in the same classrooms now, so stay together and be careful."

"What about when Jasmine uses the bathroom?" John asked, concerned about her being alone.

"You have the power to turn invisible. I suggest you use it and follow her in."

"Okay, I've got to go, but you guys remember to stay together." Gabriel said, nodding his approval at them before turning to leave.

"We will," Jasmine said.

"What about Marcus's body?" Is there any way that you can at least recover it?" John pleaded.

"No," Gabriel answered firmly. "You wouldn't want it. While your friend Marcus is dead to the human race, he is alive in the world of the wolves."

John bristled. "Okay, well, you lose then. I will not fight until Marcus is fixed. He didn't ask to be in this battle—none of us did!"

"I will go and talk to The Father about it and see if he will show grace," Gabriel sighed as he spoke to indicate he really did not want to bother with it.

Gabriel left and was back within seconds. "He said Marcus cannot live again, but he will cure him of the affliction and allow him passage into heaven once the tournaments are completely finished."

"Thank you, and I am sorry for talking like that. It's just that Marcus is my friend, and I cannot even try to comprehend him living on as a werewolf."

"I understand," Gabriel said, as he vanished.

"John, that was really brave," Jasmine said, hugging him close. "I don't think I would have spoken to Gabriel like that, but you did what you felt was right, and I can definitely respect that."

"We need to get some sleep. We won't be able to hold a ceremony until this war is over. We've made far too many mistakes up to this point. We can't afford to make any with Leviathan."

After spending the night in the hotel, they teleported back to their hometown and things were immediately suspicious. One of their teachers had been mysteriously fired, and they had a sub until their new teacher showed up.

Coincidentally, their new teacher wasn't due to show up for two more days, a day after Leviathan would be free. The sub kept his eyes on John, Jasmine, and Ho Young for most of the class. John and Jasmine got into a whispering argument as to whether or not the sub was a monster working for Lucifer and Zeus.

"So you haven't noticed that we're the only ones he is watching in the class?" John said to Jasmine

"Well, I can imagine that it would be kind of hard not to notice the three of us all bandaged up."

"Okay, then we'll have to test him," John replied defiantly—he had a point to prove.

"How?" It was in times like these that Jasmine wished John didn't have the power to block her from his mind.

"It will be easy," he replied. "While he's not looking at us, I knock him over using my powers and if he looks around at everyone or at the windows then I'll drop the subject, but if he looks straight at me, he knows."

"So, if he looks at us, he knows?"

"No, only if he looks at me, because I'm the one with the power to do that. As a matter of fact, you go on that side of the room and fiddle with some paper, and Ho Young, you go on the other side of the classroom and just stand there." He waited until they agreed. "So, I'm going to hit him from your side, Jasmine. If he looks at me directly and not the direction from which the wind comes, he knows."

"Agreed." Jasmine was confident John was wrong.

The sub noticed Jasmine and Ho Young moving around the room, and Jasmine fumbled around looking through extra credit assignments to maintain discretion.

Ho Young, however, looked beyond suspicious. He kept peeking at the teacher and looking away quickly before the teacher could return his gaze. John kept his head focused, reading his book. He looked up as the teacher was focused on Ho Young and, with quick *swoosh* of his hand, the teacher flew against the wall. John looked down before the teacher could recover and continued reading his book quietly as if nothing had happened.

Moments later, Jasmine and Ho Young returned to John's side. "You were right," Jasmine said. "He didn't just look at you—he glared with hate."

"I told you," John said as he winked at her, pointing at her with his right pointer finger. "And I am not playing these games anymore." John stood up and lifted the teacher off of the ground with his powers and slammed him back and forth between the ceiling and ground. The whole class jumped back in fear and a few of the girls screamed. Jasmine steadied them, offering calming smiles and gentle words.

She explained the situation to everybody and showed them her powers, as only the kids who also shared Mrs Norton's class with them knew their secret. The fear melted into palpable excitement as Jasmine explained that their new teacher was most likely Leviathan, the great dragon.

"Wow," Dené said. "So dragons are real?"

"You have to act like you don't know, because he's likely to start the battle here in the school and kill anyone he thinks might matter to us," John replied to Dené.

Dené and John had been childhood friends. John had even lived with her and her family for a while. Dené' looked at John and Jasmine with amazement. "This is pretty cool," she said, smiling.

"Not as cool as it sounds. These beasts are dangerous. Marcus was killed by Fenrir the werewolf before we were able to kill him."

"Marcus is dead?" Dené' said, as her face scrunched up to fight back her tears.

"Yeah," Ho Young answered her as John swallowed. "Well, not dead…" Ho Young was about to continue, but stopped when John gave him a shushing look.

"What do you mean, not dead?" Another boy in the class, named Dustin, asked.

"It's Ho Young," John replied to Dustin, hoping to skip over the question quickly.

"Yeah, gotcha," Dustin said, knowing Ho Young said off-the-wall stuff sometimes.

"Now, when this new teacher comes, nobody give him any problems. I don't want anyone getting hurt." The class agreed, mostly because none of them wanted to get themselves hurt, either.

The next two days went by too fast and the first day of the new teacher dawned quickly. John was ready. He sat patiently in class with Jasmine and Ho Young, waiting for the teacher to walk in.

"Hello class," he greeted them as he entered five minutes after the bell rang. "My name is Professor Borland. I apologize for my tardiness—this school is impossible to navigate."

A few of the students acknowledged him, looking up from their desks and muttering a brief "hello."

The class went well—much better than any of them could have predicted. Mr Borland was passionate about history, and after a few days, even John began doubting whether he was actually Leviathan. He was a tall man, with brown hair and brown eyes, and looked nothing like a dragon. If he was, why wasn't he attacking?

It wasn't long before the class was talking amongst themselves about how much they liked him, and they would've given up their suspicions if Jasmine hadn't remembered Gabriel's warning—Leviathan was crafty; he would learn all about them before making any moves. She knew that if he was the beast, he would only attack them after he finished studying them; finished toying with them.

One afternoon while the three of them walked to Jasmine's house—which was where they'd decided to stay until the battle was over—she decided to call on Gabriel.

The anxiety of not knowing had been building, and she wanted to put an end to it.

He appeared instantly and, not for the first time, John wondered if helping them was all the angels did.

"What can I help you with?" Gabriel asked.

"Gabriel, please, no messing around. I want a straightforward answer, or we're pulling out," she pleaded.

"If you choose to pull out, girl, your deaths, and the deaths of your parents, will be on your heads." He gave her a stern look to convey his disappointment.

"That's fine," John said, getting upset about Gabriel's treatment of Jasmine. "Guess you better get ready to re-accept those fallen angels into heaven." Gabriel glared at John, but he didn't care. "And I'm sure that they'll show us mercy, rather than punish us, if we just quit and let them win the tournament." Gabriel's eyes flared. He could not believe the boldness that John and Jasmine were offering.

"Look," Jasmine continued. "This isn't fair. The dragon knows who we are, so, it's only fair that we get to know who he is."

Gabriel disappeared without a word. They started walking again, thinking that they had upset the angel, but he reappeared in front of them a moment later.

"Leviathan is your new teacher at school, and he is studying your every move," he said, though his expression made it clear that he didn't really want to.

"I figured it might be him," Jasmine said, without looking at John and Ho Young. "Because I couldn't see his future or his past."

"I hate this. This dragon is really irritating. He knows who we are, and he's studying us. We need to mess with his patience a bit—enough to irritate him, but not enough for him to attack us when we aren't ready."

"I know. I personally think we should transfer out of his class so he can't continue studying us."

"That sounds good in theory," John said. "But if we leave his class, he might just decide to attack us sooner. I'm sure he knows we're hurting at the moment, and that he can beat us right now."

"No, we need to study him as well," Jasmine said. "As a matter of fact, let's go to the library."

*****

"How may I help you?" asked one of the three librarians. She had gray hair and was wearing a 1920's dress with a floral design all over it. On her head, she wore a pair of giant 1970's style glasses.

"I'm looking for a book on dragons," John said, confident that she was going to take them right to the book that would help them the most.

"I'm not sure exactly what type of book you're after, but there are plenty of books with dragons in them. The Harry Potter books have dragons in them. The Percy Jackson books have dragons in them. *How To Train Your Dragon* has dragons in it. *Dragon Hearts* is also about dragons. Really, there are many books with dragons in them. Do any of those seem like something you'd like?"

"No," John said, stepping away from the counter in disappointment. "This was useless."

"It really was," Jasmine agreed. "Let's ask Michael."

"Hey, that is a good idea," Ho Young said.

"Well, we have nothing to lose." John said as they left the library, feeling dejected.

*****

"You called?" Michael said grumpily, as he appeared in Jasmine's living room moments after they arrived.

"You already know what's up," John said, glaring at the angel, not interested in playing games.

Michael laughed and gave them an answer that they didn't want to hear. "Well, really, there is no actual book written on how to kill a dragon, especially since no man has ever really done it. The only angel to ever kill a dragon was my distant cousin, Thor, and he's still in the process of gaining his form and powers back. Right now, he is nothing more than essence, so as of yet, he cannot speak."

"Do you know how he did it?" John asked Michael.

"Well, it's simple, yet impossible. You can't really drown a dragon that lives in the ocean, now, can you?"

"No," Jasmine replied, looking disappointed.

"And oxygen feeds fire, so trying to block the dragon's fire with air, again, is useless."

It was now John's turn to express his disappointment, "So it's up to Ho Young then?"

"No, it is not up to any one person. A part-time dragon going head to head with the original dragon—who's been around since creation? I doubt you want to see how that ends.

"Okay, so we quit then. If there's no way to win, what are we doing fighting? Either tell us how to kill the dragon or stop wasting our time," John said angrily.

"Just because I don't know how to do it, doesn't mean it can't be done," Michael said, trying to instill some confidence in them.

John rubbed his chin, "I have an idea. I bet the dark elves would know how to beat a dragon."

Michael looked at John sharply. Fire blazed in his eyes. "What do you know about the dark elves?"

"Well, I know I saw a lot of YouTube videos about people spotting the elves or hearing them in the rocks, talking, in Iceland. I even saw one where a very famous missing scientist lady was found, naked, in the caves that were said to be the entrance into the world of the dark elves. They say that sometimes the elves get mad and punish the people, but most of the time the elves leave them alone."

"You have learned correctly, but your assumptions that you can negotiate with those elves are past crazy."

"All we have to do is use our powers if they attack us."

"So, you're going to use your little pieces of power against forty thousand dark elves, all of whom have great magic. Think about it… They break the rules of the realms all the time, yet Leviathan, who hated rule breakers, and also hated the dark elves, never attacked them."

"Because they could have beaten him?" Ho Young asked nervously, shifting from one foot to the other.

"They are powerful and can't be trusted. They are the ones who lured Thor away from Asgard on purpose, so that Fenrir and Leviathan could attack Asgard. Thor and Odin couldn't fight together side by side as they always had—if they had, I'm sure the battle would have turned out differently." Michael looked almost nostalgic for a moment.

"Wait, I thought the Greek gods planned that, after they found out that Thor was gone?" Jasmine asked.

As Jasmine spoke, Gabriel appeared beside Michael and joined in the conversation.

"It is not as simple as planning. The dark elves had heard a prophecy about it and so they, knowing the fallen angels on Earth were planning on attacking, drew Thor away by attacking the elves of light. In the prophecy, it stated that if Thor and Odin fought together side by side, they would triumph, but if they didn't, Asgard would fall,"

"Okay then, so we can go ask The Creator how to defeat a dragon, because he knows all things," Ho Young suggested, eager to find the answer.

"Yeah, very good point, Ho Young," Jasmine said, giving him a high five.

Gabriel was getting ready to speak, but John cut in. "How is it fair," he asked, "that he can study books and find information about how to beat us, but we can't find any information on how to beat him?"

Gabriel disappeared to go and see if God would tell him the answer and as always, he reappeared within a couple of seconds. He did not have good news.

*****

"Ok, so the dragon is impossible to beat." Jasmine stated, once the angels had left. "If we can't figure out Leviathan's weakness, we have to run for it."

"We can't," John replied. "His mission is to study us and then fight us. If we run, he will not rest until he finds us, and I'm sure Zeus or another fallen angel will be able to find us with no problems, no matter where we hide. They'll tell him where we are. Not to mention there is also the possibility of him going after our families as well."

Jasmine started crying, "John, I don't think I want to do this anymore."

He reached for her and held her tight as they stood there, her tears drenching the top of his shirt on his left shoulder where her head was resting. It was a lot to take in, and they'd had very little time to adjust. John was nervous too, but not as nervous as he had been with Fenrir. He stroked her back and whispered to her, encouraging her to draw on the strength he knew she possessed.

*****

The next day at school, John acted out of impulse and a bit of desperation. "Mr Borland, can I talk to you?" he said, as he entered the classroom in between his classes.

"Sure thing," Mr Borland answered. "And is it about the homework?"

"Well, I guess it sort of is, but not the homework you think it's about."

"Okay… how can I help you?"

John braced himself. "I'm going to get to the point rather than beat around the bush," he said.

"I appreciate that," Mr Borland replied.

"We know you are Leviathan and that you are studying us, and I'm sure the date of your attack is coming soon, since you feel you have to win the cowardly way."

"How do you mean?" Mr Borland asked, not bothered a bit that John knew he was the dragon.

"Well, you have the resources to study us, but I bet if we had equal resources to study you, we would be able to beat you—easy," John taunted, knowing he wouldn't be able to help himself.

"Okay, well, what resources do you need? I think we could reach a deal, of sorts. I have only been beaten once, by a very powerful angel… I killed him too, you know—took him with me… so I'll take that bet, since your powers are nowhere near what his were."

"I want access to see that battle. I want to be able to see details about every second of the fight in book form, showing me Thor's thoughts and actions, and yours."

"Anything else?" Mr Borland asked, seemingly completely unfazed.

"Yeah, to make things really fair, I need a list of your strengths and your weaknesses—as you have of us."

Mr Borland grabbed a piece of paper and, after thinking for a long second, began writing. When he finished writing, he handed John the piece of paper. John looked at and discovered the dragon had written only a few words. They were *pride* and *too intelligent*.

"Oh yeah," John added, tucking the little list into a pocket. "And you have to swear on the River Styx that you won't follow us anymore."

"Deal," Mr Borland said, turning back to the pile of paperwork on his desk.

*****

John made it to class just a few moments after the bell rang, and it was all Jasmine could do not to wrap her arms around him in relief. He sat down between her and Ho Young, promising to explain after school.

"Wow, so he's going to actually leave us alone to study him?" Jasmine asked, as they walked to her house. She was shocked that John had done what he had done.

"Yup, and he has to find a way to show me his battle with Thor, too."

"Nice," Jasmine said. Ho Young nodded his head like he was thinking of something, but John didn't dare to ask him what it was. He didn't have it in him to handle anymore nonsense after everything they had been through. They walked home together and began to make guesses.

THIRTY-FOUR

The next morning John, Ho Young and Jasmine went to school more relaxed, knowing that they had time to get a plan together. As they sat in Mr Borland's class, the topic on the board had been changed from the civil war to dragons—much to their surprise.

"Okay, class," Mr Borland addressed them after taking roll. "I am sure that many of you have seen, by now, that we are changing subjects from the civil war to dragons."

The class eyed Mr Borland suspiciously. They all wondered why he was switching their history subject to dragons. The class had just started believing that there was no way that Mr Borland could be Leviathan the dragon, but the change in subjects put their minds right back to thinking that it was a possibility.

"Why are we changing the subjects to dragons?" Jenny asked.

"Well, I figured it would be an interesting switch up from reading about the civil war. Okay, so who knows anything about dragons?" Mr Borland asked.

John's hand shot up quickly. He was going to seize this opportunity to drag out all the information he could about how Thor died, as well as how he killed Leviathan in The Battle of Ragnarok, which the angels called The Battle in Asgard.

"Yes," Mr Borland said, as he pointed to John. An evil glint showed in his eyes and he smiled wickedly.

"Well," John began. "I've heard of this dragon, and I have a question. Leviathan barely beat Thor, who isn't as well equipped as Michael. So… the dragon does have one weakness, which means that Michael is right. Leviathan has one fear, and it is him."

"Michael said that, did he now?" Mr Borland said as he sat back in his chair, obviously considering what was just said. John could tell he said the right thing and that it struck a nerve with Leviathan. "Well, if Michael wanted to test his skills, he would be more than welcome to fight Leviathan. I am sure Leviathan won't mind. It's unlikely that Michael is the toughest angel. He is one of them, but there are a few whom I believe can beat him."

"You can stop talking in third person," Dené' said, without raising her hand. "We all know that you're Leviathan. We knew before you even became our teacher."

"Interesting," Leviathan said. "I was hoping it would be a surprise. Unfortunately for you, my deal to not attack until they have studied me was with the three demigods; everyone else in this class is fair game." Mr Borland shimmered and twisted, and the dragon that stood in his place was so large that it filled the room. "So," it said. "I am afraid I must kill you all. And, if any of you three interfere, the deal is off and I kill you now." It stared at John, Jasmine, and Ho Young.

"What about Michael," John asked, attempting to trick Leviathan into inviting Michael into the battle. "I noticed you left his name out. From the looks of things, it does seem like you're a bit scared of him."

"Nice try demigod, but I am no fool. I will fight Michael if he wishes, but only when I am through with you three and your classmates."

John didn't have time to be disappointed that his plan to get Leviathan to invite Michael into the fight didn't work. He had to immediately work out how to protect the class and carry out whatever plan he came up with.

"Everyone, I know how to beat Leviathan!" John said, hoping Leviathan hadn't lied about pride being his weakness. It must have been partly true because he delayed his attack to turn and look at John as he issued an order to the class.

Everyone quickly huddled up, much to Leviathan's amusement. "Okay," John continued. "Everyone, grab a hold of the person's hand next to you," John said, keeping his eyes on the beast before him.

Leviathan laughed. "What is this, some kind of prayer meeting? Is that how you think you can beat me?" His laughter was dreadful. It sounded like howler monkeys, thunder, and the worst tuba players in the world, all mixed together to create an awful noise.

"Not quite, but it's the next best thing—"

Before John could finish his sentence, he teleported to the group and placed his hand on the shoulders of one of his classmates just as Leviathan reared back in rage to blow fire on the class. The whole class disappeared with John in an instant, and the fire hit the wall. Flames erupted in the classroom and the fire alarm rang out loudly.

Leviathan, seeing the class gone, turned his attention to Jasmine and Ho Young, who had not been part of the huddle. Jasmine wasn't mad at John for leaving her in harm's way—she too was concerned for the class, because they had no powers to defend themselves. With John gone, Leviathan became all the more frightening, and Jasmine waved her hands in terror. The water in the pipes swelled and swelled until they burst, and the flood exploded towards Leviathan's eyes. The water flowed in circles around Leviathan's head, blocking his vision so that he was unable to see Jasmine and Ho Young escape out of the window. He roared with rage and blew a fire hotter than the Lake of Fire itself out of his mouth to evaporate the water.

Once he was able to survey his surroundings, he saw that the demigods were gone. He looked out of the window and saw them running madly across the field, trying to get away. He grinned at their idiocy. They would never escape him on foot.

Leviathan leapt out of the window after them and quickly grew to his full size. He was one hundred feet in height, with a mass greater than a full-sized football field.

Jasmine looked back and saw Leviathan flying towards them with a speed that should have been impossible for something of his bulk. "Ho Young!" Jasmine cried as her heart thudded madly in her chest. She fell over in the grass as she lost her footing, and when she looked up, she expected her last vision to be teeth bearing down on her or a great wave of fire engulfing her. Instead, she saw two dragons fighting. They were about the same size, but things soon began to go very badly for Ho Young.

Leviathan clawed Ho Young's chest and blood gushed out as he fell to his knees. Leviathan, not wasting any time, sunk his teeth into the front of his neck and ripped it out with a sickening squelch. Ho Young fell to the ground in his human form, floundering in a pool of bright red blood.

"No!" Jasmine cried. "Noooo!"

Leviathan turned his attention towards Jasmine and began to move swiftly towards her.

THIRTY-FIVE

John appeared back in the classroom, but nobody was there. It didn't take him long to see where they had gone, and the scene before him made his heart plummet. Ho Young—dear Ho Young—was dead on the ground and Leviathan was advancing on Jasmine. John teleported to her and, without a word, teleported her to the same place he had taken the class. They were in Hanna, Hawaii, and all sat on the beach waiting for his return.

When only John and Jasmine appeared next to the class, they immediately noticed Ho Young's absence. "Where is Ho Young?" Evan asked with a worried look. He was ringing his hands nervously.

John didn't even have to answer. Jasmine fell to the ground, screaming "nooo!" over and over again, hysterically. She had snapped. They were not trained warriors—they learned how to use their powers in combat the night before it all began, and it was too much.

John scanned the area, looking at his classmates who all seemed to be a bit shaken up. A few of the kids were sitting on the beach burying their heads into their arms as they leaned forward, using their knees as cushions.

He wanted Jasmine to be safe, even if it would probably ensure his own death. The island was beautiful. It was a sunny day with few clouds in the sky, yet everyone was filled with sorrow because of the death of Ho Young.

Without saying a word to the class—or to Jasmine—John teleported back to the spot where he had left Leviathan and Ho Young.

*****

Keith Blackburn was the first to notice that John was gone. He rubbed his hand across the gun that he had holstered along the front of his pants. The bulge was covered by his oversized t-shirt and thick blue hoodie. He didn't know if John was coming back or not, but if the dragon came, he was glad he at least had some protection. He figured that if it came to it, maybe, he could shoot Leviathan in the eye or somewhere soft on his body.

*****

When John reappeared, Leviathan had transformed into a much smaller dragon and was feasting on Ho Young's body. The crunching of bones was gruesome, and John nearly threw up.

"Come back to die like your friend here, have you?" Leviathan asked without looking up. John teleported close enough to touch Ho Young's body, and teleported him away before the beast knew what he was doing. When he returned, he looked at Leviathan with absolute hatred as he prepared an attack strategy in his mind.

The best plan he could come up with was to keep attacking in spurts, and somehow tire the dragon.

John hoped that just maybe, the great dragon—who had resumed his massive size—would at some point get careless and make a fatal mistake in his anger. After several rounds of niggling back and forth, Leviathan's wisdom went out the window, just as John had hoped. Never before had any demigod ever dared to toy with him as John was. Thor himself had fought Leviathan with everything he had.

Who does this demigod think he is? Leviathan thought in outrage. *I will kill this disgusting excuse for a human and squish him like the bug that he is.*

Leviathan blew a sizzling flame of blue, gold, purple and white, and rather than block it, John used his wind and rage to push it to the side. It was a good plan, except that the grass caught on fire. John had no time nor inclination to put the fire out.

*****

On the island, Jasmine was distraught. She sat on the beach as her schoolmates tried to comfort her, but she knew John had gone back to fight Leviathan alone, and she was pissed off. She understood why he had done it, but in the end she felt that John's actions were selfish. She had already lost Ho Young and Marcus—two people she cared dearly about. She was in love with John, and if he died too, she was never going to forgive him.

*****

Leviathan paused for a moment. He was, for the first time, realizing John wasn't just any demigod, but a very intelligent one. "Your grades in school don't speak on behalf of your actual intellect," Leviathan said, slowly circling him.

He wasn't in the mood to talk. He figured if he teleported again that Leviathan would expect him to use the same move, which was to teleport right in front of him, land a hit, and then teleport away.

Instead, John stopped teleporting close to Leviathan but kept popping up all around him, never setting a pattern that the dragon could figure out. As John teleported one last time before he planned on going in for his great, bulging eyes, the dragon shot a lucky flame right in front of him. He barely got a wind barrier up before the flames hit. The barrier held but the heat from the flames was enough to make him collapse, and John lay faint on the ground, his eyes barely staying open.

THIRTY-SIX

Leviathan drew nearer and nearer, aiming for the kill. His massive claws gouged at the ground beneath him as he walked, and the snarl on his face was ferocious. His teeth looked as angry as his eyes as he barred them, growling and moving towards John. It was time to end the battle once and for all.

Twenty yards away from the nearly unconscious demigod, he drew a deep breath and released a flame just as hot as the previous one, which had incapacitated his opponent. John, still dazed, felt a wave of scorching heat against his skin and saw a blur of purplish light growing brighter and brighter as it drew closer to him. Without stopping to think, he teleported himself back to his house.

Leviathan raged in a child-like fury. Where there should have been the charred ashes of a demigod, there was nothing but burning grass. He had been cheated of his victory. Again, a demigod had survived on luck alone.

*****

Jasmine had finally stopped crying, and the class was all gathering close together. Night was drawing in on them, and the fresh chill of darkness was approaching. They needed to find a way to stay warm, so they huddled up tightly. Just as the sun began to set in Hanna, John appeared next to them. He was drifting in and out of consciousness, weakened by the incredible heat of the fire that had downed him. He was sweating and feverish, and barely had enough strength to get back to Jasmine.

"I'm sorry," he murmured as he reached her. "I failed to beat him." He passed out before he could explain.

"No!" Jasmine screamed. Her hands caressed his face of their own accord, fingers clenching knots in his hair as she rocked in place.

She couldn't take it.

John was dead, just like the others. Her heart was broken and now she was the only demigod left. There was no way that she could win, or protect her classmates. A few of them forced her away from John, wrapping her in comforting arms and dragging her shaking body from his so that they could assess the situation. Dené approached

John with tears streaming down her face, but upon checking his pulse, she found that he was still alive.

"He is still alive!" she' yelled. "But we need to cool him down. He has a fever. A really bad one."

Jasmine rose to her feet, stumbling over herself to get to him. She dropped to her knees beside him, her thumb tracing desperate, soothing circles against his forehead. The anger and hurt that she had felt at his decision to fight alone fled—for now, it didn't matter.

THIRTY-SEVEN

John rested for three days. With the gentle and reverent care from Jasmine and his classmates, he surprised them all and made a full recovery.

The group rested for three more days on the beach, but John knew they didn't have much time before Leviathan showed up. "We need to hit the library," he said to them finally. "I need to find out how dragons breathe fire. If there are any books on it, even fairy tales, there might be some truth there which could help us."

Dené volunteered and led most of the class to the library, while John and Jasmine stayed behind at the beach to discuss battle strategies.

"Okay," John said. "For the most part, I can handle him. I was beating him easily, but then he started blowing those huge flames in random directions. He missed me with a lot of them, but the last one was dead on target. It was lucky I got that shield up or… It was lucky." He couldn't quite bring himself to recount any further. "I'm hoping it's some sort of liquid process that makes the flames, because you can control all liquids, and if we can keep him from breathing fire, we have a good chance at winning."

Jasmine was buoyed by the idea and nodded along. "Yeah, that's a good plan, and hopefully it works," she said, but she still didn't crack a smile. Marcus and Ho Young were dead, and John barely escaped death himself. The stakes were real, and they had already lost too much.

"Also, I plan to take out his eyes, so we need to keep the battle right here by the ocean so we can—"

He didn't get to finish his sentence. In the distance, a large flying object was looming over the horizon, racing towards them.

"Well, at least Dené' and the others aren't here." John said as his stomach clenched. He grabbed Jasmine by the shoulders, kissed her on the top of her head, and steadily met her gaze. "Go and hide in the ocean—please," he begged. "I'll handle him on land."

Before she could protest, John touched her hand and teleported her right out to where the water was close to twenty feet deep and motioned for her to wait three minutes before surfacing.

When he reappeared back on land, many police vehicles had already begun to arrive. It seemed that the locals had also noticed the hundred-foot dragon heading their way and had called it in. The police tried to get John to leave the beach, but he refused. When they tried to force him, he caused a great wind to blow on the land, picking all the police up off their feet and dropping them onto the middle of the island. He couldn't be worrying about them and fighting Leviathan at the same time.

THIRTY-EIGHT

Leviathan landed on the beach. "So, you thought you could escape me, did you?"

Before John could answer, a hard wave from the ocean hit the beast in the face. Jasmine had sprung into action the moment he landed—she wasn't about to let her far-off position prevent her from helping John.

Leviathan stepped back, snorting and coughing as the water shot up his nostrils. He tried to blow it out but couldn't, because Jasmine was holding it firm. While Leviathan was distracted and trying to sneeze, John teleported as close as he could to his right eye. He touched it, crossed his fingers, and teleported away. He was incredibly to grateful to see that his intense focus had led him to transport only the eye, and not the entire dragon.

He wanted to go in for the other one but thought it best to wait a moment. Leviathan was in a rage, staring at John with deadly focus. He had to avoid falling into the trap and doing exactly what the beast expected of him. Thirty feet away from him, Leviathan tried desperately to blow fire towards him, but nothing came out. As the great dragon raged, John looked toward the ocean. Jasmine was walking onto the beach, focusing intently on Leviathan. The dragon turned to look at her for a split second, and the short moment of distraction gave John the opportunity he needed. Within seconds, John was back at the same spot on the beach with Leviathan's left eye. Leviathan was now blind and couldn't smell, because Jasmine was clogging his nose with water.

He reared back and screamed in fury as he tried again and again to produce fire to no avail. In a moment of vicious spite, John made the decision to toy with their tormentor. In two quick, successive moves, he removed two of the dragon's wings and rendered the most ferocious of the beasts useless—unable to see, smell, or fly.

Leviathan was not a quitter, and clawed blindly at the air, assuming John would come for him again.

The crowds on the beach had grown, and every single person in Maui had come out with their children and families to see the mighty battle unfold. There was a great roar from the crowd when they realized what John had done, and he was heartened by their spirit.

Even with Leviathan blind and unable to fly, they still couldn't kill him. His scales were sealed tight and were harder than any weapon known to man. For a frightening moment, it seemed as though they had run out of options, but then an idea struck.

"Jasmine, walk with me real fast," John said as he made his way away from his collected pieces of the dragon. "Look," he said. "I figured out that I can focus on parts of something, and teleport just that part, without the rest of it."

"Yeah, I can see that," Jasmine said, gesturing at the pile of Leviathan's body parts.

"Well, what if I can do even more than that? What if I can actually focus on objects and teleport them without even touching them?"

"What are you planning?" Jasmine asked, giving him a questioning look, her eyebrows raised. She could tell he was up to something but wanted to know exactly what.

"Well, we can't kill him from the outside. His body is stronger than steel. When I punched him in our last fight, I dang near broke my hand."

"Okay?" Jasmine said, hinting for John to hurry up and get to the point.

"Well, what if I can teleport his heart out of his body? All we'd have to do then would be to find something to stab his it with." He glowed with excitement at the prospect.

"It's worth a try," Jasmine replied, smiling. She was happy that, so far, the battle was going in their favor.

"Go and ask some of the whalers over there if they have any long spears," John suggested, pointing at a bunch of fishermen who had left their whale ships and were rowing towards the shore, likely to assist them on the beach. John focused his mind on Leviathan's heart while the dragon was still clawing the air in case John teleported himself in again. He continued roaring very loudly, as if it would change the outcome of the battle. It was bone chilling, but no longer enough to secure him a win. Now that he was blind and couldn't breathe fire, he was nothing but practice for John, as he attempted to do things with his powers that he had never done before.

John tried, with all of his might and energy, to teleport Leviathan's heart out of his body for a full twenty minutes before finally giving up.

"Damnit!" he yelled. "I can't do it. Forget this. I'm done with this stupid tournament. We can't kill him, and he can't kill us. In my book, that means the tournament is a stalemate and ends in a draw."

"John, we have to kill him, or the tournament won't end," Jasmine said, sensing his frustration. She wanted to keep him focused on finding a way to kill Leviathan, rather than focusing on ways that he couldn't.

"What do you want me to do, Jasmine?" John asked in despair. He was ready to walk away. He was pissed off that nothing was working.

"Why don't you just take his body apart piece by piece, like you did his eyes and wings?" Jasmine suggested, as she visualized him doing just that.

John stopped pacing to look at her.

"You know what? That actually could work." He rubbed his chin with his thumb and pointer, thinking.

"That's a really good idea," he continued. "That should have been common sense for me. Thanks!"

"You're welcome," she said, giving him a hug. "Now do us all a favor and go and finish that dragon off!"

It took John less than five minutes to have the beach filled with parts of Leviathan's body, and his heart was now exposed. The inside of Leviathan's body looked disgusting, and the smell coming from him almost made them want to throw up.

He died very quickly.

Michael appeared next to John and Jasmine, beaming at them with great pride.

"Well done you two," he said. "I can't lie. I was nervous in that last battle." He turned to John. "When you went to fight him alone—but you guys managed to pull it off. It's… It's actually quite astounding."

Jasmine didn't respond. She was thinking about Ho Young and Marcus. Michael bowed his head—he could tell what she was thinking about.

"No, God will not bring them back, because then he would then have to be fair and bring all the beasts back. I know it is a sad loss for you, but you need to rest now."

"Wait, rest?" John said, tensing up.

"He means get rested up from the impossible challenge that we just finished up." Jasmine said, assuming that she understood.

"No, I don't think that is what he meant," John said, eyeballing Michael in angry anticipation.

"I'm confused," Jasmine said. "What do you mean?"

"The way he said *rest*… it wasn't in a '*you are finished with everything*' type of sentence. It was more of a '*get rested up in between challenges*' type of statement. He said it like a boss says it at the end of a hard shift when you have to come back and work hard again the next day."

"Please, tell me we're done?" Jasmine said, looking at Michael. She tried hard to contain herself, but the tears of exhaustion were spilling gently down her face.

"I wish I could, but all I can tell you is to rest for now."

THIRTY-NINE

Lucifer appeared in the throne room. "We have lost the first challenge," he addressed them gravely. "But the next challenge will prove to be much more difficult. These two meddling demigods will have to go on any mission that we send them on… We will have to vote, but I don't see anyone not liking my idea. I say we send them through the catacombs. With all the monsters down there, including Arachne and her many spiders, there is no way they will survive."

"Well, that depends," Athena said. "There are a lot of exits, and if all they have to do is make it to an exit, then it is still possible for them to live. It will not be easy, but it will be possible, especially with as crafty as those two are.

"They will have to free Apollo, who I imprisoned in Tartarus after he freed me from the bottomless pit."

"Wait, what do you mean? He freed you from the bottomless pit?" Zeus stood up, outraged at Lucifer's confession to imprisoning his son. Everyone had been wondering why Apollo was not present at this momentous occasion, but none expected that he'd been imprisoned.

"Before we fought the final battle in heaven and were cast down to Earth, Apollo switched sides—he has been working for The Creator. He has been here among us, on Michael's orders, as a spy."

Zeus wanted to argue, but he, himself, had had suspicions during that war in heaven about his son Apollo being a traitor, and it did make sense.

"Well, if he is such a traitor, why exactly do you want him freed?" Hades asked, confused but attempting to understand Lucifer's plan.

"I don't want him freed," Lucifer said with a rumbling chuckle. "I'm just raising the stakes of the journey; making it more impossible. If they can get past my sons, then they meet the catacombs. There is no way they can make it in and out of Tartarus with Apollo."

All of the fallen angels could see Lucifer's point. This challenge definitely seemed to skew further in their favor than the last one. They all voted in the affirmative, so Lucifer went back to The Creator to tell him the plan.

*****

John, Jasmine and their classmates went back to Chicago. Even though they didn't have the bodies they, along with the families, held a joint funeral for Marcus and Ho Young. Gabriel altered the memories of everyone except for John and Jasmine, so that everyone remembered Marcus and Ho Young being killed in an explosion. When the group ceremony was complete, John and Jasmine held their own private funeral for their friends, honoring them properly.

"I'm going to miss them," John said out loud, as he and Jasmine sat in the moonlight.

"Yeah, me too," Jasmine replied, resting her head on John's chest. They didn't want to think too much about what was coming next. They knew whatever it was, it was most likely going to be even harder.

ABOUT THE AUTHOR

Jonathan Gatsby was transported from his troubled youth into unknown lands and the exciting tales of our favorite heroes when two of his early high school teachers broke from the mold to encourage him. They instigated a voracious love of reading that opened up new worlds and opportunities that had previously felt unreachable.

Born in America on August 4th, 1984, Jonathan's youth was rife with the difficulties of the time. He is dedicated to using his experiences to nurture and care for others through the various passions that have spanned the course of his life and inform his writing today. He has spent time as a professional boxer, recording artist, preacher, church pianist and, most importantly, a dad.

Jonathan's love of boxing and music led him to open a boxing gym and piano school. Having been a writer since the age of fifteen, it was a natural progression for his love of words to eventually lead him into authorship and the inclusive and escapist fantasy worlds he inhabits today. Despite his colorful life, Jonathan still feels he doesn't fit in much anywhere, so he keeps to himself, entwined in a world that he has created.

CAN'T WAIT TO FIND OUT WHAT JONATHAN AND THE GROUP ARE UP TO NEXT?

The Wars between Angels and Gods: Book Two

Forced Into Heaven's War

Out Soon!

World War III: Book One

Nationberg, Gatsby, and the Execution Camp

Two years after his capture, Gatsby watches on with mounting anxiety as a fellow prisoner is slaughtered each month. His turn must be near, and he grows desperate to escape, but surrounded by jungle with no knowledge of his location, leaving looks just as dangerous as staying. A hard-headed young man from Fairbanks, Alaska, with a history of finding himself in trouble with the law, Gatsby steels himself against the conditions and grapples with the possibilities.

Sergeant Dunham and his troops, searching for the rumored execution camps, are plagued by the extremities of a world at war. It seems as though all of the power houses are squarely on the other side, but America is the Land of Hope, and only time will tell if that will be enough.

Nationberg, Gatsby, & the Execution camp is a tale of the strength, hope, and romance that must endure the relentless trial that is World War III.

Coming Soon!

www.ingramcontent.com/pod-product-compliance
Lightning Source LLC
Chambersburg PA
CBHW060612310726
48982CB00003B/538
* 9 7 8 1 7 3 6 1 7 6 9 0 0 *